DIVINE
SANCTUARY

Cheryl Kaye Tardif

DIVINE SANCTUARY
Book 3 in the Divine Trilogy

http://www.cherylktardif.com

FIRST EDITION Trade Paperback

Imajin Books - http://www.imajinbooks.com

June 18, 2014

ISBN: 978-1-927792-68-1

Cover designed by Ryan Doan — http://www.ryandoan.com

If you haven't read *DIVINE INTERVENTION* and *DIVINE JUSTICE* (the first two books in this trilogy), please visit your favorite retailer before reading *DIVINE SANCTUARY*. Thank you.

Praise for DIVINE SANCTUARY

"An excellent last installment to this psychic mystery/thriller series! Fast-paced action from cover to cover!" —Dale Mayer, international bestselling author of the *Psychic Vision* series

"Dark and compelling with details so vivid the reader can smell the smoldering corpse as he follows Pyro-Psychic, Jasi McLellan, who has the ungodly ability to enter the mind of a serial arsonist. This Canadian FBI psychic team moves like wildfire in the hands of consummate thriller author, Cheryl Kaye Tardif." —Barbara Silkstone, international bestselling author of *Miami Mummies*

If you haven't read *DIVINE INTERVENTION* and *DIVINE JUSTICE* (the first two books in this trilogy), please visit your favorite retailer before reading *DIVINE SANCTUARY*. Thank you.

Dedication

This book is dedicated to all the fans of my Divine series, for their patience and enthusiasm. Jasi and her team would be nonexistent without you.

Acknowledgements

Special thanks to my husband, Marc, for always supporting me, my writing and my career.

Character contest winners:

I often hold special character contests where winners can become a character or choose a character's name from a family or friend.

Thank you to "PutiPato" (Todd Barselow) and "Prescott," two bloggers who entered my Create a Corpse Contest and won. They are responsible for the names of two corpses, "Jennifer Phillips" and "Cooper Prescott", in this novel. Ironically, Todd became my editor about two years later.

Thanks to Nannetta Cook, who answered a Facebook call and suggested her name for the chief pathologist. This was an impromptu contest I held just for fun, and it received over 30 entries within a couple of hours.

During my *SUBMERGED* Army promotion, I held more character contests, and the winners were able to choose to have their name featured or another name of their choice. These winners were: Sheral Downham, Kaye Killgore, Stefan Gathmann, Kristen Howe, Jesse Giles Christiansen and Paxton Helling. Thank you all for allowing me the use of your name or one you selected.

Family life itself, that safest, most traditional, most approved of female choices, is not a sanctuary: It is, perpetually, a dangerous place.
—Margaret Drabble

Prologue

Emily emerged from the shadows of Jasi's closet. She drifted forward, her feet barely touching the floor. Her head, with its long blonde hair, lolled at an awkward—strangled—angle.

In this dream, an adult Jasi gasped in surprise.

The pink skipping rope noose was gone.

"You're ready, Jasmine."

"Ready for what?"

"To start looking for me."

Jasi stood still, mesmerized by the bruises around the girl's neck. They were fading before her eyes.

"The skipping rope is gone," she said finally. "And your bruises are disappearing."

"Yours will too," Emily said.

"I don't have any bruises."

Emily led Jasi to the mirror. When she peered into it, her image shifted from a young Jasmine back to her adult reflection. One arm was bent in front of her, throbbing as though someone was squeezing it hard then letting it go. Yellowed bruises dotted her arm.

Emily tried to smile. "In time all your bruises will fade. But first, ya have to set things right."

"And how do I do that? Oh, right, I have to find you."

"Yes. Find me." The dead girl floated backward.

"Wait!" Jasi cried out. "Why did your bruises fade?"

"Because you're one step closer to finding me."

"How? I don't know anything more than I did before."

Emily blended into the shadows. Before they swallowed her, she said, "You may think you aren't any closer to finding me, but trust me, you are." Darkness closed in around her.

Jasi took an anxious step forward. "Emily?"

Silence greeted her.
And a mystery.
She took a deep breath. "I'll find you, Emily."

Sanctuary: (1): a place of refuge and protection (2): a refuge for wildlife where predators are controlled and hunting is illegal
—Merriam-Webster Dictionary

1

In the smoky ruins of what had once been a flophouse for methamphetamine tweakers just off Hastings Street in downtown Vancouver, CFBI agent Jasmine McLellan stared at what was left of Tara Kincaid's smoldering corpse. The young woman's body had been reduced to a twisted, blackened mass of tendons and bone. From the gaping hole that was once the victim's mouth, Jasi deduced that twenty-one-year-old Tara had been alive when her killer poured some kind of accelerant on her and set her on fire.

"Ready?"

The question came from Benjamin Roberts, a Psychometric Empath and the only Psychic Skills Investigator—*PSI*—who could pull off wearing a well-fitted Armani suit to a crime scene.

Her lips tightened. "As ready as I'll ever be, Ben."

Beside Ben stood Natassia Prushenko, a former Russian SVR agent and gifted Victim Empath, and Brandon Walsh, an arson expert they'd met during a previous case. Brandon was the only member of their team who did not have a psychic gift. He had other *gifts* though, ones she preferred to think of in the privacy of her bedroom.

Focus!

The corpse beckoned her closer. Though the Oxy-Mask protected her, she knew the smell of death permeated her own hair, skin and the very air around her. It was a pungent scent, like no other, and she knew it all too well. Some smells were impossible to wash away, no matter how much bleach one used.

"When you take off the mask, inhale slowly," Brandon said. "Don't rush it."

"This ain't my first rodeo, you know."

"No, but I know how badly you want this guy. I don't want you passing out."

For Jasi, the scent of a fire set by a killer triggered something mysterious—a psychic gift, the ability to view a scene from a killer's mind and memories. A Pyro-Psychic and covert government agent for the Canadian Federal Bureau of Investigation, she knew these killers more intimately than anyone else. Sometimes the visions were so strong they knocked her unconscious for a few minutes.

"Not this time," she murmured.

She inhaled the smoke-free air from the mask, gave her team the thumbs-up signal and tucked her auburn hair behind her ears. *Okay, give me something—anything—so we can confine this bastard to a windowless cell in Matsqui Institution.*

She removed the Oxy-Mask, inhaled two shots of OxyBlast from a mini-can she'd strapped to her chest and tentatively sniffed the smoky air. "I'm fine. It's Shake 'n Bake time."

Breathe…in…out…in—

The vision hit her hard, knocking the air from her lungs.

"No!" the young woman screamed. "Please don't! I'll go back. I'm sorry. Let me go back!"

Didn't she know how pathetic she looked? I'd bound her legs and hands, trussed her up like a calf waiting to be slaughtered. Poor little cow.

"It's too late, Tara," I said. "You know the rules."

"But I can do better. I'll do what I'm told. I can be useful. You'll see. Someone will want me."

I smiled at the stupid child. "No one wants you. Not your parents, not any of us, no one. You are weak. You are a traitor." I spat the last word at her.

"Please!" she begged, her face dirty except for the path her tears took down her cheeks. "Forgive me."

"I told you when you joined us that it was a life choice. You chose."

I reached for the gasoline can, unscrewed the cap and began to pour it over her body as she lay writhing on the ground. She was shivering from the cold night air and her lips had a bluish tinge to them. It's not difficult to get hypothermia when you're practically naked and lying in the middle of a clearing at two in the morning.

"Mercy!" she cried.

I had shown her mercy. I hadn't let the others have her first.

"I'll do anything!"

I scowled at her. It was too late. "Soon you won't feel a thing."

Tara coughed and sputtered as I poured gasoline over her head. When I lit a match, she screamed and the sound echoed in the night.

With barely a backward glance, I headed to the nondescript gray sedan I had borrowed, lifted the trunk, pushed aside a small white bag and removed the blanket I'd used to wrap around Tara's unconscious body. I returned to the hellish mass that was once Tara and tossed the blood-soaked blanket into the fire. I watched it smolder and ignite.

After a minute or so, I returned to the car and climbed inside. Against my will, I peered into the rearview mirror. Behind me, several yards away, flames scratched at the air like hungry claws grasping for food.

Lighting a joint, I took a long drag. The deed was done.

I drove away, knowing I had made my point, one the others would clearly get. There was only one way out.

Jasi gasped as hands secured the Oxy-Mask over her head once more and her vision cleared. Blinking back tears, she said, "We've got him."

"Are you sure," Natassia asked, her sapphire eyes widening.

Jasi clenched her teeth and stared down at her hands. "I saw his hands. And I saw his vehicle and his eyes in the rearview mirror." She described everything she'd seen.

Ben handed her a folder containing an assortment of suspect photos. It took her seconds to find the killer, a beefy guy with thick arms and an oversized bald head.

"Him."

"Boris Lipinski?"

She nodded. "I saw his tattoo, a cobra, inside left wrist."

Lipinski was one of the head guys of the Black Cobras, a ruthless gang originally from Denmark that had set up camp in the Vancouver area. He'd been investigated multiple times for theft, illegal weapons and drugs. A few cold murder cases were thought to be his work, but no one had been able to gather enough evidence to prosecute him. Until now.

"He drove a gray Ford Fairmont, late '70s or early '80s," she said. "BC plates, but I didn't get the number. There will be trace evidence in the trunk. He was sloppy."

Natassia glanced up from the palm-sized, government-issued data-communicator and brushed aside jet-black bangs. "According to my data-com search, Lipinski doesn't own a car. I checked vehicle registrations Canada-wide."

"Look for one of his older relatives. Someone on heart medication. I saw a pharmacy bag in the trunk. I only caught the last name. Same as his. You'll find blood on the bag too, so tell forensics to check the relative's garbage if they don't find the bag in the relative's house."

"Got it!" Natassia said. "A 1979 Ford Fairmont is registered to a Regina Lipinski, age 83. Boris's mother. She underwent heart surgery a week ago."

"I'm positive this is the vehicle he used for all four body dumps. He would've had access to it while his mother was in the hospital. We've got him." Jasi threw Brandon a sad smile. "The four women that were lured into this gang will be avenged."

"You always said Boris was the enforcer," Brandon said.

She shrugged. "He had that look. Kind of like Schwarzenegger meets Stallone—on elephant steroids."

With the task at hand completed, she headed toward the SUV parked on a side road near the secured crime scene. She removed the Oxy-Mask and stowed it in a backpack along with two cans of OxyBlast. After gathering her smoke-infused hair into a ponytail, she withdrew a small photo of Tara Kincaid. The woman's mother had given it to her a week ago when Tara hadn't shown up for a planned family get-together. In the photo, Tara was smiling.

"This is how you'll be remembered," Jasi whispered.

She dreaded the visit she'd have to make later—the one where she got to tell a mother that her child was dead. There was no easy way to break that kind of news.

Brandon loomed over her. "Are you okay?"

"Yeah."

"You seem rather quiet."

"I was thinking about Tara's mom. Her life is going to change completely."

"It's going to be tough, but at least she'll have closure. She won't be wondering if her daughter is out there somewhere, in pain or alone."

She thought of Emily, the dead girl in her closet, and blinked back a tear. "I guess there's that. We found Tara." *But will I ever find Emily?*

Though she had shared many things with Brandon, she hadn't gathered the courage to tell him about her dreams. They were too horrific. And she couldn't admit to him that she'd seen a ghost while she'd been wide awake either. He was still getting accustomed to her psychic abilities.

"How often does it happen this fast?" he asked.

"Clear visions? Not often. I'm not sure why this case was an easy one, but I'm glad it was. You and I still have that date you promised. And don't think you're going to get out of that."

Brandon gave her a half grimace, half smile. "I can hardly wait."

"I'm not water-boarding you, so stop acting like you're being tortured."

"I was expecting a different kind of date. One with less—"

"What, culture? This is going to be the best date ever."

"If you say so," he mumbled.

She almost laughed out loud at his downtrodden face. They had been dating for just over a year now, ever since they'd been thrown together in an arson investigation. He'd annoyed the hell out of her when they'd first met, but he'd proven his loyalty to a fault. And although he didn't have a psychic talent, his expertise in arson investigation was advantageous, and her feelings for him had blossomed into something she'd never before experienced—something more than pheromones and physical attraction.

They didn't always see eye-to-eye on what constituted a "date." He'd dragged her to many a hockey game and monster truck event, and she suspected they may have permanently affected her hearing. Now it was her turn to plan a date. She'd eventually convinced him to see *Phantom of the Opera*. He'd even bought the tickets. For tonight. But when Matthew Divine had called them in to consult on a string of four brutal killings, she was pretty sure Brandon had been relieved.

She looked at her watch. "We have lots of time to get ready for Phantom."

"I don't know, Jasi. What about our reports?"

"Ben and I'll write them up," Natassia called out as she and Ben joined them. "What? Not my fault you two were talking so loudly that I could hear."

Jasi laughed. "I swear you'd hear a leaf fall in the woods from five miles away, Natassia."

"Seriously, I don't mind. You two go out and have fun. Ben and I will take care of the reports. After all, you did crack this case wide open with a single vision. Didn't even need me to read the victim. Not that I mind."

"Didn't need me either," Ben said, adjusting his black gloves to ensure his skin was fully covered.

Jasi knew what he was doing—preventing the chance of an unexpected vision. As a Psychometric Empath, he had visions when he touched an object or person. But the visions were symbolic and enigmatic, and translating them wasn't always easy.

"No," she said, "but you did get us closer to finding Lipinski. You were the one that picked up the gang connection on the second victim when you touched the necklace she'd been wearing."

Ben patted her shoulder. "I think we all agree that this win is really yours."

"We're PSIs. Credit goes to everyone on this team, not just me. Now, go write your reports."

She watched as he and Natassia drove off with a city detective.

She climbed into the passenger seat of the SUV. "Come on, Brandon. We have one stop to make. After that, we've got a date with the Phantom and some champagne."

He gave her a mocking salute. "Yes, ma'am."

Sitting on the sofa in Jasi's living room, Brandon raised his champagne glass. "To an evening of mystery…without serial killers or corpses."

"Amen to that." She clinked her glass against his. "Cheers to two days of downtime and a night out like a real couple."

His pale blue eyes twinkled with mischief. "We've still got about two hours until the show starts."

She arched a brow. "Any ideas on how we can fill the time?"

"A few. One involves a long, hot…" he grinned, "shower."

"That works for me. And we can discuss that…uh, *thing* I mentioned a few days ago."

He frowned. "What—oh, right. The living in sin idea."

She set her glass down and leaned in for a kiss. "If this is sin, I'll go to confession later." Her lips met his.

On the coffee table, her data-com rang.

"Ignore it," Brandon murmured against her mouth. His tongue traced her lips then swept inside, searching.

The ringing persisted.

"You changed the ring tone," he said.

"I thought the buzz was more irritating."

Ring-ring! Ring-ring!

She scowled. "I guess I was wrong."

The 'com went silent, the call directed to voicemail.

"There," she said. "Now where were we?"

"Getting ready for our shower. You have too many clothes on."

His tanned fingers moved to the button on her blouse. Bit by bit, he exposed more skin, leaving a trail of kisses from her neck down to the top of her breasts.

She moaned. Lifting his face, she traced the zigzag of the scar that crossed his right brow. She kissed it.

Her data-com rang again, but they both ignored it.

Brandon peeled the blouse away, unhooked her bra and flung it behind him. With her breasts free, he caressed them, teasing her nipples until they were hard.

Jasi grabbed the sides of his shirt. "Take this off." Her fingers couldn't move fast enough. When his chest was bared, she reached for the snap of his jeans.

They rose as one—mouths and limbs entwined.

Somehow they made it to the bathroom, where they quickly shed the last of their clothing. Naked, their bodies collided, their passion primal and urgent. It had been too long.

She reached for him.

"Jasi," Brandon said with a grimace.

"Am I hurting you?"

"No. I wish that were all it was. Your 'com is ringing again."

"I'm off duty. It's probably Natassia wanting to know if you've managed to worm your way out of going tonight. She'll figure out we're otherwise occupied."

The 'com began another round of ringing.

He playfully nipped at her bottom lip. "Whoever it is, sounds like they're going to keep calling until you pick up."

She groaned now. "Fine. I'll make it quick, especially if it's a telemarketer. Then we can get back to discussing your living arrangements."

She wrapped her robe around her and headed for the living room, thinking about her offer to Brandon. A few days ago, before they'd been called in on the gang case, she'd asked him to move in. It made sense. To her, at least. Her apartment was more secure and much larger, one of the perks of being in the CFBI. And it was closer to Divine Ops, making it an easier commute to work for both of them now that Brandon was a permanent addition to her PSI team.

But he seemed hesitant about the idea. She wasn't sure why. He practically lived there already anyway. What was the big deal? They always used her place for overnights—which had turned into most nights.

Maybe he doesn't want to commit.

She fumbled for her data-com and listened to her messages. There were three frantic messages, all from the same person. Cameron Prescott. Cameron was a television reporter for *CTBC News*, and she had a nasty habit of getting involved in some tight situations.

Jasi called her right away.

"I really need your help!" Cameron's voice was shaky, frightened. "My friend Sheral Downham is missing. She's a reporter for *The Vancouver Sun*, covers the Lifestyle section. She's involved in something…dangerous." She lowered her voice. "I can't talk about it on the phone."

"Where are you?"

"Parked across the street from your apartment building."

Brandon entered the room, dressed in the ratty white robe he'd brought over after their first overnight. As soon as he saw her serious expression, the sexy grin was wiped from his face. "Ah, damn…"

She gave him an apologetic look. "Come on up, Cameron. Brandon is here too."

2

When Cameron entered Jasi's loft apartment, she gave Brandon a brief nod and then sank into the sofa as though she hoped it would swallow her whole. Her face was pale, her blonde hair a tangled mess and the shadows under her eyes suggested she hadn't slept in days.

"Start from the beginning," Jasi said, handing her a glass of water. "And tell us everything."

Twisting the straps of her handbag, Cameron let out a slow breath. "Okay, I need you both to understand that I tried talking Sheral out of this. I knew it would be too dangerous, and she had no backup except me. But she told me she *had* to do it." She stared down at her purse and bit her lip.

Jasi sat down beside her. "Do what?"

"Go undercover."

"Where?"

"Sanctuary."

That one word, though spoken as a whisper, made Jasi shiver. Sanctuary was rumored to be a safe harbor for rapists and pedophiles. A cult for the damned, created by the damned.

"Sheral went in without any backup," Cameron said, her voice breaking.

"Shit."

Cameron sighed. "Yeah."

Brandon sat in the chair across from them. "Since I'm not originally from here, what's Sanctuary?"

"A cult," Jasi said. "It's located on an acreage just outside Mission, about an hour's drive from here."

"Religion based?"

"If you count Father Jeremiah's beliefs as religion."

"I think I've heard his name before."

"Father Jeremiah has been in the news before," Cameron said. "Most recently he was advocating rehabilitation for addicts, no matter their predilections."

"His real name is Giles Christiansen," Jasi added.

"Interesting last name for a religious zealot," Brandon said.

"I know. It's ironic. Christiansen has been suspected of having his hand in a number of criminal activities, but no one's found any concrete evidence against him."

"That's why Sheral went in," Cameron said. "Said she wanted to sink her teeth into a story that would give her a top priority byline, maybe even front page. Journalism is a tough industry, and if you don't get ahead of everyone else, you end up on page sixty—or worse."

"When did your friend infiltrate the cult?" Brandon asked.

Cameron let out a soft sob. "Twelve days ago."

"I know this is difficult," Jasi said, reaching for her hand, "but the more we know, the more we can help."

"Thank you."

Jasi took out her 'com. "Voice record on. I hope you don't mind, but we need to be thorough and do this right."

"We can't go public with this." Cameron stood up and paced the room. "None of what I'm telling you can be made public. Not yet. If Christiansen gets wind that she's there undercover, who knows what he'll do to her. Maybe her data-com died and that's why she hasn't contacted me."

"I don't think you really believe that. Otherwise, you wouldn't be here."

"I just don't want to do anything to make it worse for her."

"You won't. I'll get Matthew Divine to agree to a discreet investigation."

"How will you do that?"

"He owes me a favor. Don't worry. We'll find out where your friend is." *If she's still alive.*

She didn't reveal her thoughts, but one look at Brandon told her he was thinking the same thing. Chances were, so was Cameron.

"Why don't you sit back down and tell us what the plan was. Start from the beginning."

Cameron sat, her shoulders sagging as though she had the weight of the world on them. "Sheral's plan was to get inside Sanctuary, get to know some of the people there, gain their trust and come back with dirt on Christiansen."

"I take it she didn't use her real name?"

"No. Too many people read her column, Jasi. That would've been suicide."

"What name did she use?"

"Nancy Davison. It's her mother's first name and her sister's last name."

"What exactly was she expecting to find?"

"People." Cameron swallowed hard. "Sheral had been investigating a number of missing persons cases. Family members had called her at the paper, begging her to look into it. Over time, she noticed that many of the cases had a common connection."

"Let me guess. Sanctuary."

"At least a dozen people have gone missing after visiting Sanctuary. Sheral thought they might be imprisoned somewhere on the property. Or worse."

"When she reported in to you," Brandon said, "did she give you any idea if she'd found anything to substantiate this idea?"

"No, but she'd done her homework before going there. Whispers on the street suggested there was something more to these disappearances and that Christiansen was involved. It's like everyone *knows* it's true, but no one can prove it."

"Who did she report to and how did she communicate?" Jasi asked.

"Only me. She had a mini spy-com, one of those new models with the camera. She called me every other day at 1:00 PM like clockwork."

"Was this her regular 'com?"

"A burner. She didn't want it traced back to her if they found it." Cameron recited the phone number. "She managed to sneak the 'com in even though they're forbidden at Sanctuary. No phones, no computers, no TVs or radios."

"Christiansen doesn't want his *sheep* to have contact with the outside world."

"Exactly. Sheral strapped the spy-com to her thigh before they picked her up. I have no idea how she kept it concealed in the complex though. I never thought to ask her." Fear flickered across her face. "I've tried calling her a half dozen times, but there's no answer."

"When was the last time you heard from your friend?" Brandon asked.

"Five days ago."

"Perhaps something happened to her 'com," Jasi said. "Maybe she lost it."

"Or someone found it," Brandon added.

Cameron flinched. "That's what I'm afraid of. She told me they have strict rules at Sanctuary, and anyone who disobeys is punished."

"How?"

"Sheral didn't know exactly, and she was afraid to ask or draw attention to herself. But she did say there was a commotion a few days after she arrived. A woman named Jennifer Phillips—Jenny—bunked in Sheral's cabin. Apparently she broke one of Sanctuary's commandments, and that was the last anyone had seen of her. Father Jeremiah said she'd be in isolation for a few days, and if she didn't learn her lesson, she'd be exiled."

"Did you see Sheral the day they picked her up?" Brandon asked.

"No. I only know she was posing as a hooker. She'd been hanging around downtown, waiting for them to notice her. You know, in the red light district. Sanctuary has a white-panel van they use to pick up recruits. People call it 'the pedo-van.' I'm not sure who drives it."

"Christiansen, maybe?"

"No. A younger guy. I saw him once when Sheral was doing her research and I camped out in her car with her. When the van stopped to pick up a young girl, we saw a guy in a navy-blue suit get out."

"Describe him," Jasi said.

"Good-looking guy, maybe in his thirties. Shoulder-length, dirty-blond hair and a moustache and goatee. He kind of reminded me of Brad Pitt. When Sheral called me the first day, she said, 'You'll never guess. Pitt picked me up.' As if it were a great thing."

"But she didn't mention the guy's real name?"

"No. Anyway, Christiansen renames all of his flock when they're reborn."

Brandon lifted a brow. "Reborn?"

"Not the typical Christian rebirth as in accepting Jesus, blah, blah. Sanctuary has their own process. Members have to pass a trial period of fourteen days. 'To cleanse them of their sins and shed them of their former lives,' according to *Father Jeremiah*. Sheral was supposed to have her 'rebirth day' in three days. At that time, she'd be introduced to everyone at Sanctuary, and she'd be given a new name for her new life." Cameron's words dripped bitterness.

Jasi touched her arm. "We'll find her. I promise."

"Thank you. I didn't know what else to do. I couldn't go to the police because I don't want this to get back to Sanctuary."

"What exactly did Sheral tell you when she called you?" Brandon asked. "Did she uncover anything that would put her in danger?"

"She said she was housed in a cabin with two other girls who had been picked up the week before. One was Jenny, the woman I already told you about. She's an addict. The other was a fourteen-year-old runaway named Katie. Every day they're given chores to do, and at meal times they have to sit together, ostracized from the other members.

They're told not to talk to anyone except Father Jeremiah."

"Part of their trial," Jasi said. "To see if they can follow orders."

"The more docile they were, the more he'd ease up on the chores and invite them to their group rituals."

"Sounds like brainwashing to me," Brandon said. "A bunch of Kool-Aid drinkers."

"You can't really blame them," Cameron said. "Most of the people who end up at Sanctuary are outcasts in one way or another, separated from their family, living on the streets, addicted to drugs, alcohol or other things. Sanctuary poses as a safe haven for anyone who wants to change their life."

"What about Sheral?"

"What do you mean?"

Brandon's expression was doubtful. "Maybe she drank the Kool-Aid too."

"Sheral is happy with her life. She'd never willingly give up everything she has, and all that she's worked for, to live in a reclusive cult."

"Cults can be pretty persuasive," Jasi said. "Especially with a charismatic leader like Christiansen."

"She went in for a story, one that could *make* her career. She's a bulldog that way. She'd never allow anyone to brainwash her." Cameron stood. "Find her, Jasi. *Please.*"

"We'll do what we can."

"Thank you."

"One more thing," Jasi said.

"Yeah?"

"Do you have a photograph of Sheral?"

Cameron rummaged around in her purse. "Here. This was taken last month at Vortex." She looked over at Brandon. "It's a popular nightclub in North Van."

Jasi studied the photo. Sheral Downham was a beautiful young woman. Tall and slender, she had the presence of a consummate and confident professional, especially when dressed in a tailored gray skirt and jacket that accentuated her curves. Rich brunette hair draped down her neck to below her shoulder blades. In one hand she held a martini glass that contained a blue liquid that glowed, and around her wrist was an amethyst-studded bracelet in either silver or white gold.

"Sheral couldn't let this go," Cameron said, her chin quivering. "She said she had to know for sure what was going on at Sanctuary."

Jasi stared at the photo. *Let's hope you didn't find yourself a victim of curiosity.* "We'll check out Sanctuary tomorrow morning, Cameron.

We'll do it discreetly, in case Sheral is still there."

Cameron looked her in the eye. "I didn't tell you quite everything."

"Go on."

"About an hour ago, the RCMP was called out to Sanctuary to investigate a suspicious death. They found human bones inside an incinerator. One of my contacts in Mission called me right away because she owes me a few favors. She said the bones are from a female, about twenty-five to twenty-eight years old." Cameron took a deep breath. "I think it's Sheral."

As soon as Cameron left the loft, Jasi and Brandon headed to Divine Ops, a top-secret warehouse that accommodated the PSI division. Situated in Vancouver's West End, Divine Ops didn't look like much from the outside. Worn signage touted it as a condemned fish-packing plant, but inside was a different story.

After handing their weapons to the tech on duty, they keyed in their security access codes, passed through Voice Recognition and the Retinal Scanner, and a full body scanner that examined the tracking devices implanted in their navels. They followed a narrow corridor to Ops One, the primary operations station, and Jasi submitted to the routine paranormal electroencephalograph scan, while Brandon's body stats were scanned and recorded. Then they took the elevator down to the PSI floor.

"Every time I come here I feel like I've been stripped naked and made to walk a runway," Brandon whispered in her ear.

With a chuckle, she pushed him away. "You'll get used to this eventually. As Matthew keeps telling us, these precautions are designed to keep us safe."

When they reached the Command Office, Matthew Divine greeted them with a grim smile, his gray hair slicked back in his customary ponytail. "I wasn't expecting to send you out again so soon, Jasmine. You both deserve some downtime."

"The Cobras' case is now closed," she said, sitting down at the conference table. "We barely got our hands dirty with that one. Besides, I promised Cameron we'd help her. After all, she's helped us in the past."

Matthew's face shuffled through a range of emotions. "The CFBI has been after Giles Christiansen for years, but the man always manages to slip through our hands."

"Did you get our warrants?"

He handed her a manila folder. "A search warrant for the property and structures within the property of Sanctuary, warrants for individual evidence collection and a faux arrest warrant for prostitute Nancy Davison. I had to do a bit of convincing to get the paperwork in Sheral

Downham's fake name." He slipped off his ancient tortoise-shell glasses and wiped them on his shirt.

"I appreciate it, sir. Thank you."

"If this woman is at Sanctuary, and if she hasn't been found out, she's putting herself in a lot of danger. I want you to convince her to leave with you."

"Unless she's the victim in the incinerator," Brandon said, taking a chair across from Jasi.

Matthew slid his glasses over his ears and sat down at the head of the table. "Christiansen told RCMP officers it was an accident, that whoever died in there must have wandered inside and couldn't get out. He says the incinerator is only turned on once a week and everyone knows the schedule."

"What does the medical examiner say?" Jasi asked.

"That's the strangest thing. When the bones were collected, no one noticed at first."

"Noticed what?"

Matthew flicked a switch on a control box in front of him and two panels in the wall slid open, exposing a mammoth video-wall. He pulled up a photograph taken inside the incinerator. It showed an assortment of bones that had been set on top of a white cloth and pieced together like a jigsaw puzzle.

"See anything missing?" he asked.

"The skull," Jasi and Brandon said in unison.

Matthew diminished the photo. "There were no other remains found inside the incinerator."

Jasi winced. "Someone cut off her head?"

"With a very sharp weapon."

"Someone didn't want us to be able to identify the victim."

"Any defensive wounds found on her?" Brandon asked.

Matthew shook his head. "Not that the ME could tell. Of course this is only the preliminary report. We'll know more once the body has been transported to the morgue."

Jasi stood and paced in small circles. "So we're looking at a murder here."

"Most definitely."

"Has anyone left Sanctuary in the past week?"

"That's what you'll have to determine. Christiansen swears he doesn't keep track of who comes or goes."

"So this victim *could* be Sheral Downham."

"Yes, it could, Jasmine. Or it could be someone entirely different."

"Perhaps Sheral left Sanctuary and is laying low somewhere,"

Brandon offered.

Jasi stared at the photo on the screen. "As with Boris Lipinski and his Black Cobras gang, there's usually only one way out of a cult like Sanctuary. In a body bag."

3

Jasi decided they would take Brandon's SUV since Sanctuary was located off the main roads and deep into the woods. She sat in the passenger seat and reviewed the RCMP report, while Brandon navigated the early morning traffic on the Trans-Canada Highway. Rush hour in downtown Vancouver was horrendous and driving time sometimes doubled. They lurched along, ignoring the honks from impatient drivers, and she sucked in a breath every time Brandon slammed on the brakes.

Behind them, Natassia and Ben followed in an unassuming and slightly rusted white panel van with tinted windows and a worn city mosquito control sticker on both sides. A year ago, the van had been confiscated in a drug bust. When it was released from police impound, the CFBI picked it up, stripped the interior and designated it as a surveillance vehicle. It now housed a high-tech audio and video monitoring system, along with storage for weapons, bulletproof vests and other supplies.

An X-Disc Pro, a circular aerial drone complete with scanners, camera and other recording devices, was mounted to one wall alongside Jasi's Oxy-Mask. The X-Disc Pro was capable of flying or hovering hundreds of feet off the ground. Powered similarly to a military drone, it could scan not only the surface of the ground but what lay beneath it. It was all a matter of how it was programmed for the task of the day.

The plan was simple: Jasi and Brandon would enter Sanctuary as CFBI agents investigating the bones in the incinerator. If the remains turned out to be another victim, they would look for Sheral. If she was nowhere to be found, they'd show Christiansen valid search and arrest warrants for prostitute Nancy Davison, thanks to Matthew Divine.

Christiansen would have no choice but to lead them to the missing woman, and he could use any excuse he needed to explain her confinement.

Jasi thought about Cameron. They'd become friends during the same arson case in which she'd met Brandon. *Friends.* She didn't have many of those outside of the CFBI. Most women her age were intimidated by her CFBI agent status—and the fact that she carried a gun and knew how to use it. And she couldn't share the part about being a PSI agent who had psychic visions whenever she smelled smoke left by an arsonist's fire. No, casual friends were something other people had.

She glanced at Brandon. *I have him. He's a friend. And Natassia and Ben. And Cameron.*

Cameron knew about Jasi's gift, and she had accepted her, though she was skeptical at first, even after everything that had happened with Cameron's brother. Cameron could have left, stayed away, hated her forever, but she'd proven to be a loyal friend, and when Jasi had returned home after a lengthy stay in the hospital, Cameron was the first person to drop by, with chocolate and three bottles of Arbor Mist Peach Chardonnay—Jasi's favorite—in hand.

And now Cameron's friend was in danger.

What if the victim at Sanctuary is Sheral Downham?

If so, she'd have to break the news to Cameron as gently as possible.

Her data-com rang and she jumped, her thoughts immediately shifting to the various crime scene photos that were being displayed on the monitor. "The RCMP's X-Disc photos from Sanctuary are in."

She shuffled through the photos to the first picture. It was an aerial view of the Sanctuary complex, which consisted of a two-story log home, some outbuildings, about twenty small cabins in a field surrounded by thick woods, and a dirt road winding over the land and leading back to a paved road. More photos zoomed in on each of the cabins, catching the odd cult member out in the open. A close-up of a quaint two-story lodge revealed a man sitting on the front porch, his face staring up at the sky as though he knew he was being photographed. A smile spread across his face, one Jasi recognized instantly. *Giles Christiansen.*

The next photo showed a younger Christiansen. He'd been brought in on charges of drug distribution. He'd spent five months in jail and was let out on good behavior. That was almost seven years ago, when he'd found God—or whoever he worshipped. Shortly after, he'd set up Sanctuary. How he'd gotten the money for the land was anyone's guess, but no one had been able to prove he'd come by it illegally. And since he promised to provide refuge to the less desirables, no one put up much of a fight.

She enlarged the photo. The man was handsome, she'd give him that. She could see why people would be drawn to him. At the time the photo was taken, he'd been thirty-two, with wavy chestnut hair that grazed his shoulders, brilliant amber eyes that seemed to stare into her very soul and an easygoing smile that radiated caring and acceptance. She wondered how the past seven years had treated him. *And what are you hiding? Because I know you're hiding something.*

She flicked the screen to the next picture. The incinerator.

"Sanctuary has one of those new waste-to-energy incinerators," she told Brandon. "The kind that converts waste into usable energy, like electricity."

"Sounds expensive."

"They are. The city uses them, as well as many of the larger farms in the interior. I wonder how Christiansen came up with the money for one."

Next up on her screen were two dozen or so photos of the human remains inside the incinerator. The bones were deeply charred. Even more horrific, there was no head attached to the body. What had happened to the severed head?

She imagined a skull that had once held flesh and eyes. *What did you see?*

The following photos were outdoor shots surrounding the incinerator. Located at the end of one of the outbuildings at the far end of the field, the massive rectangular structure had two doors at one end about three feet from the ground and a smaller door at the other.

She scrolled through the next set of interior shots taken by the RCMP. "A person could definitely walk inside the incinerator. But there's a safety lever near the door. On the *inside*."

"So if she had been forced inside prior to her death, she could have escaped," Brandon said.

"Exactly. All she had to do was lift the lever and the system would have automatically shut down." She considered this for a moment. "So she was already dead when she was placed inside."

"Or unconscious."

"And now Sheral Downham is missing. She may have witnessed the murder. We have to find her, Brandon. Hopefully alive."

She gazed out the window and studied the street signs as the SUV passed through Coquitlam, Port Coquitlam and into Maple Ridge. It had been years since she'd driven this far east of the Greater Vancouver area. One of Pop's old cop buddies lived in a mobile home on the west side of Mission. When she and Brady were young, they used to visit him often—

before someone broke into their home and murdered her mother.

After that horrific event, everything changed. Except Jasi's bone-deep desire to find her mother's killer.

Don't think about that right now!

Her thoughts drifted from her mother to Emily, the dead girl who appeared in her dreams and sometimes her waking moments. After her experience in the woods so long ago, when Emily had shown her the way, there was no way Jasi could deny the ghost's existence. Like Sheral, Emily needed to be found.

What didn't make sense was why Emily had contacted Jasi. She wasn't the only psychic in town, and her gift had nothing to do with seeing or hearing ghosts. The thought of digging up a young girl's remains wasn't appealing either. And what about Emily's claims that someone was trying to hurt her? How could someone hurt a dead girl? Another ghost, perhaps? Most likely it was the remnant of a memory.

Jasi was haunted, not just by Emily but by the mystery that surrounded the girl. And by her promise to help find the girl. Every corpse deserved a decent burial. Jasi could at least do that much.

Tapping her 'com, she opened a folder marker 'Emily' and examined the notes. There weren't many. She'd spent hours combing through missing persons reports to ascertain the identity of Emily. Nothing. She'd need more clues, and only the dead girl in her closet could give her those.

Emily, where are you?

She hadn't seen her in weeks.

"You sleeping over there?" Brandon asked.

"I wish." Maybe then she'd get some answers.

Passing through Mission's east side, Jasi spotted the Mission Golf and Country Club. She never could understand why people got so hung up on the game of golf. As far as she was concerned, all it offered was a lot of walking around, chasing after a little ball.

Brandon slowed the car just before Fraser River Heritage Park and turned left onto Stave Lake Street. Sanctuary was north of their position and east of Allan Lake.

Ten minutes later, he turned off onto a dirt road. "Sanctuary should be about two miles down this road." He glanced at the clock on the display. "Took us just over ninety minutes."

Like the X-Disc photo, the road curved through the landscape, a serpentine path that took them deeper into an ominous, overgrown forest of cedar and spruce trees. At times the sun fizzled from view, leaving them shrouded in a shadowy cloak of oppressing woodland. Dust spit from the tires as they found traction in the worn ruts from vehicles gone by. An occasional branch swiped at the SUV, and Brandon cursed under his breath.

"The truck is insured," Jasi said.

"I know."

She stifled a laugh. He was such a guy, babying the SUV as though he, and not the CFBI, owned it.

The road narrowed until bushes scraped both sides of the SUV. They veered around a curve and lurched to a stop. They had arrived at Sanctuary.

Up ahead, a heavy, black wrought-iron gate indicated they'd reached their destination. The vertical bars were black with sharp spikes on top. An arched panel spread above the top of both sides with raised letters in gilded silver metal that spelled out *SANCTUARY*. The T was larger than the other letters and split in two, one half on each side of the gate doors.

Brandon stopped the vehicle. "What do we do now?"

"Matthew said he'd phone ahead to let Christiansen know we—" She broke off as the gate doors groaned and creaked open.

"We're being watched," Brandon said. "There's someone standing behind the brick post on the right."

"He must have opened the gate."

The man, dressed in mud-splattered coveralls and rubber boots, watched them with curiosity as they crawled past him.

She waved and forced a smile. "What I'd like to know is whether the gate is there to keep strangers out or to keep Father Jeremiah's flock from leaving."

In the distance, she could make out Christiansen's foreboding two-story lodge, as well as several smaller cabins and outbuildings of all shapes and sizes. The property sprawled over acres of ground, and part of the land had been planted with neat rows of fruits, vegetables and grains.

"Drive in slowly," she said. "I don't want any surprises."

Women in pale-colored, ankle-length dresses stepped onto their porches, their eyes darting nervously from the road to the field. The men there stopped all tasks and moved protectively toward their families. Older children wordlessly lined up along the road, their faces smudged with dirt. Toddlers gathered around their mothers' skirts, unusually quiet and well-behaved.

No one smiled. No one waved a hand in greeting or welcome.

As the SUV ambled down the road, the children shuffled behind the vehicle.

"Children of the corn," Brandon mumbled.

"Stop it. I'm already creeped out as it is. This place makes me nervous."

"I admit this isn't the greeting I was hoping for, but at least they're not coming at us with pitchforks."

"Wait for it. Normal, sane people don't join cults."

"Seriously, Jasi, not all of these people came to Sanctuary for illicit reasons. Some merely needed a place where they'd be accepted, fed and sheltered."

"I know you're right. We can't judge them all, at least not the innocent ones." But a murderer was hiding somewhere among these people. She was sure of it.

A giant of a man in his late thirties stepped out onto the porch of the lodge. Jasi recognized him immediately. Giles Christiansen. From the look of him, the past seven years had treated the man very well.

"Let's go meet Father Jeremiah," she said with a sigh of resolution.

They stepped from the vehicle and waited.

Watching Christiansen—AKA *Jeremiah*—cross the distance between them was like watching a lion carefully stalk its prey. The man moved languidly but with determination, circling around them. His deliberate movements sent a shudder down Jasi's spine, especially when his gaze caught hers.

"You must be from the CFBI," Christiansen proclaimed, his full lips stretching into a wide smile. "Welcome to Sanctuary, home of the homeless and friend to the friendless."

She flashed her badge. "Agent Jasmine McLellan and Special Consultant Brandon Walsh."

"Come, let me show you what Sanctuary has to offer…even for the disbelieving."

She flicked a look at Brandon and mouthed, *"Can't wait."*

"Let's go inside," Christiansen said. "It's going to rain."

She studied the cloudless sky. "So you're a prophet now?"

"No, Agent McLellan. I was listening to the radio when you arrived. There's a storm front coming in from the south."

"I was under the impression you didn't have technology here."

Christiansen's hand wavered on the doorknob. "I have a radio and cell phone for personal use. I like to stay informed of current events. And the phone is for emergencies."

"What about the other people living here?" she said as they entered the lodge. "Shouldn't they be informed too?"

"They prefer to live a simple life, Agent McLellan, and they trust that I'll alert them if they need to know more. Now, please…follow me."

Brandon gave her a warning look.

"What?" she said beneath her breath.

"Play nice. We want him to cooperate."

Christiansen led them to a cozy sitting room. It was furnished in warm beiges and chocolate brown, a definite man cave appearance— without a huge flat screen television or bar. Sculptures and paintings adorned the walls and shelves. A mammoth albino moose head was mounted on the wall above the fireplace.

"You hunt?" she asked, her fingers trailing across the cedar mantle.

"No."

"Albino moose are rare," Brandon said.

"It was a gift from a friend. He likes to hunt, and I like to collect the occasional rare item." Christiansen nudged his head in the direction of the sofa. "Please, have a seat. Would you care for a glass of ice tea?"

"We're good," Jasi said.

She remained standing, while Brandon took the chair opposite Christiansen.

"How many people live at Sanctuary?" she asked.

"About three dozen. But it changes every week."

"Because you're recruiting off the streets," she said, holding back a scowl.

Christiansen crossed his legs and leaned back. "I sense you're not a supporter of my methods, Agent McLellan."

"I don't know what your methods are exactly. Care to explain them?"

"As I told the RCMP this morning, we don't have anything to hide here. Everyone who joins us at Sanctuary comes here of their own free will. And they can leave whenever they choose, but most are truly happier here than anywhere else." He looked at Brandon. "They're searching for acceptance. And a home. They find both here."

She withdrew the search warrant from her jacket pocket and handed it to Christiansen. "I believe you have promised your full cooperation."

"Of course. I am shocked by what was found in our incinerator. I have no idea how that poor woman got in there."

"The search includes every building on your land," she said.

Christiansen stood. "Where would you like to start?"

"Here is fine," Brandon said. "We'd like to search your lodge first, then the incinerator. Then we'll move on to the other cabins and outbuildings."

"I will be happy to personally escort you around, Agent Walsh."

"Special Consultant, actually."

"Right. My apologies." He skimmed a look over Jasi. "I must say, I was surprised when the CFBI notified me of your interest in this tragedy. I thought you handled the more serious cases—serial killers, terrorism and such—and left simple accidents to the police or RCMP."

"We haven't yet confirmed this was a simple accident," she said. "After all, a woman was beheaded."

"Trust me, none of my family here would harm another intentionally. I suspect someone planted that body to implicate us. Not everyone supports our vision. We aim for a peaceful life, without the conflicts and inundation of modern society."

"Yet you have a headless corpse in your incinerator."

"You're very abrupt, Agent McLellan. Feel free to search my home. Please knock on any closed door. And do be respectful. My wives are nervous about your presence."

"Wives?"

"Yes, I have four wives. We believe no man should be limited in love. It's not in our nature for humans to be monogamous. So here at Sanctuary we have many unions, which I personally conduct. And before you ask, I am licensed to perform marriages. Of course, our government won't recognize my multiple marriages as legal."

"How many people have you married?"

"Other than my own, I have married eight other couples. All consenting adults. All legal."

She made a mental note to check into his credentials.

"Polygamy is still illegal in Canada," she said. "You're breaking the law."

Christiansen raised his chin in defiance. "No law has the right to judge our unions of the heart. We are the navigators of our own destinies."

"We'd like to navigate the rooms in your house now." She shot him a saccharine smile. "We'll be gentle with your *wives*."

"I would expect nothing less."

Christiansen took a step toward the hall, but she grabbed his arm. "Stay here. We may have questions for you after."

With an annoyed huff, he settled into a plush armchair. "Fine."

When Jasi and Brandon were nearly out of earshot, Christiansen called out, "Search away. I guarantee you'll find nothing out of the ordinary here."

4

Sanctuary, outside Mission, BC

As they searched the ground floor, Brandon couldn't help but admire the handiwork of the building's construction. Each log that made up the exterior was hand-hewn, bolted and mudded between to insulate the house. Much of the artwork was artisan created and handmade, from fabric wall hangings to oil paintings to carvings in wood, copper and stone. Rich ambers, bronze and gold adorned every wall, and when the sun streamed through a window, it created a lavish atmosphere, which conflicted with such humble ornamentations.

"Expensive décor," Jasi commented.

"Most likely financed by his investors."

"Father Jeremiah has *investors*?"

"Some very wealthy ones. A couple of CEOs, a few politicians."

He had spent some time the night before investigating Sanctuary's financials. Giles Christiansen had managed to acquire some hefty contributions from some of Canada's wealthiest CEOs, including Marco Bernardi, owner of Bernardi Cable. Bernardi was somewhat of a recluse, though paparazzi had recently hunted him on his travels through France.

"I guess supporting a cult posing as a rehabilitation center like Sanctuary looks good on a resume or portfolio," Jasi said.

They inspected every room on the lower level, but found nothing out of place.

Jasi shot him a look of disappointment. "This kitchen is spotless. You could eat off the floors, it's so clean."

He flashed a grin. "Something to be said for having four wives." She elbowed him and he grunted. "Lucky for me, I only have my eye on one."

The look in Jasi's emerald eyes was priceless. Part shock, part horror.

"We're talking about you moving in with me," she said. "Living in sin and all that. Who said anything about marriage?"

He shrugged, knowing he'd hit a nerve. "Relax. It was a joke."

But it wasn't. Not really. The more he was with Jasi, the more he realized he never wanted to be without her. He loved her beyond all logical reason, even when she sometimes exasperated him.

"Let's go meet the wives," she said, charging up the stairs.

"Maybe I should ask the questions."

Pausing, Jasi swiveled on one heel. "What, you don't think I can handle questioning a bunch of women?"

"I think you're pissed off about Christiansen and his way of life, and that might color your questions. If his wives feel you disagree or are judging them, they may not open up."

She lifted her chin. "So you're the wife whisperer now."

"Jasi, for once, please let me do the talking."

She murmured something indecipherable, and he took that as agreement. He should've known better.

At the top the stairs, the hallway veered off to the left and right, wrapping along both sides of the stairs and framed by cedar posts and handrails. Four doors on the left and four on the right, with a set of French doors adjacent to the top of the stairs.

"Master bedroom," Brandon guessed, indicating the French doors.

"Let's do that room last."

"Okay. Shall we start on the left then? Last door and work our way back?"

"Sounds good to me."

The first room they entered was empty except for sparse furnishings—a bed, chair, nightstand and dresser. The bed was unmade. There were no clothes in the closet, not one thing to indicate anyone was staying in that bedroom.

"Must be waiting for his next victim," Jasi said. "I mean, wife."

"The drawers are empty. Nothing here."

The next two rooms were also unoccupied. Both had the same standard furniture, as well as handmade oak cribs.

"Christiansen has a fixation on having more children," Jasi said.

"Most men in his position do. Children mean more followers. More followers mean more power. Especially over the women."

"It's just sick."

"I'm pretty sure Christiansen wouldn't have brought Sheral Downham into his home. She was new, and we know she was assigned a cabin with two other women."

"Unless he had his sights on her being his new baby mama."

"We won't find her here, Jasi."

"I know. I was hoping this would be easy, but I understand it won't be. If he has her here, *if* she's still alive, he'll have hidden her from us. Just keep your eyes open. Sheral could have been in the house at some point."

He reached out and brushed a strand of hair from her eyes. "We'll find her one way or the other."

"Unless the RCMP previously did and those are her remains."

The final room on that side of the house was a massive bathroom with five stalls, a wall of showers and two vintage porcelain clawfoot bathtubs. They did a quick check but found no sign of Sheral Downham. Like the kitchen, the bathroom was spotless.

"Not even hair in the shower drain," Jasi said. "And the RCMP already dusted the entire place for fingerprints."

"Someone must have cleaned up afterward."

They veered down the opposite hallway. A sign on the door at the end of the hall read: *Rachel.*

Brandon knocked. "Rachel Christiansen?"

"Yes?" a soft voice answered.

"We're with the CFBI. We need to talk to you."

"You may come in."

Brandon opened the door and blinked. The room was decorated in pink tones, some bright and some muted. Stuffed animals lined a white bookshelf. Drawings of horses and butterflies were tacked to the walls. *A kid's room?*

"How may I help you?" the blonde woman in the rocking chair asked without getting up. She was petite, fragile looking with pale skin and big brown eyes. And she was very pregnant.

"You're Jeremiah's wife?" Jasi asked.

"I know I look like I'm not even sixteen, but I can assure you I am twenty." Rachel rose carefully, as though she were afraid her bones would break. "Would you like to see my birth certificate?"

"No, ma'am," Brandon said. "That won't be necessary."

Rachel sat back down slowly, her dress draping in layers over her rounded stomach. "I understand you're asking our family members about the bones found in the incinerator."

"Do you have any idea who they could belong to?" Brandon asked.

"No."

"Where do these doors lead?" Jasi indicated the double doors on one side of the room.

"My children's room. Jacob and Oliver are in the field working with the men, and my youngest, Samuel, is napping."

"May I?" Jasi asked.

Rachel hitched in a breath. "Please don't wake him. He's had colic."

"We'll be very quiet," Brandon promised.

He followed Jasi into the adjoining room, taking in the crib with sheer lace draped over it and the bunk beds in the opposite corner. The room was the exact opposite of Rachel's room, all blue tones.

"The favored child bride?" Jasi said.

"What do you mean?"

"She's given Christiansen three sons and she's only twenty. If two are helping in the field, they must be at least five or six. Do the math."

"Nothing we can do about it now that she's of legal age."

"Something should have been done earlier. These women are being exploited."

They peeked inside the closet and found only toys and bedding.

"There's zilch here, Jasi. Let's move on."

As they moved toward the door, he saw Jasi take a step toward the crib and part the netting. She leaned down, her hand drifting inside the crib, caressing the child nestled within. It was a simple maternal gesture that twisted his insides. For all of Jasi's tough exterior, she had a soft heart.

Back in Rachel's room, he said, "We appreciate your cooperation, ma'am."

"We have nothing to hide here." The woman stood again, this time placing both hands on her stomach. "Excuse me, please. This one is more active than the others so I can't sit for long spells."

"When are you due?" Jasi asked.

For the first time, Rachel smiled. "Any day now. God has looked upon me favorably and blessed me. I am a fortunate woman."

Jasi opened her mouth to say something, but Brandon nudged her. With an awkward nod, he steered her from the room, praying she'd stay quiet.

"Why did you do that?" she demanded in the hall.

"I didn't want you to say anything to upset her. She doesn't know anything."

"How can you be so sure?"

"Rachel isn't a healthy woman. Didn't you notice?"

"I was too busy taking in all that blinding pink. I was half expecting Barbie and her friends to join us."

"Rachel Christiansen is ill, Jasi."

"That makes it a high risk pregnancy."

"And that means..." He waited.

"She's restricted to her room for the duration of her pregnancy. And if she's been there for any length of time, she probably doesn't know much."

He knocked on the next door labeled *Hannah.* The dark-haired, slightly plump woman who opened the door appeared to be in her late-thirties. With one hand, she pushed black-framed eyeglasses along the ridge of her nose and held the side of the door with the other.

"Hannah," he began, "we're with the CFBI—"

"I know who you are," the woman snapped. "It's bad enough that those RCMP officers were here since dawn, traipsing through our homes and fields, scaring our kids, and now they have to bring in you hotshots." Hannah swiveled on one heel and stomped to the window that overlooked the front of the house. "Do whatever you gotta do and be done with it. We're not hiding anything."

While Jasi poked around the woman's blandly decorated room and peered inside the closet, Brandon pointed to a beige armchair by the window. "Mind if I sit?"

Without looking at him, Hannah shrugged. "You're gonna do what you wanna do."

"Have you been here a while?"

"Since I was twenty-one. Seven years."

Brandon did a quick recalculation. Hannah was only twenty-eight, but her haggard face showed far more years on it. Before she had crossed her arms, he'd noticed the faint pinpoint scars. Hannah Christiansen was a drug addict.

Her gaze clashed with his, and her lips stretched into either a grimace or a smile. He couldn't tell which.

"Jeremiah rescued me from a life of crack houses and whoring."

The way she said it, he figured she was trying to shock him, but he kept his face blank.

"Brought me to Sanctuary and gave me back my life. Made me whole again."

"Sounds like a real hero," Jasi said.

"He is." The woman gave Jasi the once-over and sneered. "Honey, you could use a man like him in your life. He'd make you see the error of your ways, rid you of your attitude."

"What do you know about the woman found in the incinerator?" Brandon said, changing the subject.

Hannah tipped her head to one side, her eyes narrowing. "How do you know it was a woman?"

"Forensics. The coroner has already examined the remains and sent us her initial report."

"I only know what my husband told me. Someone got stuck in the 'cinerator and they got burned. Grace, one of my sister wives, found the body. She's still shook up about it, but I told her what's done is done. You can't bring back the dead."

"Yeah, shit happens," Jasi mumbled.

"Don't I know it," Hannah said. "Fas as I know, all our family is here 'cept those who left on their own."

"How does that work exactly?" he asked.

"What, leaving? They pick up their feet and walk through the gate. Just like *everyone* who doesn't belong does…eventually."

Brandon took the hint, stood and made for the door. "Thank you for your cooperation."

"We just want y'all gone so we can get back to our lives." Hannah reached into a drawer near her bed and retrieved a joint. She lit up and inhaled deeply. "Medical marijuana. I've got a prescription."

Pausing in the doorway, he indicated the single bed on the other side of the room. "Who sleeps there?"

"My daughter, Amanda."

"How old is she?"

"Thirteen next week. And in case you're gonna ask, she ain't Jeremiah's. But he accepted her like she was his. Just like he accepts us all."

"Where is Amanda now?"

"She's doing laundry, down by the creek. You wanna talk to her too? She's just a kid. She doesn't know nothing. But you go right ahead and talk to her if you have to."

"You have no children with Jeremiah?" he asked.

Hannah clenched her jaw, her eyes locking on his. "I had four miscarriages. But my husband is forgiving and says we're gonna try again. I'm a very fortunate woman."

"Thank you for your time," Jasi cut in.

The door closed firmly behind them and Brandon let out a sigh. "We're not getting anywhere with the wives."

"Two more to go."

The third wife, Beth, was just a girl. She let them into her room without hesitation. Her smile was broad, as though it had been a long time since she'd seen anyone outside of the complex.

"Sit," she said, pointing to three chairs by the window. "Can I get you some ice tea? I have a fresh pitcher. I was just teaching Jebediah his ABCs."

Beth's toddler sat in one corner of the room, a bunch of flashcards set out before him on the floor.

"Thank you," Jasi said, accepting a glass of tea.

Brandon passed on the refreshment and focused on the girl. Though seemingly cheerful, her hands were shaking. Blonde, blue-eyed and quite pretty, Beth chewed on her bottom lip.

His eyes narrowed. *Why is she so damned nervous?*

"When did you come to Sanctuary?" he asked.

"Just over three years ago."

"How old were you?"

"Sixteen," came the quick reply.

Brandon did the math. She certainly didn't look nineteen. Then again, his age meter had proved defective with the first two wives because he hadn't been right about their ages either.

"And Jebediah?"

Beth beamed. "Jeremiah's son."

The boy played quietly in the corner, occasionally glancing up at them. His jet-black hair and green eyes seemed out of place against his mother's pale beauty and his father's brown hair and amber eyes. Beth might be passing Jebediah off as Jeremiah's son but Brandon had his doubts.

"Jeb and I sit here with Jeremiah almost every evening," Beth said, her smile fading. "Isn't it amazing how God has blessed us on this land?"

Brandon stared out the window for a moment. The view of the fields and forest was spectacular, with rocky hills in the distance. "Beth, did you see anything suspicious last night. Anything at all out of place?"

"No." She glanced at her son. "I went to bed early last night. Jeb was a handful yesterday. He wore me right out."

"So you saw and heard nothing strange?"

"That's correct."

"Do you have any idea who died in the incinerator?"

Beth shook her head. "I don't."

"Did you see all the women this morning at breakfast?"

"I didn't go down this morning. I…wasn't feeling well." She placed a hand over her flat stomach.

"Stomach flu?"

"She's pregnant," Jasi whispered in his ear.

"Shh!" Beth said. "I haven't told my husband yet."

Brandon felt a twinge of irritation. Christiansen was repopulating the earth at an alarming rate. And this poor girl had been suckered in yet again.

"There's zip here," Jasi said quietly.

"I'm sorry I couldn't help you," the girl said.

"Thank you for answering our questions," he replied. "And congrats on the new baby."

"Thank you. I am a very fortunate woman."

Out in the hallway, Brandon said, "I know you're pissed at this Christiansen character and everything he stands for, but you need to tone it down, Jasi. We need these people to trust us."

"I know. But something about this place has my skin crawling. And I can't figure out why exactly."

"See no evil, hear no evil, speak no evil."

"Exactly. And they all seem to be living up to that motto quite well."

The last door on that side of the house led to the bedroom of Grace. She looked even younger than Beth. The girl had luxurious black hair swept up into a high ponytail. She was petite but healthy looking, with traces of native heritage in her brown eyes and high cheekbones. The dress she wore was a shimmering mauve concoction, and the high empire waistband accentuated her pregnant belly.

"My husband is thrilled to be a father again," Grace said, stroking her stomach as she rocked in a chair by the window.

"How far along are you?" Brandon asked.

"Almost six months."

"How long have you been married?"

Grace hesitated. "Five months. Jeremiah rescued me from a life of abuse and brought me here about a year ago. He is very good to me, especially since I am the new wife. And my sister wives all treat me with respect. Especially now." She looked down at her belly. "God has blessed me. I am a—"

"Don't say it," Jasi interrupted, holding a hand up. "You're a very fortunate woman."

Grace lifted a brow in surprise. "Yes. How did you know?"

"Just a lucky guess. You were the one who found the body?"

The woman shivered. "It's something I'll never forget. I woke up early and decided to clean out the incinerator—it's my weekly chore—and when I opened the door, I couldn't believe what I saw." She swallowed. "I can't get the image out of my head."

"Did you see anything suspicious last night?" Brandon asked. "Anyone hanging around the incinerator that shouldn't be?"

Grace shook her head.

"Is anyone you know missing from Sanctuary?"

"No, sir. I can't say for sure who is here today and who isn't. Sometimes a group of us go on excursions into the city. Occasionally we stay overnight. And we often have new members who don't stay here long. It can be hard to keep track of the newcomers."

"So you have no idea whose remains are in the incinerator?"

A slight pause. "None."

Brandon eyed her for a long moment. Pressing Grace now would only alienate her, but clearly she had something on her mind. "Thank you. You've been very helpful."

"Have I?" Grace smiled. "I'm glad to help."

He glanced at Jasi. "We're done here."

They left Grace's room with no more than they'd had when they'd gone in. He was disappointed. From the look of things, no one at Sanctuary was going to admit they'd seen or heard anything.

"Okay, on to Christiansen's room," Jasi said.

"I think we'll find the same thing in here. Absolutely nothing."

Giles Christiansen's bedroom suite consisted of three rooms—a separate sitting area with a wall of bookshelves and two large plush armchairs by the fireplace, the bedroom with a regal, king-sized canopy bed framed by rich amber chiffon drapes, and a skylight-lit en suite bathroom with a Jacuzzi tub and an oversized steam shower with showerheads at both ends.

"I'll take the sitting room," he said. "What about you?"

"Bathroom." Jasi proceeded into the en suite.

He wandered over to the bookshelf and skimmed the spines of the hardcover titles that packed each row. He wouldn't have taken Christiansen for a well-educated man, but based on the reading material on his shelves, the guy had an inquisitive mind and weird taste in literature. Amidst thrillers by Christopher Rice, Jonas Saul, and a variety of other names he recognized, he discovered a number of non-fiction works by popular self-help gurus, including Van Harvard's latest, *Wealth & Health: It's Your Choice!*

When Jasi reentered the room, they searched the bedroom together, peeked in his closet and under the bed.

"Nothing," she said with a sigh.

No sign of Sheral Downham. Nothing unusual or out of place.

Yet something irked Brandon. He just couldn't put his finger on it.

"Incinerator time," Jasi said, interrupting his thoughts.

"I'll be with you every second."

Brandon was still uncomfortable with her gift, and the fact that the scent of smoke could trigger a psychic vision sent alarm bells off daily in his head. When she assured him that this only happened when a fire was set by a killer, he had relaxed. Just a bit.

But it didn't stop him from worrying about her.

5

With trepidation, Jasi made her way toward the incinerator. Encompassed by a tall fence, it stood a few yards away from a metal-sheeted outbuilding, just as she'd seen in the photos. It was much larger than she'd expected, a commercial grade waste disposal unit that could handle the needs of a small community even larger than Sanctuary's.

Kind of overkill?

Her Oxy-Mask was in place, filtering the air around her. She kept her breathing slow and steady.

"Ready?" Brandon asked. He stood a couple of feet away, his handsome face lined with worry. Beside him stood Christiansen, who seemed to have no care in the world.

"Ready." She looked at Christiansen. "How does this thing work?"

"Waste can be shoveled or dropped in through the double doors. After that, it moves through the chamber by reciprocating grates."

"Then what?"

"The resulting ash drops down onto the conveyor belt and is dumped into the storage chamber at the end where it can be scooped out and used as compost for our gardens."

"Is that safe?" Brandon asked. "What about gases from material being burned?"

"This baby is designed to burn off all waste gases, and the subsequent energy produced from the process is converted and stored." He pointed to the outbuilding. "That barn houses our main generator. It stores the energy converted, which is then used to run most of our electrical system. Sanctuary is as green as it gets. Fresh well water, no chemicals added. Green energy. No pesticides on our fields. We grow all our own vegetables and fruits. We have chickens in another barn."

"Sounds like heaven," Jasi said, not even attempting to hide her sarcasm. "Thank you for the sales pitch, but it's time you step back now."

With a polite smile, Christiansen gave a nod and walked over to the two RCMP officers who had been assigned to guard the incinerator until the CFBI arrived.

She peered over her shoulder. "Okay, Brandon, it's shake 'n bake time."

Behind her, she heard Christiansen say, "Why is she wearing that mask? I just explained there are no gases remaining inside."

She didn't wait to hear Brandon's explanation. She took two deep breaths, stepped inside the incinerator and pulled the doors half closed, partly for privacy but also because she didn't want to be left in total darkness.

"Brandon, can you hear me?"

"Yes." His voice came from the earpiece she'd activated.

Seconds later, she emerged from the incinerator. "We have a problem, Brandon."

"What's wrong?"

"Someone's moved the remains."

"What?"

"The bones are gone." Her voice was muffled by the mask.

Brandon scowled at Christiansen. "Where are they?"

Christiansen shrugged. "Apparently there was some kind of miscommunication between the local RCMP detachment and the CFBI. The body was transported to the morgue in Vancouver an hour ago."

Brandon pulled Jasi aside. "You can still get a read in there without the remains, right?"

"I should be able to. Remember, it's the smoke that triggers my gift, not a body. But Natassia will have to go back to the city to read the victim." She clenched her jaw. "Shit. She's not going to be happy about that."

Jasi strode back inside the incinerator, once again half-closing the doors behind her. "I'm taking off the mask, Brandon."

"Be safe."

"Stop worrying. I've done this a hundred times." Actually, it was closer to two hundred, but he didn't need to know that.

"Voice record on," she said, activating a recording feature on her data-com that would capture anything she said while under.

She removed the Oxy-Mask and slowly released her breath. Next, she breathed in a long shot of OxyBlast. Then she exhaled and breathed the incinerator air. It had a faint smoky odor. *In...out...in...*

The killer's mind collided with hers, a force that sucked her in, causing her to stumble against the steel wall. Suddenly she could see everything through someone else's eyes. In essence, she *became* the killer.

She was running through the woods. Was she being chased? No. She was pursuing someone. A shadow up ahead darted between the trees. She ran faster, her heart racing as rage filled her heart.

I have to catch her! She's going to ruin everything!

"You can't escape!" I screamed. "And when I find you, you will wish to God you had never come here."

Where did she go? I can't see her anywhere. Shit!

I tripped over a tree root and my glove scraped against the trunk as I grappled for support. Righting myself, I scoured the forest. I raised my rifle and peered through the night scope. Ah, there she is.

"There's nowhere to hide!" I yelled.

I chuckled. The bitch has only made things worse. First, her sneaking around. Then her interference. She had to be stopped. And I would make her pay dearly for her transgressions.

I veered off to the left where the ground flattened ahead of me. Perhaps I could cut her off before she reached the road. If I didn't make it in time, then maybe the bitch would be mowed down by a car.

As I pushed myself ahead, I was sure I'd beaten her. I paused and listened.

Nothing.

Where is she?

I heard crackling sounds. Behind me.

Shit! She's heading back to Sanctuary.

Knowing I couldn't let her seek shelter there with the others, I set off once again, following the sounds of a desperate, injured twit who had to stick her nose where it didn't belong.

My throat burned with each breath as I pressed on. Up ahead I heard a sharp crackling of brush, a soft thud and a muffled whimper. I smiled. Had my luck finally changed?

I moved with precision. I'd been here a thousand times before. I leapt over a fallen tree in my path, paused and listened. To my left, I heard another soft cry. She was hiding behind a thick-trunked cedar, about five yards away. I approached as quietly as possible.

I whipped around the tree and came face to face with my prey.

"No," she cried.

She slumped against the tree, quivering in fear, her face veiled by shadows, her hand pressed against her side while blood seeped between her fingers and coated a bracelet on her wrist.

The first shot hadn't killed her, lucky for me.

"Hope is lost," I said. "Nothing can save you now."

"Please..."

"The hunt is over. I win, you lose."

I raised my rifle and aimed it at her. The night exhaled the shot like a sudden, hot breath.

Then all was calm.

Lifting my prize over my shoulder, I glimpsed the lights from Sanctuary between the trees. I knew the perfect place to eliminate the body.

Jasi opened her eyes. It took a few seconds for her surroundings to register. She was inside the incinerator, but in her mind she could still see the forest and the woman. As the remnants of emotions from her vision faded, she slipped the Oxy-Mask back over her head and cleared her throat. "I'm out, Brandon. Did you get everything?"

"Heard you perfectly."

"Give me another minute or two, then I'll be out."

She rested against the wall and released a tired breath. Though she hadn't seen Sheral's face in the vision, she'd recognized the bracelet from the photo.

How am I going to tell Cameron that her friend is dead—murdered?

Brandon poked his head inside. "Everything okay?"

She nodded, not trusting her voice. When he held the door open for her, she climbed out.

Christiansen rushed toward her. "Is something wrong, Agent McLellan?"

"You mean other than someone dying in your incinerator?"

"Perhaps you need to sit down and—"

"What I need, Mr. Christiansen, is the truth."

He flinched at the mention of his name. "Please respect that here at Sanctuary, I am simply Jeremiah. I have been completely honest with you. I do not know who died last night."

"Please escort *Jeremiah* back to his residence," she said to the officers.

She watched them walk away, her heart full of dread.

"I think it's Sheral Downham," she said to Brandon minutes later.

"Are you positive?"

"I didn't see her face, but the woman in my vision wore an amethyst bracelet."

"Any sense of whether we're dealing with a male or female suspect?"

She shook her head. "It was dark, and I didn't see much in the way of clothing. And he or she wore gloves, so it could be either."

"Think it's time to show Sheral's picture?"

"Not yet. I want as much cooperation as possible from the people here. Right now they think we're only here about the remains in the incinerator. They want this wrapped up as quickly as possible. Besides, we still don't have a suspect, and I don't want anyone else disappearing from Sanctuary."

"Whoever did this may already be gone."

"I know. If that's the case, someone here will know something. We have to be patient." She stared up at him. "I have a feeling this case is going to take longer than the Cobras case."

Above them, the skies darkened.

"Christiansen was right," Brandon said. "It's going to rain. Let's head back to the house."

Her 'com rang.

"Damn. It's Cameron."

"What are you going to tell her?"

Jasi swallowed hard. "The only thing I can. The truth."

6

Ben removed his gloves and adjusted the sound on the recording equipment. He'd spent the last hour cleaning up the feed from Jasi's data-com record for the latest report. They'd already listened to it twice, but something was off. Hell, the entire investigation had turned into a farce.

"I still can't believe someone screwed up and let the coroner leave with our evidence," he muttered. "Matthew says it was a jurisdictional error."

Natassia let out a huff. "Jurisdictional error, my ass. I bet that nut job Christiansen had something to do with it."

Ben caught her gaze. "Why do you say that?"

"Because I don't like him."

"You haven't even met the man."

"I don't need to. There's something very weird about a man who spends all his energy *rescuing* other people and then living with them."

"So you think he has a God complex."

"Don't you?"

"I don't know. Ask me that in a few days."

Natassia looked at her watch. "My ride should be here soon."

Matthew had made arrangements for a rookie Mission-based agent to pick her up and drive her back to the city morgue.

"You sure you're okay with me leaving you here with no backup, Ben?"

"Things are quiet. I don't anticipate much happening in the next few hours. And I've got Jasi and Brandon. Plus Matthew promised a full support team, if we need one."

"What if there's not enough left of the body for me to make a connection? What if I can't conclusively ID her?"

He scooted the chair closer to her, slipped his gloves back on and took her hands. "It's not always about identifying the victim, Natassia.

You could see something important. Something that'll lead us to the bastard who killed her."

"I hope so."

A car horn beeped outside the van.

"Your ride's here," he said.

"Jeez, now you sound like you're trying to get rid of me."

He leaned over and kissed her cheek. "The sooner you leave, the sooner you get back. Oh, and can you bring me some Timbits and fill up the coffee thermos?"

She chuckled. "So I'm the coffee bitch now, am I?"

"We'll need to stay awake tonight." When he saw the twinkle in her eye, he added, "We'll be *working*, so don't go getting any ideas."

"Some days you're just no fun, Benjamin Roberts."

He followed Natassia outside and watched as a CFBI-issued SUV meandered toward them at the pace of longstanding ketchup in a bottle. The vehicle eventually stopped, and a copper-haired young man climbed out.

"You're the driver?" Ben said, taken aback.

"Yes, sir."

Ben shouldn't have expected Matthew to send anyone other than a kid for driver duty, but still.

Freckles danced across the young man's red cheeks. "I'm here for an Agent Prushenko."

Natassia sauntered forward. "That would be me."

Ben would have laughed out loud at the stunned expression on the kid's face if Natassia hadn't whipped around and said, "Not one word." She fastened her gaze back on the young agent. "What's your name?"

"Uh…A-agent Jason Anthony."

"I'll just call you Jay?"

"Uh…well, really my…" The kid's voice trailed off, his face lost in a frown.

"Come on, Jay."

Ben stifled a chuckle when Natassia reached for the driver's door at the same time as her new driver.

"I, um…I…sorry," Agent Anthony stammered.

Natassia cocked her head. "Listen, Jay, no offense but you look like you're still in high school. I'm driving. We'll get there faster. Trust me."

Without a word, Agent Anthony walked around the vehicle and climbed in beside her. Even his freckles had paled. As they sped away from Sanctuary, he gripped the door for support.

Ben had mixed feelings as he watched them leave. He had a feeling that by the time Natassia was through with her escort, the young driver would be smitten. She had a way about her. She exuded sexual chemistry everywhere she went, and underneath that hardened exterior was a woman with a soft heart. He knew her well.

"Ben?" Jasi's voice came through the speaker.

"I'm here."

"We came up empty in the lodge."

"Did you speak to the wives?"

"Yeah, no one knows anything and Father Jeremiah is a God among men." Jasi's sarcasm came across loud and clear.

"You going to use the warrant?"

"Not yet. So far, people are cooperating. Once we pull that warrant, they could close ranks. Even if Sheral Downham wasn't a full-fledged member, these kinds of cults are very protective of their own."

"I agree. Keep pushing the murder investigation angle. Someone has to know something."

"All we need is to gain their trust so they'll talk."

"Seems Christiansen has no problem in that department. We've got enough sound bites on him to put together an audiobook."

"Yeah, he's arrogant and ambitious, to say the least. He loves the power of being the leader here. He tries to hide it beneath all his piousness and self-sacrifice, but the control-freak angle resonates from him loud and clear." Jasi paused. "Wonder what else he's hiding."

Ben adjusted the microphone attached to his earpiece. "I have a feeling we're going to unearth plenty of secrets at Sanctuary. And we may not like what we find."

Jasi sighed. "As long as we find out what happened to Sheral Downham."

"You still think the remains are hers?"

"I don't know. Seems like it. The same age and size. And the victim was wearing a bracelet with amethyst stones, just like Sheral had in the photo Cameron showed us."

"Did the RCMP find the bracelet?"

"They found a twisted chunk of yellow stone with the remains. Amethyst turns yellow when exposed to very high heat. I believe the bracelet got bagged and tagged with the remains. Must be on its way to the downtown lab."

"Damn. What happened to no one touching anything until we got here?"

"I don't know. Have you heard from Matthew?"

"He's in a meeting now. But I left him a message."

"He's not going to be happy about the evidence and chain of custody issue, Ben."

"Yeah, I have a feeling some PD knuckles are going to get slapped."

"As long as they aren't ours."

"Speaking of slapping knuckles, how did you manage to restrain yourself around the good Father Jeremiah?"

"Who says I've restrained myself?"

He laughed. "He doesn't know what he's in for."

"Christiansen showed Brandon and me the incinerator. Seemed awfully proud of a piece of machinery that burns garbage."

"Listen, Jasi, I'm going to try to track down that bracelet. Maybe I'll have a chance to check it out, get a read from it."

"Okay. Brandon and I will continue our interviews. Let me know when Natassia is back."

"Will do."

Ben signed off and set the audio device to record all transmissions recorded on Jasi or Brandon's data-coms. That way he could conduct his own investigation into the bracelet's whereabouts and check the recordings later on.

He stretched, releasing a soft groan. The van seemed to mimic him. He needed fresh air. Grabbing his jacket and the small stack of crime scene photos from the printer, he opened the van door and stepped outside.

One by one, he examined the photos as he strode down the gravel road. Nothing stood out in any of the pictures. Other than the corpse in the incinerator, there was no evidence of a crime on Sanctuary grounds. And no clues.

Damn. We need that bracelet.

He was halfway to the gate to Sanctuary when an approaching RCMP vehicle slowed. The driver, an officer in his fifties with a receding hairline and deep fissures under weary brown eyes, rolled down the window. "Can I help you?"

A smear of what looked like mustard invaded the crack on the officer's butt chin, and Ben tried hard not to stare as he held up his badge. "CFBI. I'm looking for the evidence that was collected at the scene."

"Let me check on that." The officer leaned through the open car window, said a few words into his radio and waited.

"Is everything all right?" Ben asked him after a moment.

"The bones were taken to the morgue."

Ben flashed the photo of what was left of the amethyst bracelet. "What about this? We believe it's the victim's bracelet."

The officer lifted his radio again. A few seconds later, he said, "That particular item *was* collected. Problem is, no one knows where it went."

"What?" Inwardly, Ben cursed. "How can you lose a key piece of evidence?"

"I didn't say it was lost, Agent Roberts. I'm sure it'll turn up."

"You and your men do understand this is a CFBI investigation, don't you? You were told to keep the scene clean, wait for us and not disturb the body."

The officer's mouth thinned. "Listen, we responded to the call and proceeded as normal. We had already processed the scene by the time anyone said anything about CFBI interfere—*involvement*. We're doing our best to cooperate with you."

Ben was not impressed. "And yet your department seems to have lost evidence, something that could potentially ID the victim."

"I'll make it my responsibility to find it for you. How's that?" From the man's tired and resolved expression, he seemed sincere.

"You find it and I'll owe you one."

As the officer drove away, Ben wondered whether someone had purposefully disposed of the bracelet, or whether it was an honest mistake and the item had been mistagged. Either way, they were screwed unless it was found.

7

Vancouver, BC

True to her word, Natassia and Jay arrived at the city morgue in record time. The morgue was housed in the basement of Vancouver General Hospital, and they passed through security without a hitch.

"You want me to go inside with you?" Jay's face was the color of fresh milk.

Natassia shook her head. "As much as I'm sure I'd enjoy watching you pass out, how about you stay here?"

"Works for me," the kid said, visibly relieved.

She left him standing outside the door to the morgue.

"You must be from the CFBI." A fortyish woman in a starched white lab coat rose from a desk and crossed the small intake room. "I'm the chief pathologist and medical examiner, Dr. Nannetta Cook."

"Agent Natassia Prushenko."

"I have the remains laid out over here."

Dr. Cook led her through double doors into a generous-sized, sterilized room that gleamed of metal. Even with a Febreeze air freshener spritzing the air as she walked past, the subtle stench of death lingered in the air, like a bad stain you couldn't get out no matter how hard you tried. On a table near the far wall, fragments of bone had been carefully laid out on a white cloth.

"Not much of her left," Dr. Cook said, "but more than we would have had if someone hadn't shut off the incinerator early."

"What's that?" Natassia asked, pointing to a long, black shard of bone.

"A fragment of the right tibia. The leg bone."

"Were you able to get an ID?"

The pathologist shook her head. "Not enough to work from."

Natassia slipped on a latex glove and picked up the bone. "What about DNA?"

"These fragments are highly degraded, and identification has been hindered further by traces of PCR inhibitors in the collagen. Most of these fragments contain no nuclear DNA whatsoever, and many of the fragments are contaminated by external DNA sources. It's my understanding that the incinerator the victim was found in was used to destroy other animal waste."

"True.

"Cross-contamination of DNA will delay identification. But I'm still hopeful." Dr. Cook moved toward a counter and pointed to a bone fragment soaking in clear liquid. "On this section of cervical vertebra, I'm attempting a DNA extraction method using cetyltrimethylammonium bromide lysis buffer and isoamyl alcohol-chloroform."

Natassia gave her a blank stare. "What about the gunshot wounds?"

"Gunshot?"

"We have reason to believe she was shot twice. Once in the left side, near her waist. The second shot to her stomach."

The doctor's eyes flared. "That explains it." With long tweezers, she removed a small, fractured rib bone from its bath and placed it under a microscope. "I couldn't tell for sure what had made these markings because we're missing the rest of the bone. But I believe this," she indicated a slight notch carved into the edge of the bone, "could have been caused by a bullet. Do you know what weapon was used?"

"We suspect a rifle."

"Hmm, large caliber. Most likely, it shattered the other side of the bone. The incinerator would've turned those particles into dust."

"And the decapitation?"

"I found that to be quite unusual." The doctor pointed to the severed spinal cord near the neck. "See? No hesitation wounds. Someone used a very sharp blade. A sword, I suspect. It cut through bone and tissue with one slice."

Dr. Cook's pager buzzed.

"Sorry," she said, "I have to sign for a new arrival. I'll be back in about fifteen minutes if you'd like to go for coffee and come back."

"I'd like to examine the bones on the table, if you don't mind."

Dr. Cook hesitated for a second. "CFBI, huh? Well, who am I to argue with the higher ups?" She moved to the double doors. "Wear gloves and don't touch anything other than the bones on the table. They've already been scanned and tagged."

"Believe me, I've handled bones before. They're safe with me."

As soon as the doctor was gone, Natassia pulled a stool up to the table. She removed the latex gloves and set them to one side. She picked up a piece of bone, stroking it softly, thinking about the victim and how afraid she must have been.

Dr. Cook knew Natassia was CFBI, but the woman had no idea that she was also a Psychic Skills Investigator—a Victim Empath, to be exact. Like most PSIs, Natassia considered her psychic abilities to be both a gift and a curse.

Her gift had appeared when she was a teen still living in Russia, after her best friend Tatyana had died from an overdose of sleeping pills. *Suicide*, the coroner in St. Petersburg had said. Natassia had never believed it. Tatyana was a strong-willed girl with everything to live for, especially once she found out she was pregnant.

Her death had hit Natassia hard. The funeral was held at the lavish St. Isaac's Cathedral in the city. But when she had touched Tatyana's cheek during the open casket ceremony, Natassia saw images of a strange man with a skeleton tattoo on his left forearm. In her vision, the man was force-feeding pills to a sobbing Tatyana.

Frightened by the terrifying images in her mind, she fled the church. Outside, she saw the same man standing beside a black limousine. Tatyana's father, Konstantin Gorokhov, said something to the man and settled in the back of the limo. The man with the tattoo glanced at Natassia, then climbed into the driver's seat. As the vehicle sped away, Natassia tried to still her pounding heart and swirling mind. She didn't know much, but she knew one thing without a doubt. The driver of the limousine had killed her best friend.

A week later, the man's body was found in the river. He'd been shot in the forehead, executed.

Yeah, Tatyana may have come from money, but Natassia, even as a teen, came from a world of connections.

Now, as she held the small bone fragment that once belonged to a living, breathing woman, Natassia thought of Tatyana. She hadn't been able to save her friend, but her gift had helped bring closure. Perhaps today it would do so again.

She closed her eyes and stroked the bone. *Who are you? Are you Sheral Downham?*

She felt the undeniable pull of the victim. Her skin tingled, her own bones seemingly melding with the one she held. In her mind, fragments of bone swirled around her, magnetically drawn together to form a skeleton. Her soul entered it, filling it, becoming it, as flesh began to grow. The ribcage expanded and contracted, breathing in life, breathing out death.

"Show me," Natassia said.

She released her breath, stopped fighting and a second later she was in…

She was surrounded by dense forest. Above her, the night sky was pitch black. She could barely see her hands, but the glint of silver on her wrist comforted her.

Somewhere behind her a predator hunted her. She fought back panic.

"Stay calm," she whispered.

She shivered, her breath burning her lungs.

Time shifted and she was running now. Running and crying.

"You can't escape!" a man screamed at her.

Now she was lying against a tree, her leg twisted and throbbing. The crunch of branches told her he was much closer. And now she couldn't run. Maybe if she were very still he'd pass by her and keep going.

He stood before her, a shadow of death and doom.

"Please…" She wanted to tell him that she wasn't the one he wanted. She wanted to beg for her life. But all that came out was a whimper.

"The hunt is over," he said in a low growl. "I win, you lose."

He raised the rifle and she closed her eyes.

The echo of the gunshot rippled through her body, which was suddenly flying on its own. Cool air breezed by her. Surely death had come to claim her with its cold touch.

Her lungs collapsed with sudden force.

Another sound, metal on metal, and then all was still.

She opened her eyes and squinted. She was in total darkness now.

A few minutes later, a door groaned and fingers of light crept toward her. Footsteps drew nearer. She raised her eyes and caught the glimmer of something shiny, metal. Then a sharp blade rushed toward her. She screamed as fiery agony sliced through her neck. Her scream echoed, the last thing she ever heard.

The sound of footsteps roused Natassia from the intense image of dying. She inhaled deeply and stood too quickly. The room spun and she grabbed the edge of the table.

"Agent Prushenko?"

Dr. Cook moved toward her, her expression one of concern until she noticed Natassia's ungloved hands. "I thought I made it perfectly clear that you had to follow protocol."

"I did. I was just leaving."

Steadying herself, Natassia crossed the room. "Thank you, Dr.

Cook. You've been most helpful."

"I'll be sure to submit my full report once I have all the results in."

Natassia pushed through the double doors and strode down the hallway, nearly colliding with a bored looking Jay.

"I waited for you."

She scowled. "I can see that."

It wasn't that she intended to be mean to him. Okay, well, maybe just a bit. In her line of work, she could use all the comic relief possible. And right now, Agent Jason Anthony would have to do.

"You all right, Agent Prushenko?"

The kid was kind of sweet.

"I'm fine." She massaged her forehead, sifting through the elements of her vision and compartmentalizing them for future reference. She couldn't wait to tell Jasi what she'd discovered.

"You get a positive ID?" Jay asked, holding the exterior door open for her.

"No. The DNA was too corrupted."

She tossed him the keys.

Jay stood there, blinking.

"You're driving," she stated.

His mouth gaped.

"If I wanted to drive, would I have given you the keys, Jay?"

"Uh, my name is Jason. Or Agent Anthony, if you'd like. Not Jay. So I'd prefer it if…"

The steel in her eyes shut him up.

They made their way to the parking lot, climbed into the SUV and the kid started the engine.

"Where to now, Agent Prushenko?" he asked.

"Where do you think, Jay?" She heard him release a sigh of resignation, before she said, "Back to Sanctuary."

8

"You really think it's Sheral?" Cameron sobbed on the other end of Jasi's data-com.

"We should know for sure in a day or two," Jasi said, pacing the small space of an unoccupied cabin Christiansen had loaned them for the day. "But everything points to the victim being your friend. I'm so sorry."

"But it could be someone else."

"The victim was wearing an amethyst bracelet."

For a long moment, all Jasi heard was the rain pouring outside.

"Yeah, that's her," Cameron finally said. "She always wore it. It was a gift from her mother." Pause. "Oh God…how am I going to tell her?"

"Promise me you won't say anything to anyone until I give you the okay."

"I won't."

"If you want, I can contact Sheral's mom for you."

"No. She should hear this from me." Sob.

Jasi chewed her bottom lip. "I'm really sorry, my friend."

"Me too. Sheral was an awesome person."

"Are you going to be all right?"

"Ask me that in a week." Cameron's voice was drained of all energy.

"Let me know if there's anything I can do for you. I might be stuck at Sanctuary for a few days, but I can get one of my team members to take over if you need me there."

"No, Jasi. You find out who did this to Sheral. That's all I want now."

Jasi disconnected the call and swore under her breath.

She picked up the photo of Sheral Downham. "I'll find out who did this to you."

Peering out a window, she was surprised to see the storm clouds had dispersed and the sun had made an appearance once again. It was an encouraging sign.

She exited the cabin and found Brandon. He had decided to wait on the porch to give her some privacy during the call to Cameron. He was sensitive that way, a quality she loved about him.

"How did it go?" he asked, wrapping one arm around her waist.

She stared into his eyes, blinked back tears and shook her head.

"We'll get the person who did this, Jasi." He kissed her forehead.

"That's what I told Cameron."

"Well, I have some interesting news to share." He jerked his head toward the cabin. "Christiansen told me we can stay here overnight instead of heading to a hotel in town."

"You want to do that?"

"I think we'd have better luck getting some answers if we stay close to Christiansen and his clan."

"You better not be drinking his Kool-Aid."

"Not on your life. I can barely handle one woman. Why would I want more than that?"

She raised a brow. "Handle?"

"You know what I mean."

"I'm not sure I do, but you can always show me later how well you *handle* me."

He grinned. "So what next?"

"Let's go find Hannah's daughter, Amanda."

"You really think a kid can help us?"

She shrugged. "Amanda is thirteen. That's a rebellious age. She could have seen something. Or she might know something that no one else is willing to share with us."

"It's worth a try."

"Her mother said she was at the river doing laundry. Think she's still there?"

"I guess we'll find out." Brandon pulled up a map of the area on his 'com. He pointed south. "This way."

A few yards from the tree line, they spotted a muddy path.

"You think this leads to the river?" Jasi asked.

"We'll find out."

It took nearly fifteen minutes of trekking through dense woods before the trees thinned and opened into a clearing. The soft gurgle of water told them they were heading in the right direction.

When the river came into view, they released a collected breath of relief. The river had narrow, rocky banks and curved out of sight around a sharp bend. The water moved lazily downstream, circling around small boulders and occasionally grasping at tree roots. A couple of younger children frolicked in their underwear in the water.

"This seems to be the swimming area," Jasi said. "If Amanda is washing clothes, she's probably downstream. When we find her, let me do the talking, okay?"

"You think I can't talk to a teenage girl? You've wounded me." Brandon placed a hand on his chest. "Don't forget, I have an eighteen-year-old sister."

"I know, but Sierra is different from these kids. She wasn't isolated like they are. She trusts adults and authority figures."

He scratched his chin. "You're right. You ask the questions."

They trudged along the shore, rounded the bend and almost knocked over a stocky, dark-haired girl carrying a basket of laundry.

"Amanda?" Jasi said softly.

The girl eyed them with suspicion. "Who're you?"

"I'm Jasi and this is Brandon. We're with the CFBI."

"Police?"

"Kind of. We spoke with your mother and she told us you were here."

Amanda lugged the basket to one hip. "I have chores to do."

"Your mom said you could talk to us for a minute."

"I don't know anything about the dead person." Amanda set the basket on the damp grass. "Except she got burned real bad."

Jasi set her data-com to record. "How old are you, Amanda?"

"Thirteen."

"How long have you lived at Sanctuary?"

"I dunno. Like forever."

"Do you like it here?"

The girl shrugged. "It's okay. Most of the time."

"You go to school here?"

"Yeah."

"Do you know everyone who lives here?"

"Most of 'em."

"Do you know if anyone has left Sanctuary in the past week? Anyone missing?"

They were interrupted by a tanned, lanky boy of about fifteen dressed in a T-shirt and coveralls, the legs rolled to his knees and his feet bare. He stomped toward them with purpose. "Hey, these people bugging you, Amanda?"

Something akin to fear emanated from the girl. "No, Eric. It's okay. They're police."

Eric's eyes narrowed. "Want me to stay with you?"

Amanda covered her mouth. "No! Go home!"

He seemed surprised by her outburst, but he turned and walked away, leaving behind a familiar waft of tobacco.

Amanda turned to Jasi. "Please don't tell my mom Eric was here. He's supposed to be working in the field."

"My lips are sealed. Is he your boyfriend?"

Amanda's face turned twenty shades of red. "No. I'm too young to have a boyfriend."

"Who are your best friends here?"

The girl hesitated. "I thought you wanted to know about the deadie in the 'cinerator."

"You know something about that?"

The girl blinked. "I...uh...no."

Jasi exchanged a knowing look with Brandon.

"If you know something, you really should tell us. You can trust me."

The girl sneered. "Can't trust anyone 'cept myself."

"Why is that?"

Amanda's face grew dark. "Because bad things happen to people who talk about things they shouldn't." She picked up the basket and made her way to the path.

"What kind of bad things?" Jasi called after her.

"Stay here long enough and you'll probably find out."

Amanda vanished into the trees.

"Well, that was cryptic," Brandon said. "Did you notice her hair and dress were dry?"

Jasi nodded. "Eric's too."

"If they'd been caught in the rain down by the river, they'd be soaked."

"So maybe they were doing something more than laundry."

"I don't know about that, but I do know Amanda is afraid of something. We need Natassia."

If Amanda had experienced any kind of trauma, especially if she'd witnessed the death of Sheral Downham, then Natassia might be able to read the girl.

"We'll proceed with caution here," she said. "I don't want to scare Amanda off. If we can get her to trust us, then maybe she'll share what she knows."

"Or you could pull the boyfriend card and threaten to tell her mother about that Eric kid."

Jasi shook her head. "No. These people think very differently. I don't want two kids to get punished for something as innocent as a crush."

"Seems like there's more than just a crush going on here."

"Smoking, you mean? Yeah, I smelled it too. But only on Eric." She grabbed his arm. "You can't say anything about that to Christiansen or Hannah."

"Wasn't planning on it."

They followed the path back to the cabins, every now and then passing some of the residents. A few smiled, but most turned their backs and ignored them.

"I'm going to talk to Christiansen," Brandon said.

"Go ahead. I want to look over the files."

It wasn't until Jasi was sitting on the bed in their assigned cabin that she realized that Amanda had never answered her question about anyone leaving or missing.

What exactly do you know, Amanda?

"We've been summoned to a barbecue tonight," Brandon said when he returned a half hour later. "Apparently Father Jeremiah is holding it in memory of the victim, though he says he has no idea who she may be."

"How caring of him," Jasi said with derision.

"And later they're having a sweat lodge, and we're invited to attend."

She squinted up at him, wondering if he'd forgotten who he was talking to. "Are you kidding me? You want me to sit in a room filled with smoke and get all sweaty?"

"Well, I do like the latter. And there's no smoke, so you won't have to worry about triggering a vision."

"How can it be a sweat lodge then?"

"It's more like a sauna. Christiansen said they use hot stones and water for steam. Supposed to cleanse you of all toxins and free your mind...and all that."

She gaped at him. "Oh...my...God."

"What?"

"You *are* drinking the damned Kool-Aid!"

He laughed. "Relax. I simply thought this would give us an opportunity to meet more of his flock. If they see us fitting in, they'll be more inclined to open up."

She wrapped her arms around his neck and kissed his lips. "Some days you are so darned smart."

He pouted. "What about the other days?"

"Let's just say it's a good thing you're incredibly attractive and sexy."

Brandon playfully swatted her rear end. "Back atcha, babe."

"Fine, dinner and a sweat lodge. Sounds like fun."

His eyes narrowed. "Okay, what are you planning?"

"I think it may be time to mention Sheral's alias, Nancy Davison. We can see what the reaction is, especially with Christiansen and Amanda."

"What about Ben and Natassia?"

"They're going to stay out of sight in the van for now. We can bring Natassia in tomorrow. See if she gets anything from Amanda."

"Ben still hasn't found the bracelet."

"I know."

"You think we'll find it?"

"Either it's an honest mistake and it was sent in with some of the other evidence—"

"Or someone with an ulterior motive has taken it," he finished.

"And if that's the case, we may have to do a cabin-to-cabin sweep and search every inch of this place."

"That could take weeks."

"We don't have weeks. There's a murderer walking around free. And he or she is either connected to Sanctuary and someone here, or still on the grounds."

"You think Sheral found something incriminating and that's why she was killed?"

"Maybe. That's why at dinner I want to pass her photo around. If everyone denies she was here, we'll know they're lying and covering something up."

"And if someone says they know her?"

"We'll find out which cabin she stayed in, who she spoke with and who might have had a beef with her. Cameron said Sheral had a recording device with a camera. Since it wasn't found with the body, it has to be around here somewhere."

"I doubt she kept it in her cabin," Brandon said. "She had roommates."

Jasi paced the room, stopping every now and then to stare out one of the windows. "Where would she hide it?" She caught sight of a barn roof. "She wouldn't keep it in any of the buildings. The risk of being caught would've been too great." She gazed beyond the buildings to the dense forest. "Somewhere in the woods or by the river."

Brandon grunted. "That's a lot of land to cover."

The trees outside rustled as if in agreement.

9

"Whatever you do, Jay, don't drop anything," Natassia said as they walked toward the surveillance van. "Or Ben will have your head on a silver platter. You can't mess with the man's food."

Jay's arms were loaded down precariously with two piping hot pizza boxes, a tray with two extra-large coffees and a family-sized box of Timbits, but Natassia had to give the kid credit. He didn't say a word as he dodged the potholes. She'd never seen him move so fast.

She reached for the side door of the van and hauled it open.

"Put everything inside," she said.

"Evening, Agent Roberts," Jay said as he set the food on the small table in the back.

Ben gave a nod, towering over the kid.

"This is Jay," Natassia said, stepping inside.

"Agent Jason Anthony, actually," came the quiet reply.

She gave him a saccharine smile. "I'll call you if we need your services again."

"Oh," Jay said, shuffling his feet. "I, uh, was hoping I could stay and help out with the investigation." He eyed the pizza boxes as though he hadn't eaten in a week.

She flicked a look over her shoulder. "We need another body tonight?"

"Nope," Ben said.

"You heard the man," she said.

The look of sheer disappointment on Jay's face made her think of a child getting socks for Christmas instead of the toy train he'd begged Santa for. She almost changed her mind. Almost.

"Okay then," Jay mumbled. "You have my number?"

"Yes, Matthew gave it to me earlier." She patted his arm. "Don't worry. I'll call if we need you."

She hovered in the van's doorway and watched as he strolled to his car and climbed inside. The SUV grumbled when the kid shifted to the wrong gear, then it spit up some rocks and lurched down the road—at the speed of sloth.

"Seems you made the right decision to do the driving," Ben observed.

"Let's hope no one gives the kid a gun."

Sliding the door shut, she sank into a chair at the back of the van and gratefully accepted a cup of coffee. She took a few sips before filling him in on her visit to the morgue.

"My vision was a bit vague," she said, sighing. "I didn't really get anything new, just confirmation that the victim was shot by a rifle." She told him everything she'd seen.

"But you did get more, Natassia. We now know for sure she was shot somewhere in the woods and brought back to the incinerator. By an unknown subject, a man. And we know the unsub considered his actions as a bet, a game."

She looked up. "What?"

"You said he told her, 'I win, you lose.' Perhaps he found out what she was up to and decided to stop her. Only he enjoyed it a bit too much."

"I think you're right. It doesn't sound like a random kill."

"No. He didn't just stumble upon the victim. It sounds…personal, like he knew her. Or spent some time with her. Perhaps at Sanctuary."

"And he could still be there."

"That's a definite possibility. If he thinks he's disposed of any traces of his crime, he'd have a false sense of security. Why leave? Sanctuary might be his only home."

"So we have a sick bastard running loose who hunted her down in cold blood and then burned her alive."

"I doubt this was his first victim. I'm running background checks on everyone currently living at Sanctuary. RCMP took photos of everyone on the property when the body was discovered. We should have the results in by tomorrow evening."

"Have you heard from Jasi and Brandon?"

"Yes. They're staying in one of the cabins."

"Overnight?"

"Christiansen persuaded them to stay."

"The proverbial leader in every way," she said with disdain.

"Makes sense though. Jasi and Brandon are gaining his trust. And they have free access to the grounds. Christiansen's not hindering the investigation so far."

"Maybe he's confident they'll find nothing because he's destroyed all the evidence."

Ben stared at her for a moment. "You really dislike this guy."

"Years ago, back in Russia, we had many persuasive leaders like Christiansen. Some of them were in government. My country suffered for it. So did my people."

"I guess there are cults in every country."

Her lips thinned. "The strong preying on the weak."

"Tomorrow I'll shake hands with him, gloves off."

Natassia arched a brow. "Reading him probably won't be easy."

"Maybe not. But we need to find out what he's hiding." Ben's data-com buzzed. "Jasi?" He listened, mumbled a few indecipherable comments, then hung up. Glancing at Natassia, he said, "I think we drew the short end of the straw."

"Why?"

"Jasi and Brandon will be feasting at a barbecue tonight, followed by relaxation in a sweat lodge."

Natassia's gaze swept across the cramped quarters of the van. "And we're stuck in here."

"Listening to them eating and sweating."

"Yeah, we got shafted."

"On a positive note, they *will* be working tonight. Jasi plans to show the photo of our missing 'hooker' to everyone at the barbecue."

"That should spark some interesting dinner conversation."

"Jasi said Sheral hid a data-com somewhere on the grounds. She thinks it's in the woods."

She raised her brows. "No one said we have to stay in here all night."

"What have you got in mind?"

"There's no better time to search the woods than when everyone at Sanctuary is otherwise engaged. We can take the X-Disc Pro. It's more efficient than the RCMP model."

Ben reached for the X-Disc and removed it from its wall mount. "Let's go."

Outside, the sky had brightened and the wind had died down.

"We have a few hours of daylight left," she said. "Tonight we can process the feed from the X-Disc."

"Let's hope we find something. We're running out of leads here. We don't want to come up empty."

The thought left a bad taste in her mouth. Last thing she wanted to tell Jasi was that they'd hit a brick wall. Something had to break in this case soon.

With a black CFBI pack slung over one shoulder, she followed Ben down the road. After twenty yards, it curved past the gate to Sanctuary and veered off away from the fence. Ben ignored the gate and kept walking.

"Shouldn't we be inside the fenced area?" she asked.

Ben studied the land. "No, it would be better if we circle around the fence line outside the property. We can activate the X-Disc and send it inside from there. Plus, the gate is monitored. If we enter, they'll know."

"Good idea."

Side by side they trudged through knee-high scrub grass, making their way toward the trees. Every now and then, she glanced toward various outbuildings on the other side of the fence. There was no one in sight.

"They must be getting ready for dinner," Ben said.

"As long as Jasi and Brandon aren't on the menu, all is well."

"They're mindless cult members, not cannibals."

But Natassia wasn't too sure that was true.

A few yards from the tree line, Ben drew to a halt. "Since the forest is so profuse up ahead, I'll set it to hover as close to the treetops as possible."

Opening his pack, he withdrew the X-Disc and set it on the ground. Flicking the activation switch, he used his data-com to program the drone. A minute later, the X-Disc whirred and beeped. They watched as it gradually rose from the ground, navigated a path upward and sped off above the trees.

"I've set it to alert us if foreign matter is found," he said.

They approached the backwoods of Sanctuary, the overgrown shrubs and imposing trees growing denser the farther they ventured in. Overhead, a waning sun struggled to reach them, narrow wisps of light filtering in like ethereal fingers caressing their hair. The air had grown cooler. Night would be upon them in a few short hours.

"You have the flashlights?" Ben asked.

"Yeah. Hold on a sec." Natassia stopped and set her pack on the ground. Unzipping a side section, she pulled out two small but powerful flashlights and handed him one. "Think we'll find anything?"

"Let's hope so. Otherwise this will become a lengthy case."

"And we'll run the risk that the RCMP will want to take over."

"Yeah, there's that."

As Natassia trekked on, she swept her flashlight across the forest floor, praying they'd discover something.

Minutes later, Ben's data-com beeped.

"The X-Disc has finished scanning inside the grounds."

"It find anything?"

Ben shook his head. "Sanctuary appears to be clean. No blood, no bodies. I'll program the X-Disc to continue with a scan back here, all along the fence and a hundred yards out."

While the drone did its thing, they pushed through the brush, looking for footprints, breakage in the underbrush or anything else suspicious. They stopped once and ate the sandwiches Natassia had procured earlier.

After nearly an hour of foraging through the woods, Ben's data-com beeped again. "The X-Disc found something. This way!"

He led her through the trees, following an invisible pathway indicated by the X-Disc's GPS. "Over here!" He pointed to a thick-trunked cedar. "Bullets."

Natassia rushed over, dropped her pack and retrieved an evidence bag from a side pocket. With tweezers, she cautiously extracted three bullets from the cedar. "Large caliber. My guess? A rifle."

"There are more," Ben said, a grim expression on his face.

Within twenty minutes they had recovered over two dozen bullets and twice as many casings. And on one tree they found something else. Blood.

"This is where it happened," Natassia said. "Sheral died here. I saw it in my vision."

"I'm not sure this is Sanctuary property," Ben replied. He dialed a number on his data-com. "Hey, Ron, can you check these GPS coordinates and tell me who the property is registered to?"

A minute passed.

"You sure?" he said. "Okay, thanks."

"Christiansen's land?" Natassia asked.

"No."

"Who owns it then?"

"It's crown land."

Her eyes widened. "Ah, that makes sense. No one would be developing this area so less chance of someone finding all this." She indicated the evidence bags and blood stain.

"That creates another problem. Christiansen can easily deny he had anything to do with this because it's not on his property. Unless we can find actual proof he or someone at Sanctuary was involved."

"Then we'll find it."

Buzz.

"The X-Disc?"

Ben stared at his data-com for a moment. "Oh God."

Natassia rushed to his side. "Did it find the victim's head?"

"Worse."

When Ben turned the 'com toward her, she saw what looked like an x-ray of an area of land to the north that showed occasional white spots scattered over the ground. He slid his finger along the screen to enlarge the area and the white spots became tinier and pixelated.

"What are they?" she asked, squinting.

"According to the analysis, bone fragments."

10

Jasi was a bit leery about their host's instructions—no weapons or data-coms during dinner or the sweat lodge. "I'm not sure we're safe here," she told Brandon while they were changing for dinner.

"I won't let anything happen to you. Trust me."

"It's not you I'm worried about."

He kissed her lightly. "Christiansen isn't going to allow any harm to come to us during such a public event. Not with the RCMP and CFBI watching. He's going out of his way to cooperate."

"That in itself is suspicious, don't you think?"

"Maybe he really has nothing to hide. If one of his flock killed Sheral, there's no guarantee he knew anything about it."

"I don't think you really believe that."

"You know me too well."

"Just to be prepared, I'm packing a little insurance." She turned and hiked up her shirt. She'd tucked a small pistol inside her pants at the small of her back. "To hell with Christiansen's rules." She slid on a gray leather jacket as extra coverage.

"What about our 'coms?"

She shrugged. "We can leave those for now. Once we're finished dinner, we'll come back and report in to Ben and Natassia. We can do the same after the sweat lodge."

For good measure, Brandon tucked both data-coms inside a pair of boots in the closet. "In case the good Father plans to have our rooms searched while we're out."

"Good thinking. Ready?"

"Let's go."

Leaving the safety of their cabin, they headed toward the lodge, only to be redirected by a good-looking guy with dirty-blond hair and a scruffy goatee.

The Brad Pitt double.

"Dinner's inside the small barn," he told them, leading the way.

"You're the driver of the Sanctuary van," Jasi said.

He blinked twice. "Uh, yeah."

"So your job is to find new members and bring them here?"

The man let out a laugh. "You make it sound so…wrong. We help those who wanna be helped."

"Look, uh…"

"Lazarus," the man volunteered.

"Lazarus?" Brandon cut in. "Like the guy in the Bible who rose from the dead?"

Lazarus pursed his lips. "That's me. Well, not the same dude exactly, but I did die and come back. Couple of years ago I overdosed on meth. Father Jeremiah found me passed out in an alley. He took me to the hospital, saved my life."

"What about the rising from the dead part?" Jasi said wryly.

"Oh, I died. Doctor said I was dead for nearly six minutes. Then— wham! Back I came."

"Lucky you."

"Damn right I was lucky. Now I get to help others turn their life around. We save people."

Jasi thought of Zane, her former boyfriend turned criminal. She was unable to save him. Now he was fish food somewhere in the Pacific Ocean.

"You can't save everyone," she murmured.

"No, ma'am. But we gotta try. Some of 'em take time. And if we fail…"

"What?"

Lazarus shrugged. "Like you said, not everyone can be saved. We accept that."

Jasi flicked a look at Brandon, then reached into her jacket pocket. "You ever see this woman before? She's a hooker from Vancouver." She handed him the photo of Sheral Downham.

Lazarus studied the picture for a second. "Nope. Never seen her before."

"Are you sure? We have an arrest warrant for her. Word on the street is that you picked her up in Vancouver two and a half weeks ago and brought her here."

"Most of the time the people I pick up are in rough shape. She sure is pretty though. I'd remember her if I seen her."

This threw Jasi off guard. She was sure Lazarus would ID Sheral. Cameron had said Sheral had been picked up by "Pitt." Yet Lazarus seemed sincere when he said he'd never seen her.

As they came within reach of the barn, they heard laughter and music.

"Sounds like a party," Brandon said.

"Naw, just our regular dinner," Lazarus said. "Father Jeremiah believes in community spirit, so we all pitch in for the evening meal. Food here is awesome. And the music is by whoever feels like playing." He looked at Brandon. "You play an instrument?"

"Some guitar, but it's been a while."

"The schedule is already set for the next three days, but maybe you'll play for us one night after that."

Jasi wanted to cut in and tell the man they weren't planning on sticking around that long, but Brandon beat her to it.

"We'll probably be gone by then," he said. "And I'm not that good, anyway."

Lazarus slapped his shoulder as though they were the best of pals. "We won't judge you. No one here's a pro. We play for fun."

Christiansen greeted them in a silver and black satin robe draped over jeans and a gray T-shirt. "Welcome, friends. We hope you'll enjoy the feast we have prepared. We're pleased to have you witness our celebrations."

"What are we celebrating?" Jasi asked. *A successful murder?*

Christiansen beamed a smile. "One of our members is being reborn tonight. There is no better way to see the salvation that Sanctuary provides than by being witness to the rebirth of a previously lost soul." He beckoned them to follow. "Please, sit here with me and my family."

Nine rectangular tables, each covered with a simple white tablecloth, had been joined lengthwise down the center of the barn. One extra-long table had been placed crosswise at the far end, forming a long "T," and it was to that table that Christiansen led them.

He sat down in the center chair. "Agent McLellan?" He indicated a chair to his left. "Please sit. Special Consultant Walsh, have a seat to my right."

Jasi saw Brandon's brows arch. He didn't like that they were separated by Christiansen. Neither did she. However, if it made their host feel more comfortable, she'd go along with it.

Sanctuary's residents filed in and took their seats. Christiansen's wives and children sat on either side of Brandon and Jasi. When Beth sat down beside her, Jasi noticed that the music and laughter in the spacious barn had subsided. Nervous whispers teased the air. What were they saying?

There was an awkward moment as everyone held hands and

Christiansen said grace, but Jasi managed to make it through without snickering in disdain at the words that were being spoken.

"Thank you for our guests," Christiansen concluded. "May they find the closure they are searching for so they can move on to other tasks."

This was said with a finality that unnerved her but also made her that much more wary. Had he just covertly warned everyone to stay quiet?

At the far end, six women and a teenaged girl stood and headed for two buffet tables that held countless dishes. With a food-laden plate in each hand, they made their way to the head table. The girl served Christiansen with her eyes down and head bowed. Two of the women served Jasi and Brandon, then Christiansen's other wives and children. When they had finished, everyone else went to the food tables to serve themselves.

"You look like you disapprove, Agent McLellan," Beth said next to her.

"Seems a bit archaic to me to have women serving like slaves."

"No one's making them do it. They *want* to serve my husband. It's their way of thanking him."

"What about the girl? What has she got to thank your husband for?"

Beth's eyes darkened. "Not what you're insinuating. Katie is extremely grateful for everything my husband has done."

Jasi scrutinized the girl.

"She was a runaway living on the streets," Beth added. "Ripe pickings for the unsavory sort. Jeremiah rescued her. And now tonight we celebrate her rebirth." A dreamy expression filled the woman's eyes. "Katie is home, as are all who come willingly to Sanctuary."

There was some small talk during the meal, which Jasi had to admit was sensational. Dinner consisted of barbecued chicken, roasted potatoes, salads of all kinds and decadent desserts that she feared would make her gain ten pounds just looking at them.

"No shortage of good food," Brandon said when Christiansen and his wives left them to refill their plates.

"Remember what we're here for," she scolded.

"Hey, can't you let a man enjoy his meal?"

She laughed. "You always act like you're famished."

"I am." He slid one hand under the table and rubbed her thigh. "For you."

"Stop!" she hissed.

Brandon withdrew his hand. "Is it my fault you're more delicious than anything they could prepare here?"

"Keep it up and I might just leave you here."

"But then who would keep your bed warm at night?"

She shot him a warning look. "You're incorrigible. I hope you noticed the cabin we're in only has single beds."

He leaned closer. "Then it's going to be a tight fit."

Thankfully, Christiansen and his harem returned, and Jasi was able to change the subject. "While we were conducting our investigation of the victim in the incinerator, we were alerted to an outstanding warrant for a prostitute who is reported to have been on your property." She showed Christiansen the photo.

"I don't recognize her. Are you sure she came here?"

"We've been told that Lazarus picked her up in the city."

Christiansen studied the photo again. "I don't know…"

The girl, Katie, took that moment to collect their empty plates, and when she saw the photo, her face paled. "That kinda looks like that new woman."

Christiansen twitched. "Who?"

"Nan. You know, the woman who came here two weeks ago." Katie looked at Jasi. "Except her hair is different."

"Ah," Christiansen said, "I see the resemblance now. Yes…Nan. She stayed with us for a few days and then decided it wasn't for her."

"So she left Sanctuary?" Jasi asked.

"Yes. Maybe a week ago."

"By herself?"

"I'll ask Lazarus if he drove her anywhere."

"Don't do that. I'll ask him myself." Jasi pushed away from the table, dropped her napkin on her chair and made her way to the far end of the room. "Lazarus, you said you didn't know the woman in the photo I showed you."

The man gave her a confused smile. "I don't."

"According to Katie and Father Jeremiah, she was here not too long ago. Nancy Davison?"

"Nancy?" His eyes brightened. "Of course. Nan! Sorry 'bout that. She changed her looks a helluva lot. I didn't recognize her." His smile faded. "Wow, that picture must've been taken a long time ago. She's not the same woman anymore. Nan's a hooker now. Gone right downhill."

"Did you take her back to the city?"

"Naw, last I saw she was telling everyone she wanted to leave."

"When was that?"

"The same night we had an emergency curfew and had to stay inside because of the killings."

Jasi perked up. "What killings?"

"One of our dogs and a barn cat. Bear killed 'em."

"Where?"

"On the other side of the fence, in the woods. When that happens, we all stay indoors until morning."

"This happen often?"

Lazarus shrugged. "Not really. There are lots of bears in the mountains. They come down once in a while to hunt. That's why we have the barbwire. Keeps the bears out."

She took a breath. "So let me get this straight. The last time you saw Nancy Davison was the same night everyone was restricted to their cabins."

"Yeah. Her roommate found a note saying Nan had gone back to the city. She must've called a cab or something."

"Without a phone?"

Lazarus gave her a dim-witted grin. "Oh yeah. Maybe not. But I never drove her, and we only have a couple of vehicles here—the van and a truck for larger supplies, so she must've walked."

"All the way to Mission?"

Lazarus shrugged again.

"Where's the note now?"

"Dunno. Guess Father Jeremiah has it."

"When was this?"

"A few days—" He stopped, his face blanching. "Just realized something. The morning Katie found the note from Nan was the same morning that body was found in the incinerator."

"And you just thought of this now?"

"Yeah. Once Grace found the body, we all forgot about Nan's note." His head snapped up. "You think it's her—Nan? In the incinerator?"

"If it is, then someone killed her and dumped her there."

"Who would do that?"

"I was hoping you'd know. Did Nancy have any enemies here? Anyone not like her?"

His gaze drifted toward his benefactor. "I shouldn't be talking about this. I don't know anything more. Talk to Father Jeremiah."

Jasi tucked the photo of Sheral back inside her jacket. "Thanks for your help."

"Sure. Lemme know if you need anything else while you're here." Lazarus eyed her up and down. "It can get lonely out here in the middle of nowhere."

"Believe me, the last thing I am is lonely."

As she walked away, she could feel his stare on her backside. "Lazarus?"

"Yes, ma'am?"

"If you don't plan on having another resurrection anytime soon, stop looking at my ass."

"Yes, ma'am. Sorry."

Inwardly, she groaned. Lazarus was a few cells short of a full brain, probably a result of his near-death experience, though maybe he'd always been this way.

Brandon made his way toward her and steered her outside. "I was about to come rescue you from old Lazarus."

"I didn't need rescuing. But *he* might have if I'd stayed there any longer."

"What did you find out?"

She told him everything.

11

As Natassia studied the boneyard on Ben's data-com screen, revulsion filled every inch of her body. "Sheral Downham isn't the only victim." She looked at Ben. "There's a serial killer in Sanctuary."

"We have to let Brandon and Jasi know."

Activating her 'com, she set it to speaker. "Call Jasi."

It rang multiple times, but no one picked up.

She swore. "She's not answering. Should we go back to Sanctuary?"

"No," Ben said. "We'll continue on to ensure the bones are human and not animal. I'll let Matthew know what we've discovered so he can get an extraction team in here. From the look of it, some of the remains are buried several feet below the surface, while others are in shallow graves. Regardless, it's going to take a substantial amount of time and manpower."

"What is going on here?"

"I suspect we may have found the missing people Sheral was searching for."

While Ben updated Matthew, Natassia sent a quick text off to Jasi and Brandon. *Possible victims found beyond Sanctuary property. Watch your back! Killer may still be there.*

"Matthew's sending in a team right away," Ben told her minutes later. "Have you heard from Jasi or Brandon yet?"

"No."

"Let's keep moving. I want to get to the gravesite before it's too dark."

It took nearly an hour of navigating through cedars, spruce and pines before they reached the area. At first glance, one would never suspect what lay beneath the mossy ground. Upon closer inspection, some of the mounds seemed to be fresher than others. And strange yellowish stains were scattered around some of the graves.

Natassia used a branch to scoop the dirt from one of the mounds. It came away coated with a yellowish mucous.

"Sodium hydroxide," Ben said, scooping a sample into a small metal container.

"Someone used lye to destroy the remains?"

"It's effective. Dissolves a body until it's nothing but liquid and a few slivers of bone, especially when water is added."

"Rain. Damn…another reason why I hate our weather."

"According to the X-Disc, we'll only find trace fragments of bone here. I'm not sure there will be enough DNA remaining for identification."

"Maybe they're not all like this one."

They spread out, removing chunks of soil from various mounds.

"Found one!" she called out, poking a dirt mound with a broken branch.

The smell of decay was overpowering. After spraying some Mentho into her nostrils, she dug into the earth, scraping away tree needles, decayed leaves and rich soil until confirmation was evident. In a shallow grave, she'd uncovered a human hand, its decayed, bony fingers clawing upward.

"My God," she whispered.

"This victim was buried alive."

Together they brushed the soil from the remains, revealing a female body. This time the head was intact.

"No lye was used on her." Passing the flashlight to Ben, she took a picture with her data-com. "I'll send this to the Missing Persons Database along with a DNA sample and see if we get a hit."

"She's maybe in her mid-thirties," he said, shining both flashlights over the corpse. "Auburn hair, about five foot four inches tall." He prodded the body with a twig. "Possible GSW." He indicated a small hole in the woman's ribcage. "Smaller caliber than the most recent vic."

"So…different weapons?"

"Definitely."

"Her body's well preserved."

"Based on the condition of her body, the depth of the grave and the dry soil, I estimate she's been out here for maybe two months. The canopy overhead is thick, and not as much rain reaches the ground here, so that helped with preservation." He sighed. "I suspect the coroner will find petechial hemorrhaging as well. She suffocated."

Natassia moved close to the body. "Okay, give me a little room here."

Ben grabbed her arm. "You want to attempt to read her now? You must be exhausted. It's been a long day. Why not wait until tomorrow?"

She shook her head. "The sooner we catch this bastard, the better. Don't worry. I can do this."

She sat cross-legged on the ground and reached out to stroke the dead woman's hand. Closing her eyes, she thought about the woman she was touching, how the victim had once been filled with life. Now, the woman's hand was limp...cold...lifeless.

She felt her own body grow lighter, as if dissolving into miniscule particles. In her mind's eye, she saw those particles invade the woman's body, melding with her.

Seconds later, Natassia was inside the woman's mind.

It was dark. So dark. And bitterly cold.

Natassia tried to move, but her body—the woman's body—was frozen in place. She let her mind drift, hoping to grasp a memory.

"Help me," whispered another voice in her head.

"I'm here," Natassia said. "Tell me. Show me."

Flickers of images bombarded her, as though someone were rapidly changing channels on a television. The gate to Sanctuary. Father Jeremiah. The inside of a cabin. The forest under a moonlit night. A shadowy figure hiding in the forest.

Suddenly she was running, breathless and afraid.

"What are we running from?" she asked.

A shot boomed, and a puff of air brushed her face.

"Run!"

Natassia, seeing everything through the woman's eyes, felt her heart pounding as she raced past trees and shrubs, branches mercilessly scraping and drawing blood along her arms and legs.

When another shot rang out, she ducked behind an uprooted tree. She made herself as small as possible and tried to calm her breathing. She was about to peek over the tree trunk when she heard the snapping of twigs.

"He's coming for me!" she whispered. "Hurry!"

But which way?

A sharp crackle made her whip around. "No. Please!"

Another shot.

Searing heat pierced her ribs, and she fell to the ground. She lay there, looking up at the moon as it peered between the cedars. A star winked nearby, and she reached out to touch it.

This was what it felt like to die.

She thought of Paige and tried to recall her sweet little face.

Struggling to keep her eyes open, she took an unsteady breath and coughed up something hot and wet.

A shadow hovered over her, blocking the moon from her view.

"I win," the shadow said. "You lose."

The shadow scooped her up in its arms, and she floated for a while, gazing up at the sky. Was this all a dream? But her dream quickly turned into a nightmare when she was lowered into a gaping hole in the earth and handfuls of moist, pungent soil landed on top of her, scattering clumps across her body and over her face.

"No! I'm still alive!" her mind screamed.

Darkness swept over her, and she heaved a sob. This was it. Her life was over. Then she embraced the peacefulness that was offered.

Time to rest. Sleep...

"Natassia?"

All she wanted to do was float like this. Forever.

"Natassia! Wake up!"

Something soft and cool caressed her cheek. When her eyes snapped open, the first thing Natassia saw was a murky silhouette leaning over her. She jerked back with a shriek, then calmed when the shape stepped back into the light from the flashlights. It was Ben, and he didn't look too happy.

"You all right?"

She nodded, unable to speak. She caught sight of the body in the dirt and shivered. She moved a few feet away and sat on a tree stump.

Ben handed her a thermos mug of coffee. "Don't say anything until you're ready."

She sipped cautiously, trying to assemble the various clues her vision had uncovered. Something niggled at her brain, begging her to remember.

"The victim was killed in the woods," she said. "Exactly like Sheral. And the killer said the same thing. 'I win, you lose.'" She paused, rubbing her forehead. "There was something else…"

"Did you see his face?"

"No." What was she forgetting? She inhaled the night air and replayed the vision. "I was in her thoughts. She mentioned someone. *Paige.* She was trying to picture Paige's face."

"What do you think?"

Natassia looked up at him. "I think we finally got lucky. All we need to do is find a missing woman who matches the victim's general stats and has a daughter or younger sister named Paige."

With a gloved hand, Ben stroked her face. "You were in deep this time. You have to be more careful."

"I'm doing my job, Ben."

"I know. It's just that I—"

"Worry? Obsess? Look, we've been over this a hundred times. I don't usually have problems separating myself."

"Usually. But it *has* happened."

"Once in a blue moon." She shrugged. "It's part of the package, and I've learned to accept it as a calculated risk. Otherwise what good would I be to the PSI Division? If I'm not going to use my gift, I may as well be a regular CFBI agent. And you know damned well I'm not transferring."

"Still…we have to work on a better method to get you back."

Standing shakily, she strode over to him and wrapped both arms around his neck. "I can think of one method that would have me out in a jiffy."

"What's that?"

"Kiss me."

Ben laughed. "You think that'll work?"

She tilted her head and gave him a mischievous grin. "Why not test that theory?"

"Natassia, we're not done here. We've got work to do."

She pursed her lips. "All work and no play makes Ben—"

"I know, I know. I'm dull. But these bodies have waited long enough."

"You're right." She released him and moved away. "What next?"

"Now," he said, "it's my turn."

Ben peeled the specially designed black leather gloves from his hands and tucked them in his pockets. She saw his hands tremble as he reached for the corpse, and she knew he already doubted his abilities. Of all their unique psychic gifts, Ben's was the most unpredictable, and she knew this wounded his pride. Would there ever come a day when he could call upon his gift and be rewarded by crystal clear images that made sense?

Minutes ticked by slowly.

Releasing a frustrated breath, Ben straightened. "Nothing."

"Let's try one more." She pointed to a mound several yards away. The thick moss that covered it suggested the body had been dumped months ago.

Ben crammed the flashlights between tree branches and angled the lights down over the mound. Using branches as shovels, they excavated the second grave. The odor was even more noxious than the first body, and Natassia willed herself not to vomit.

"This one's male," she observed. "Ebonic."

The body was in a state of severe decomposition, with most of the coffee-colored flesh obliterated by time and voracious bugs. And like Sheral, the head was missing, a clean slice with no hesitation marks.

"You think this man was killed by the same guy who murdered Sheral?" she asked.

"Similar slice marks," Ben said with a nod. "And two bullet holes in the chest. Everything is identical—except this victim is male."

"Seems our killer doesn't discriminate." She chewed her bottom lip, thinking.

"What's wrong, Natassia?"

"He's been here awhile."

"Yeah, I'd say close maybe four months."

"The corpse is too old." When he stopped digging, she added, "His spirit has long since moved on. I won't get anything from him."

Ben pushed aside a clump of earth. "I found a button." He scooped it up with a leaf and showed it to her. The button was small, plain and black, the kind one would find on a men's dress shirt.

"Think it belongs to the killer?"

"It has to belong to someone involved. It was buried with the body. And the vic is wearing a sweatshirt, so it's likely not his."

Ben picked up the button with a bare hand. As his fingers traced edges, he closed his eyes and slowed his breathing, while Natassia waited, anxious yet hopeful.

Minutes passed without a word from him.

Should she say something, call his name?

Ben blinked and opened his eyes. "I'm afraid I won't be much help, Natassia."

Shit. "What did you see?"

"Six zeroes, an illegible signature and a small black animal."

"The zeroes could be a bank account number or money related."

Ben shrugged.

"And the signature?"

"Could be anyone's," he said with a sigh.

"How big was the animal?"

"Maybe the size of a rat." He shook his head. "But it wasn't a rat. You know how my visions work. They're never exact but symbolic."

"So the question of the day is: how do six zeroes, a signature and a black animal the size of a rat connect to a murder victim buried in the middle of nowhere?"

He dropped the button into a small evidence bag. "I have no answer for that."

"You did great, Ben. We know more about this victim now than we did before."

As the sun said its final farewell and dipped beyond the horizon, Natassia retrieved one of the flashlights, and they spent the next half hour flagging the mounds indicated by the X-Disc. They photographed both bodies and sent the photos to Jasi, Brandon and Matthew.

"We don't have perimeter beacons," Ben said, "so let's cordon off the area with tape for now. Matthew and his team will take it from here. They're coming in by helicopter, so they'll probably be here in less than an hour."

"You're sure Jasi and Brandon are in no danger?"

"They don't fit the killer's profile. Plus our presence here is too high profile."

She continued to inspect the forest floor. "What does your profiler instinct tell you?"

"That we have three definite murder victims, two buried here and one dumped in the incinerator at Sanctuary. And from the look of the X-Disc scan, we're sitting at close to a dozen victims. Two have been decapitated, most likely with the same weapon, which suggests the same killer. He chose this method either out of rage or to hinder an ID. He's intelligent, well organized and can react well under pressure. He always has a backup plan."

"And he's strong enough to drag these bodies deep into the woods."

"I agree. He's physically fit. Probably works out regularly."

"Unless he has another mode of transportation," she said, her flashlight capturing two faint indents in the earth. "Check out what I just found."

Ben made a beeline for her. Crouching, he examined the tire tracks. "The X-Disc didn't pick these up because the rain we had earlier washed most of the tracks away, but the grove of trees here sheltered them." He removed the X-Disc from the backpack. "I'm setting it to do a 3-D scan. That way if it rains tonight, we won't lose the imprints."

"What do you think? Wheelbarrow?"

"No. Four wheels. See? My guess is an all-terrain vehicle."

"An ATV?"

He rubbed his chin. "One of the photos the RCMP took of Sanctuary showed a dilapidated red barn with two ATVs parked outside."

Excitement coursed through Natassia's veins. "If we can match the treads, we'll have enough evidence to shut Sanctuary down while we conduct a thorough investigation. His cult followers won't be happy about that. They believe they're safe from everything evil."

"I'm thinking the last place on earth that any of them will want to be is at Sanctuary."

12

Jasi circulated Sheral's photo to the forty or so cult members in the barn, but only three claimed to have any interaction with Nancy Davison prior to her disappearance—Christiansen, Lazarus and Katie.

Frowning, Jasi studied the room. "Brandon, have you seen Jenny, the other roommate?"

"No. Didn't Cameron say that she was sent to some kind of isolation?"

"Right." She pondered that for a minute. "You'd think she'd be back by now. How long does punishment last? And don't you think it seems strange that no one has even mentioned Jenny?"

"Jenny?"

Katie stood a few feet away, her eyes filled with dread.

"Where's your other roommate?" Jasi demanded.

"Jenny left a few days ago, before Nan."

"Where did she go?"

"You'll have to ask Father Jeremiah. All I know is she broke a commandment and was exiled." The girl chewed her lower lip. "I have no idea where she went after that."

"Did she ever talk about her family?"

"She said her parents disowned her when she was my age. She has a brother and sister though. I think she said they lived in Prince Rupert."

Jasi glanced at Brandon. "Go back to the cabin and contact Ops. Have someone check out the siblings. I'm going to talk to Christiansen."

She spotted Christiansen talking with Lazarus near the buffet tables. It appeared to be a heated conversation. As she drew nearer, they made a quick recovery and feigned smiles.

"Agent McLellan?" Christiansen said. "Coming back for seconds?"

"Yes, but not food. I have more questions."

Lazarus shifted his feet and attempted to leave, but Jasi gripped his arm. "You can stay."

"Please let him go," Christiansen cut in. "He has business to attend to. We're doing everything to cooperate with your investigation."

"Fine. Take up thy feet, Lazarus, and get lost." She watched the younger man skulk off into the shadows. Turning to Christiansen, she said, "You conveniently forgot to tell us about the note that was found in Nan's room."

"I'm sorry, but I don't see what that has to do with anything. Nan left us of her own accord. Her note simply said she was going home. Wherever that may be."

"I'd like to see it."

"That's impossible."

"So you *are* impeding my investigation."

Christiansen's lips thinned. "After I read Nan's note, I tossed it in the recycle bin last night, and everything in that bin was incinerated this morning."

Jasi almost swore aloud. Why was it that every time they had a clue, something prevented them from examining it? First, Sheral's bracelet mysteriously vanished. Now the note?

"If I had known how essential that note was," Christiansen said, his voice softening, "I never would have thrown it away."

"What about Jenny, Nancy's roommate?"

"Jenny Phillips is a sad soul, Agent McLellan. We did everything to try to help get her back on the path to righteousness. She was only with us for about a week. She left of her own accord. She accepted exile with grace."

"Like Nancy Davison."

"Exactly. Who knows? Perhaps they're together somewhere. Bad seeds attract one another."

"I thought you were supposed to be the forgiving kind," she said dryly.

Christiansen folded his arms across his chest. "I can forgive. But I'll always protect Sanctuary."

"Is that why you exiled Jenny?"

"Sometimes we have to make tough decisions. Enforcing exile is never easy for me."

"What did she do that was so terrible?"

"If you must know, Jenny slept with one of the men. Physical interaction between a man and woman is strictly forbidden here, unless the union of marriage has been performed first."

"It takes two people to have sexual intercourse."

"The man involved has also been reprimanded."

"But not exiled?"

"No."

"Isn't that a double standard?"

"Kenneth has been with us for three years. He's engaged to my wife's daughter, Amanda."

"But she's only a child!"

Christiansen raised his hands in surrender. "Hold on, Agent McLellan. I said *engaged*. Kenneth and Amanda won't be married until she turns eighteen. And before you ask, she is happy about the union."

Jasi didn't even attempt to hide her contempt. "But Kenneth slept with Jenny. How happy can Amanda be about that?"

"She wasn't pleased at first, but she's come around. Amanda knows that her fiancé gave into temptation, as is the way of man. Forgiveness, remember?" Christiansen's expression turned serious as he gazed over her head. "Now if you'll excuse me, I must prepare for tonight's ceremony. I hope you'll join us."

"I wouldn't miss it for the world," she said, hurrying off to find her partner.

She located Brandon outside Christiansen's lodge and filled him in on everything she had learned, including the fact that Sheral's note had been destroyed—if the note had ever existed in the first place.

"Damn, I didn't get much either," he said. "Jennifer Phillips, twenty-six, was raised in Prince Rupert. Both parents dead. Her sister is married, two kids. Her brother is single and unemployed. Neither of them has heard from Jennifer in months."

"Were they aware of her addiction problem?"

"They were. Her sister said Jennifer got hooked on cocaine in high school. Got in with the wrong crowd. Her life spiraled out of control after that."

"If we could find her, maybe she could tell us more about Sanctuary and Father Jeremiah."

"That won't happen tonight. Lazarus is waving at us."

Jasi peeked over her shoulder. "That guy acts like one of those vacant-eyed zombies in *The Walking Dead*."

"A walker?"

She snickered. "Yeah. He mindlessly follows Christiansen everywhere."

"By the way, Matthew is sending reinforcements tonight."

She stopped. "What? Why not wait until morning?"

"Apparently Natassia and Ben found something in the woods. More bodies."

"Oh God. How many?"

"A dozen maybe. All buried."

Jasi raised a brow. "Buried?"

"I know. Different MO. However, one of the corpses is missing a head."

"That matches our vic. They find anything else?"

"A button and ATV tracks."

Jasi's gaze snapped toward the larger barn. "Like those?" She nudged her head in the direction of two ATVs that were parked beside the barn. "During tonight's ceremony, I'll try to sneak away so I can obtain soil samples from the tires."

"So where's this life-changing event supposed to take place?"

"We're about to find out, Brandon."

Tribal drums echoed in the night air as the moon rose gracefully above them. The tempo increased with every step Jasi took, lending a sense of urgency to her actions.

"They really know how to put on a show," Brandon said.

"Reminds me of that scene in *King Kong*, when Jessica Lange is tied up and left as an offering to Kong."

"There won't be any human sacrifices tonight."

But Jasi wasn't so sure. "If this turns freaky, we're out of here. Okay?"

Brandon squeezed her hand. "In an instant."

"I believe we've reached our destination." She paused hesitantly, taking in the scene before her.

In a clearing east of the largest barn, sat a massive teepee with open door flaps. Outside, two men drummed, the tempo reverberating in the otherwise peaceful night air. One by one, members of Sanctuary filed inside.

"It's already freaky," she muttered.

"We're gaining their trust, Jasi. Eventually someone's going to talk to us, give us a clue."

Inhaling deeply, she headed toward the teepee. "We'll see."

A second later she was swallowed up by the cavernous mouth of the teepee.

She shivered, though it was anything but cold inside. Wooden benches lined the sides of the teepee, graduating in height toward the back. In the center, a metal pit contraption held hot stones that gleamed like red eyes. The stones hissed when a man in a black hooded cloak flicked a few drops of water over them.

She sniffed. *No indication of smoke.* Reassured, she let out a slow breath.

"You good?" Brandon asked as they sat in the back row close to the exit.

A bead of sweat trickled down her brow. "I'll survive."

In the hazy light cast only by the glowing stones and the scant rays of the moon that filtered in through the doorway, she tried to make out some familiar faces. Christiansen's wives sat up front. Amanda sat next to her mother and occasionally peeked over her shoulder at Eric, who sat three rows behind.

Jasi felt sympathy for them. With Amanda's impending engagement to an older man, poor Eric didn't stand a chance. She wondered what would happen if Christiansen found out they had feelings for one another.

"Christiansen's right-hand man is here," Brandon whispered.

She spotted Lazarus a few feet away, on the other side of the opening. Was he guarding the door to ensure no one left?

The drums outside ceased, and the drummers entered the teepee and closed the flaps. Thrown into almost complete darkness, Jasi waited, anxious to ease the rush of unexpected claustrophobia. After a second, her hand drifted of its own accord toward Brandon, and she felt immediate relief when he grasped it.

One by one, the room was illuminated by the glow of a dozen candles that circled the stone pit, and her confidence returned—until the figure in the center of the room dropped his hood.

Christiansen.

Something about the way he stood—the supreme arrogance that emanated from him—combined with the gullible adoration of the cult members made her blood curdle.

"Welcome, my family." Christiansen smiled and spread his arms. "And a special greeting to our esteemed guests from the CFBI. Tonight we celebrate the rebirth of one of our children. Katie, please join me."

As the girl made her way to Christiansen, Jasi noted that Katie's expression was one of pride and happiness. She'd found a new family to replace the one she'd left behind. But did the girl really understand the implications of her actions? By joining Sanctuary, Katie would be expected to give up all communication with her birth parents and any other natural family members—forever.

Jasi couldn't imagine being permanently separated from Pop and her brother, Brady. It was hard enough knowing she'd never see her beautiful mother again.

"Katie, have you chosen your name?" Christiansen asked.

"Yes, Father. My new name is Mia." She spelled it.

Jasi clued in immediately. Mia...as in Jere*mia*h.

Christiansen's eyes registered surprise, and pride washed over him. "Then *Mia* it shall be."

Lazarus approached them, a rough burlap sack in his hands. With the help of Christiansen, he proceeded to pull the sack over Katie's body.

Jasi hissed in a breath. *What the hell?*

When the girl was completely encapsulated by the sack, they picked her up and positioned her on the ground, tying the sack beneath her feet. Christiansen and Lazarus stepped back and a hush fell over the room.

The sack twitched.

"It's time to be born, Mia," Christiansen said.

The sack rolled and twisted.

"Let me out!" Katie's muffled voice cried. "I don't like this!"

"Push, Mia!"

"Push!" the crowd chanted.

"I can't breathe!" the girl said, sobbing. "Let me out! Please!"

"We can't just sit here," Jasi whispered to Brandon.

He patted her hand. "We can't interfere unless there's imminent danger. Otherwise everything we've worked for here will be lost."

Brandon was right, but it didn't make it any easier to witness the girl's distress. The sack jerked back and forth, and Katie's sobs grew more panicked with every passing minute. When her hand reappeared from the opening of the sack, the cheering began.

"Push, Mia!" Christiansen commanded.

Without warning, the sack opened and Katie emerged, her eyes streaming with tears. Christiansen gathered her in his arms, comforting her.

"This is the beginning of your new life." He placed his hands on her shoulders and turned her to face the room. "From tonight forth, we acknowledge the existence of our new daughter and sister, Mia."

A murmur of "Welcome, Mia" swept through the teepee.

Jasi caught herself saying the words and clamped her mouth closed.

Katie returned to her seat near the front, a wide grin on her face.

Christiansen gave a nod. The drummers began to softly beat their drums, while all but one candle was extinguished and the room darkened. A hiss of steam rose from the stones.

"And now we prepare our hearts and minds for the ritual of release," the obscured figure that was Christiansen said. "I ask you, dear family and friends, to close your eyes and focus on the beating drums. Imagine them as your own heartbeat, strong and full of life."

"No way I'm closing my eyes," Jasi said to Brandon.

"Trust me. Nothing's going to happen here. They wouldn't risk it."

Still, she didn't trust anyone in the teepee, except Brandon.

The steady beating made her tired. She let her eyes wander around the room, but she couldn't make out anything other than obscure blobs. No one made a sound, not even a cough.

The drums were mesmerizing, lulling her. It had been a long, tiring day. She inhaled hot, damp air and leaned against Brandon. Sweat rolled down her skin, over her cheeks, between her breasts. She felt as though she were on fire, from the inside.

Against her will, her eyes drifted shut. *Just for a moment.*

"Jasi?"

Her eyes flickered open. "What?"

Beside her, Brandon whispered, "I didn't say a thing."

She closed her eyes again.

"Jasi? Can you hear me? It's Emily?"

She had to be imagining things. Emily only came to her at night, in her dreams. Except that other time…when she helped her in the woods.

I dreamt that too.

Hadn't she?

Emily stood before her, blonde hair shimmering over her shoulders and blue eyes filled with terror. But she looked very different from Jasi's usual dreams. Emily was older, in her late teens. All traces of her normal bluish lips, mottled bruises and the jagged bruise across her neck had disappeared.

"You're not dreaming, Jasi. I'm here, but I only have a few minutes."

"Emily? What's wrong?"

"There's not much time left. He's going to kill me. I overheard him say it."

"To who?"

"No one. I think he was just muttering out loud. He's losing it, and I'm scared."

"Can you tell me who has you?"

Emily shook her head. "There's some kind of block. Whenever I try to say his name, I can't."

"Do you have any idea where you are?"

"No. He brought me here, blindfolded, years ago."

"But you're in a house?"

"I think so. I'm in the basement."

"Any windows?"

"None. I have a light, water…food sometimes."

"And you have no idea where this house is?"

"Somewhere in BC, about half an hour, I think, from the last place I was living. He moves me every so often."

"Are you sure you're in BC?"

"Yes. The furnace has a sticker with a 604 phone number on it."

"What else?"

"The house is near a river. I heard rushing water when we were arriving. And maybe a bridge. The car traveled over something hard, then gravel."

"Any neighbors?"

"I don't think so. I can't hear anything outside other than his car."

"How long have you been at this place?"

"I don't know. A year, maybe longer."

"And how long have you lived with him?"

Emily's eyes filled with tears. "Ever since I can remember."

"Why haven't you contacted me sooner?"

"He's been drugging me to keep me compliant. Today I poured the jug of water he brought me down the drain."

"You need water to survive, Emily."

"I'm okay. I cut into the water line, and I'm using it to fill the jug."

Emily reached out, and when her hand touched Jasi's face it sent a tremor down Jasi's spine. Every nerve in her body sizzled. She had somehow felt Emily's touch.

"So you're not a dream or nightmare?"

Emily shook her head and swiped at a tear. "No."

"But how is this possible? How can you be communicating with me like this?"

"I have no idea. Whenever I've tried to reach out, I've only connected with you." Emily let out a sharp gasp. "He's coming, Jasi!"

"You said you overheard him talking earlier. What did he say exactly?"

"He said I'd let him down. And that I'd be dead by my birthday."

"When's that?"

"He said it was in three days."

As the pounding of drums infiltrated Jasi's mind, Emily's body began to dissolve, atom by atom. "I'll find you, Emily."

"You have to. You're my only hope."

13

As everyone filed out of the teepee, most of them withdrawn and covered in a sheen of sweat, Jasi watched their faces for furtive looks or glances, hoping someone would reveal something. No one said a word.

"Well, that was fun," Brandon said dryly.

"You have any out-of-body experiences?" she asked, arching a brow.

"No. The only experience I had was one of discomfort."

She laughed. "Wait 'til I tell you mine."

The drummers had resumed their positions outside the flaps and were beating a somber rhythm. One of them, an older man with piercing black eyes, stared at Jasi. She trembled, unsure if this was a result of the cold night air hitting her hot, wet skin, or the man's intense gaze.

"Come on," she urged. "I need to put on some dry clothes."

"Agent McLellan," a voice said behind her.

Turning, she recognized Beth, one of Christiansen's wives

"Mrs. Christiansen."

"Beth, please."

Jasi waited while the young woman gathered her courage.

"I just wanted to thank you."

"What for?"

Beth shrugged. "Hannah's daughter told us you talked to her. That you were nice to Amanda."

It seemed odd that the woman was so interested in the treatment of one of the other wives' children.

"I'm just doing my job, Beth."

"Where I come from, police don't treat anyone with respect. So I just wanted to thank you. Oh, and that woman who died?"

"Yes?"

"Nan wasn't liked around here."

"Why do you say that?"

Beth chewed on her lower lip. "She was supposed to do her silence with dignity, but kept asking questions. Too many, if you ask me."

Jasi thought about Sheral Downham. The woman was a reporter pretending to be a hooker. It couldn't have been easy switching roles. "Maybe she was trying to get to know you, make friends?"

"Being nosy isn't the way to do that. Not around here. And she kept sneaking off to the river when she thought no one was looking."

Jasi attempted an indifferent shrug. "Perhaps she wanted to take a bath."

Beth's eyes flared. "That's a kind of indecency you *won't* find here."

Jasi studied her. *What other kinds of indecencies* will *we find?* "Did you talk to Nancy Davison?"

"Not after she started asking me about my husband." Beth lifted her chin. "It's not right to show interest in another woman's man unless you're married to him."

Jasi exchanged looks with Brandon.

"Beth!"

The woman whipped around, her eyes wide with fear. Christiansen stood a few feet away, glaring at her as though she'd committed a terrible crime.

"Coming, Husband," Beth said as she scurried toward him, almost shrinking in stature with each step.

Jasi caught Brandon's eye. "Don't ever think you can command me like that."

He chuckled. "I learned a long time ago to let you take the lead. I quite enjoy following you." Smirking, he lowered his gaze to her rear end.

She elbowed him, and he grunted.

She watched as Christiansen leaned down and whispered something in Beth's ear. The woman's face blanched. With a nod and downcast eyes, she gathered her skirt and rushed off.

Christiansen made a beeline toward them. "Tonight is a time for celebration. I thought I made that clear."

"We still have an investigation to conduct," Brandon said.

"We have been more than cooperative. But tonight is Mia's night and a time for peaceful reflection, not to harass the innocent."

Jasi almost told him the sweat lodge had been anything but peaceful. Instead she said, "We'll need samples of DNA from everyone over the age of thirteen."

Christiansen blinked. "Is that really necessary?"

"We want to rule out the innocent, don't we?" She gave him a sweet smile.

He sighed with exaggerated impatience. "Fine. Can we do this in the morning? I promise. No one will be leaving Sanctuary tonight."

"Morning it is." Turning to Brandon, she said, "Come on. I'm freezing."

Back in the cabin they changed into warm, dry clothes and sat down on the sofa to process the evening's events. When Jasi told him about Emily, she could see his analytical mind churning. He still found it difficult at times to grasp the power of her mind. Hell, so did she.

"I know it sounds crazy, Brandon. I wasn't sleeping so I couldn't have been dreaming. The only way I can describe it is that Emily…reached out to me."

She tried to make sense of her vision in the teepee. Without doubt, any sane person would chalk her little chat with Emily up to extreme heat and humidity, lack of sleep and undeniable stress from the case. But nothing seemed sane where Emily was concerned.

"I have three days, Brandon. What am I supposed to do?"

"You could ask Matthew to remove you from this case, assign someone else."

"I can't do that. It's not fair to Sheral Downham. She deserves justice."

"What about Emily?"

"Her too." She groaned. "I am so torn, Brandon. I want to find the bastard who killed Sheral, and I have to find Emily before she turns up dead too."

"And you're positive she exists?"

She gawked at him. "Of course I'm positive. My conversations with her have been far too detailed for them to be anything other than real. I don't understand this connection I have with Emily. This kind of…gift has never surfaced before with any PSI I know. And I never had any signs of it until Emily first appeared when I was a kid."

"Could be she's the only one you share this with." He rubbed his chin. "That's weird in itself. Why her?"

She shrugged. "Perhaps she's a Level 1 like me."

All psychics evaluated by the CFBI for entry into the PSI Division were evaluated on the strength and reliability of their psychic skills and assigned a level rank accordingly. Jasi was one of few Level 1 psychics. Natassia was another.

"How about this?" Brandon said. "We'll work the Sanctuary case, but in between we'll try to figure out where Emily is."

"I was hoping you'd say that. So you'll help me?"

He gave a nod. "Just tell me what you need."

She leapt from the sofa, ran to his side and threw her arms around him. "What I need?" Her lips met his and warmth flowed through her body. "All I need is you. And the knowledge that you believe me and don't think I've completely lost it."

He stroked her face with both hands. "Not completely."

She swatted him. "Okay. Where do we start?"

He jerked his head toward the bedroom.

"With Emily, I mean," she said, laughing.

"We make a list of everything you know about her."

"Let's begin. It shouldn't take very long."

An hour later, Jasi had her list. There wasn't much to go on, but she had more now than she did a year ago. Still, some things didn't quite make sense. Like why Emily had a southern accent when Jasi had first heard her speak, yet now that accent was gone. And why had the girl's wounds vanished? Emily had first come to her as a ghostly-white dead girl, and now she appeared almost the picture of health.

"What do you think?" Jasi asked Brandon.

"Maybe you've prevented those injuries from happening somehow because of something you've said or done. Or even the fact that you and Emily have this mind-meld thing going."

"That's a positive thing then."

He reached out and touched her arm. "You'll find her. I have faith in you."

"I don't have a choice. I *have* to find her. Someone plans to murder her in three days."

She glanced down at her data-com. She'd already set a countdown timer and it was ticking down minute by minute.

"I sent Ops a request for a search for any girl or woman named Emily who has been missing for the past twenty years," Brandon said. "I think by widening the field parameters we may have more luck."

"Good idea." She headed for her backpack and withdrew a comprehensive map of British Columbia, which she then tacked to one wall. "We can use this to help us narrow the land search."

Brandon examined the map for a few minutes.

"That's a substantial area to cover, Jasi," he said finally. "You're talking the entire province."

"I know, but with support from Divine Ops we should be able to refine the search area to certain locations that have ranger towers and rivers nearby. Then we can ask Matthew to send in a team to search for her."

She could tell by the doubtful look on his face that he wasn't convinced.

"It's all we can do," she said, heaving a weary sigh, "unless I get more info from Emily."

"Have you tried creating an image of her face using the FRP and running that through the Missing Persons Database?"

"No, but that's an awesome idea."

The FRP was a Facial Reconstruction Program used by the CFBI and other agencies. Jasi could reconstruct Emily's face from memory, even age it, and they'd have a better chance of finding a match.

Jasi sat at the table, opened her laptop and said a silent thank you when she noticed the battery display indicated she had full power. Logging into the CFBI website, she entered her ID code and password, selected "FRP" from the navigation options and began the task of bringing Emily's face to life.

Brandon sat down beside her. "What kind of face shape does she have?"

She closed her eyes. *Emily's face shape? Roundish.*

Opening her eyes, she scrolled through the options.

"Cheekbones?" she read aloud. "High."

It took just over a half hour before she had an image on the screen that resembled the girl that haunted her dreams. A few tweaks here and there, and voila!

"That's her," Jasi whispered. "That's Emily."

"Save that picture," Brandon said. "Then we'll age it and save that one too."

As the FRP interpreted and assembled the data, the pixels within Emily's image contorted until the child morphed into an adult woman.

"She's very pretty," Brandon said.

Jasi had to agree. Emily had beautiful features.

"Her eyes look sad though," she said. "That's one part of her that has never changed in all my visions." She stared wistfully at the woman on the screen. *I'm getting closer, Emily.*

Brandon glanced at his watch. "It's getting late. We should call it a night. I have a feeling tomorrow's going to be a very long day."

She yawned. "I'm beat."

"Want to push two of these beds together?" he asked, grinning.

"Nothing's happening here, Brandon." The disappointment on his face made her add, "This place might be a sanctuary for some, but I'm not feeling particularly safe. In fact," she flicked a look over her shoulder, "I need to do something." She strode toward the door with the intention of locking it. "Damn."

"What's wrong?"

"There's no lock." She swore again.

"I guess they figure they don't need locks here. Everyone is *family*."

"Well, I need a lock." She grabbed a wooden chair and jammed it beneath the doorknob. "There. No one's getting here without us knowing it."

For good measure she checked all the windows, which thankfully came with standard manufacturer-installed locks. By the time she was done, Brandon had stripped to his boxers and climbed into one of the single beds.

"You sure you don't want to join me?" he asked, peeling back the covers to expose tanned skin and defined muscles. "Last chance."

It wasn't easy resisting temptation. And he was *very* tempting.

Jasi smiled. "Goodnight, Brandon."

She selected the bed next to his and shed her clothes, leaving her panties and bra on. Tucking the non-government-issued Beretta her father had given her beneath the pillow, she slid beneath rough cotton sheets and released a pent-up sigh. Going over the day's events in her mind, she made mental notes of follow-up interviews they'd need to conduct tomorrow.

She let her mind drift to Emily. Fear coursed through her, and she shivered. *What if I don't find her in time?*

A few feet away, Brandon snored softly. The sound reminded her of Pop. He'd fall asleep at the drop of a hat the second he plopped down in front of the television after a hard day's work. Sometimes he'd drop off while holding his coffee mug.

Although Mission wasn't far from Vancouver, Pop seemed a million miles away. She missed him. Last time she'd chatted with him he'd mentioned he was getting the boys together for cards—and by "boys" he meant his old cop buddies. She was happy Pop was staying active. After he'd retired, she'd worried about him. A cop's life expectancy after retirement wasn't promising.

Flashes of poignant memories played before her like a movie on the big screen. Pop beaming like he'd won the lottery when her mother came home. Her mother grinning, while Pop cursed because the sun was in his eyes, no matter where he sat in the living room. Her parents kissing when they thought they were alone.

Mom...

Calista McLellan—"Cali" to everyone who knew her well—had been brutally murdered, left for dead on the kitchen floor. Traumatized eight-year-old Jasi was the only witness to the crime. The odd thing was she didn't recall much about her life *before* that horrible day. And the event itself? Hazy and intangible.

For almost twenty years, authorities had assumed her mother's murder was a case of a home invasion gone wrong. They'd never caught the person responsible, and the case had grown cold. The files were probably locked away in a dank basement somewhere until new evidence surfaced.

She scrunched her eyes, trying to recollect that fateful day. The images slithered in sluggishly at first. It was Brady's second birthday. Pop had taken her brother out for the afternoon, leaving Jasi and her mother at the house.

Her mother told her someone was coming over. Something about "business." That in itself was unusual, now that Jasi was old enough to comprehend. Her mother had been a stay-at-home mom. What possible "business" would she have been involved in?

Someone had knocked on the door.

Everything changed after that.

Disobeying her mother, who had ordered her to go outside, Jasi hid in a closet. She heard a man's low voice, and he didn't sound happy.

"Where's the kid?"

"She's not here," her mother said.

The man swore. More yelling.

Sitting on the closet floor, Jasi peeked through the slat in the door. Her mother's slippers rushed past, followed by a blur of evil, its voice exploding with rage. He wore a baseball cap low over his face. She glanced down and saw shiny black boots. They reminded her of Pop's work boots and they had the same chemical scent. Shoe polish.

The man proceeded down the hall, and she heard glass shattering. She held back tears, afraid she'd make a sound and the bad man would find her.

Her mother screamed, followed by an ear-splitting crack. The air smelled weird, like burnt toast.

Jasi remained in the closet, shaking with fear. Footsteps approached, and she saw the man carrying something shiny and metallic. A gun.

She shrank back into the shadows. *Please don't find me. Please.*

The man jerked his head as if he heard something. "It didn't have to be this way, Cali. But you left me no choice. I'm sorry, Cali."

The black shoes clicked across the floor, out of view.

Jasi fought back tears. She was so scared.

Another loud bang echoed through the house. Then all was silent.

When she'd finally gathered the courage to leave the closet, she discovered her mother's body on the kitchen floor, one hand stretched out. Her bright green eyes and mouth were wide open, frozen in a silent scream, and it was that image that haunted Jasi all her life. That and the pool of crimson blood that stained the floor.

Lying in bed in the cabin at Sanctuary, Jasi embraced the tendrils of memory that had always eluded her. She'd gone over them a hundred times during the years that followed, without ever seeing anything new. But in the cobwebbed recesses of her brain, she knew she'd seen more.

What am I forgetting?

She remembered the pungent scent that had wafted from the wound in her mother's forehead, how she'd coughed and struggled to catch her breath, how her vision had grown distorted and her body light.

My first psychic vision.

How terrified she'd been when she realized she was seeing everything from the killer's eyes, feeling him, touching his malevolent mind.

Remember...

She recalled the man's powerful rage coursing through her body as she connected with him. She could almost hear his thoughts. He wanted something. He *craved* something. And he'd do anything to get it. He'd done far worse to Cali in the past. He couldn't think of that now. He had to get the...

There! Something new.

Now she knew why her mother's killer had come to their house that day. He hadn't asked about Jasi because he was concerned she was home and would see something. He'd come to take her away. For some reason he thought Cali would allow Jasi to leave with him. Was he insane? And why had he wanted her? Was he trying to kidnap her or take her away for a few hours?

And another thing—the man had known her mother *well* and for a long time. Had he been in love with her? Was he stalking her? Had her mother taken a lover?

No, that's not possible.

Jasi summoned more of that first vision.

Before her death, her mother had scratched her attacker, drawing blood. Yet the police report clearly stated that no traces of foreign DNA were found on her body or in the house. Now Jasi knew why. The killer had meticulously eliminated all incriminating evidence, other than leaving behind a body.

Muffling a gasp, Jasi sat up in bed.

Had her mother's killer been incarcerated? Is that where she'd find the answers—in some stark prison cell?

Reaching for her data-com, she opened a familiar file titled "Mom" and entered everything she'd just recalled. Her pulse fluttered with anticipation. Between this new information on her mother and everything she'd learned about Emily in the past day, she was more confident now than ever before. Ironic how these breakthroughs had come right in the middle of a case and while she was sequestered inside a cult.

Perhaps Sanctuary isn't so bad after all.

With every intention of going to sleep, she rolled onto her stomach, but the constant buzzing of random thoughts pissed her off. She wanted to scream, *"Will you please shut the hell up and let me sleep?"*

She spent the next ten minutes repositioning her body to avoid the wayward springs that jabbed her rib. There was no escape. She pounded the pillow to make it less bricklike, but that made no difference. Half an hour later, she gave up on the notion of sleep. With stealthy movements, she escaped the confinement of the torturous slab that some fool had mistakenly labeled a bed.

Dressing with haste, she tiptoed to the table and palmed Brandon's data-com. She'd leave a message in case he woke up before she returned.

'Can't sleep. Gone for walk to test ATVs.'

She mentally kicked herself. She'd been so distracted by her vision of Emily that she'd forgotten to complete the one significant task that had been on her agenda—retrieving the soil samples.

She grabbed the Beretta from beneath the pillow, securing it in the shoulder harness she wore. She found a flashlight in the front pocket of her backpack, which she eased over her shoulder. With a backward glance, she hesitated. Should she wake Brandon and ask him to join her?

No. It'll be a quick in-and-out mission. He'll never even know I left.

Jasi moved the chair, opened the door and slipped out into the night.

14

Back in the surveillance van, Ben activated the cameras he and Natassia had positioned inconspicuously around Sanctuary's fence earlier that evening. It was a few minutes after midnight. If anyone headed into the forest or came close to the gravesites, they'd know it. He doubted anyone would be foolish enough to engage in illegal activities while Sanctuary was under the CFBI's magnifying glass, but one thing he'd learned in his years of investigating criminals, most weren't that intelligent. They always slipped up at some point.

The computer monitor flickered and split into six separate screens.

"Cameras are ready," he said.

Natassia peered over his shoulder. "You set the parameters?"

He nodded. "We won't be notified unless something larger than a dog crosses any of them."

"Good. I still wish we'd set up cameras inside Sanctuary."

"No warrant for that."

Natassia yawned. "So how are we going to do this?"

"We'll take turns on surveillance. I doubt we'll see much action tonight. Everyone at Sanctuary appears to have hunkered down for the night." He arranged chair cushions on the storage bin at the back of the van. "I know it's not much, but you should get some rest."

Natassia eyed the cushions. "I still don't get why we couldn't stay in a cabin like Jasi and Brandon."

"Matthew could only get authorization for two agents inside. There's not enough evidence to suggest someone from Sanctuary committed the crime. Evidently, Christiansen spouted that he had the right to a peaceful assembly, blah, blah, blah, according to the Charter of Rights and

Freedoms. Seems he has friends in high places, and they agreed."

"Doesn't that seem weird to you?"

He thought about this for a moment. "Giles Christiansen runs a non-denominational cult that practices polygamy. I can see why he'd want to make nice with the top brass in certain sectors." He opened his data-com's browser and activated a file search. "The good Father Jeremiah has connections to the Vancouver Police Department, at least three law firms and a handful of politicians. Not to mention, he's heavily financed by three multinational corporations, two well-known philanthropists and a popular motivational speaker."

"But that's what I mean. Why would they invest in Sanctuary? What do they get out of giving him money?"

"A huge tax write-off for one. And the appearance that they are out-of-the-box thinkers who are interested in helping others escape their addictions and find a peaceful existence."

Natassia shook her head. "That doesn't make sense to me. Tax write-offs aside, these investors all live relatively *normal* lives, with one wife, kids, the white picket fence around their mansions."

"Maybe they're closet cultists. You know, they fantasize about having the lifestyle Christiansen has." As he scrolled over the report, he paused. "Hmm, says here many of these investors have visited Sanctuary often throughout the years. Perhaps they want to escape the pressures of their *normal* lives."

"Maybe they're coming here to hook up?"

"You think Christiansen's pimping out the women?"

"And maybe the girls."

The thought made Ben sick. "We haven't uncovered any signs of sexual abuse."

"Maybe because the women are too afraid to come forward."

"You think this is what Sheral discovered, what got her killed?"

"Could be. Something is going on behind Sanctuary's doors and I doubt it's all sweat lodges, barbecues and 'Namaste.'" Natassia stretched out on the cushions, then groaned and changed positions.

"We'll be allowed inside tomorrow," he said. "Since we found the bodies buried so close to Sanctuary, Christiansen has to open the gates to us. Sanctuary will be swarming with CFBI agents come sunrise."

"So maybe we'll get that cabin?"

He chuckled. "We still can't stay overnight on the property."

"Damn…"

"Get some sleep, Natassia. I'll wake you up in four hours."

While his partner floundered on the makeshift bed, Ben continued to study the reports on Giles Christiansen, with a focus on the economic aspect of Sanctuary. The whole investor entity seemed suspect. These men had donated substantial amounts of money. Some had transferred funds via wire transfers. The further he dug into Sanctuary's financials, the more convinced he became that the money was the key.

Follow the money.

He made a note on his data-com. *'Possible reasons for donations: buying women/sex; trafficking women/children.'*

He recognized many of the investor's names. If they were involved in something illegal, they'd lose more than tax deductions.

If the truth ever came out.

He thought about the bodies buried in the forest. Some were men. Surely they weren't being sold or abused. Had they threatened to reveal Sanctuary's sinister secret? If so, that could have led to their deaths.

What about Sheral Downham?

He suspected she had seen or heard something incriminating, perhaps even captured it on film. Then she'd been caught. And murdered. But why had the killer dumped her body in the incinerator instead of burying it with the others? If he had done the latter, the CFBI wouldn't be scrutinizing Sanctuary so closely, and the victims would be decomposing without anyone being the wiser.

The night of the murder, the residents of Sanctuary were told to stay indoors because of a bear sighting. The order may have been issued to allow the killer time to eliminate the body. But perhaps not everyone obeyed.

What if someone else was prowling around in the woods? Maybe that's why the killer disposed of Sheral's body in the incinerator and not out in the woods. He had no time.

"All we need is one witness," he whispered, staring at the photo of what was left of Cameron Prescott's friend. *If only those bones could speak...*

In some way they had. Natassia had received a clear but short vision.

He removed the gloves and stared at his fingers, flexing them with caution. His pale but well-shaped hands hadn't seen sun in years. He couldn't risk it. If he touched an object or a person, he'd often be inundated with symbolic visions.

He remembered the day Matthew Divine had found him. Ben was only twenty-one, and his parents had confined him to a psychiatric hospital. He didn't blame them really. They had no idea what was going on inside his head at the time. Hell, he hadn't even had a clue. All he knew was that sometime after his sixteenth birthday, his brain had become assaulted by thoughts and images whenever he touched specific items or people. He'd thought he was going insane—until some of his visions proved to be accurate.

Like the time he'd touched a co-worker's arm and envisioned money, only for the company to discover a week later that the co-worker had been embezzling funds.

Or the time Ben had touched a pawn shop necklace he'd wanted to buy for his girlfriend at the time, only to see images of a dead blonde woman with a knife in her back. A few days later, he saw the same woman on the news. She'd been stabbed in the back multiple times, her body discovered on the kitchen floor by the weekly cleaning company she'd hired. When he reported the necklace to the police, they questioned him for hours, curious to learn how he'd recognized the necklace as the victim's. The next thing he knew, Ben was the key suspect in the investigation.

And that's how he met Matthew. Soon after, Ben joined the CFBI, enlisted in the PSI Division, and he'd never looked back.

He rubbed his face, which only made his fingertips hypersensitive.

What would I see if I touched Natassia?

They had an unspoken rule—gloves on, *always*, even when they were intimate. But one day, they may be able to break that rule. Matthew had a team of scientists working on a special hand spray that would allow Ben to touch everything, yet it would block the sensations that triggered his visions.

He smiled. He couldn't wait for that day to arrive.

Slipping his hands back into the gloves, he played a few games on Facebook while keeping an eye on the screens before him, which showed no movement in the forest. Once in a while, he checked for a signal from Jasi or Brandon's 'coms. Both were silent.

Just after two in the morning, the monitor beeped. The cameras had picked up movement. He deactivated the warning so the noise wouldn't wake Natassia and watched as six CFBI agents—identified by fluorescent lettering on the back of their jackets—approached the forest gravesites. He watched as the agents spread out around the cordoned off crime scene. They took positions several feet from one another and sat down on their backpacks. One of the men spotted the camera Natassia had attached to a cedar trunk, and he waved.

Ben watched them for a while but grew bored after about fifteen minutes. What was the point? Only an idiot would go near a crime scene surrounded by CFBI agents. That left only Jasi and Brandon to worry about, and he was quite positive they were sleeping.

His watch read: *3:22.* It was almost time to switch off with Natassia, but she was sleeping so soundly he didn't want to wake her.

A red light flashed on the monitor. One of the cameras on the perimeter of the fence had caught something. Two figures moved swiftly through the trees.

He tried zooming in, but the figures vanished. *Shit.*

A minute later he saw a slightly larger figure following the first two. *Jasi!* He recognized her movements, how she took cover behind trees while keeping her prey in sight. She held her right hand firmly at her side, weapon drawn.

"Natassia," he called out.

Natassia jerked awake and sat up. "What's wrong?"

"Jasi's tracking someone in the woods."

Natassia moved to his side. "Is Brandon with her?"

"No, she's alone. I'm going after her. I need you to watch the cameras. Make sure everything is recorded. I don't want any surprises."

"You want me to call Brandon?"

"No. We don't know she's in any real danger, and last thing we want to do is piss off Christiansen and his clan. Let's keep this quiet for now. Chances are someone saw her and is curious what she's doing out so late."

"I'm wondering the same thing."

He secured an earpiece to his ear. "I'll use Jasi's tracker to find her."

All CFBI agents had a microscopic tracking device, compliments of nanotechnology, implanted in their navels. These tiny computers used a GPS and mapping system similar to one found in a modern vehicle, only far more detailed and always up-to-date. Unfortunately, trackers were most often activated when an agent had gone missing. Sometimes it was the only way they could identify the unrecognizable body of someone in the CFBI.

He shivered. *That won't be the case tonight.*

He keyed in Jasi's identification code, and his data-com brought up a map of the area, with a small green light indicating her position. "Got her."

Natassia hauled open the van door and passed him a flashlight and his gun. "Need anything else?"

"I'm good. Let me know if anyone else decides to take a stroll through the woods at three-thirty in the morning."

"I will. Stay safe, Ben."

He jumped down from the van and took in the bleakness of the night. The sky was overcast. No moon or stars. No streetlights. Not one light on in any of the cabins.

For a second he felt lost in time and space.

He turned on the flashlight. Inhaling deeply, he strode toward the trees.

15

With only her flashlight to guide her, Jasi eyed the derelict barn with its peeling red paint. Situated at the northeastern edge of the property, the small building backed onto the razor wire fence.

She veered around the corner of the building and surveyed the other side.

The ATVs were nowhere to be seen.

Has someone taken them into the woods?

If that were the case, Ben and Natassia would notify her.

She released a pent-up breath. *The ATVs must be inside.*

The doors were unlocked, so she pushed on one. It belched in mutiny, but she was able to get it open without waking the entire community. Standing in the doorway, she shone the flashlight over the various humps and bumps. As neglected as the exterior, the interior of the barn accommodated various crop machines, most in a state of rust and disrepair.

To the left of a plow sat the two ATVs.

She took a quick look over her shoulder then proceeded into the barn. From the wild mewing that came from the loft above, she deduced that a few resident barn cats had made the place their home. She hoped that was all that resided here.

She removed an evidence kit from her backpack and crouched next to one of the ATVs. With sterile disposable plastic tweezers, she flaked off the damp soil particles trapped between the treads of the front tire and dropped them into the evidence bag. Sealing the bag, she wrote the serial number of the ATV on the front. She repeated her actions with the second vehicle. She shone the flashlight over every inch of the ATVs, hoping to find other trace evidence—like blood. Both machines were clean. She swabbed the seats, clutch handle and throttle for DNA and secured each in its own labeled container. She'd have an agent bring the samples directly to Ops in the morning.

She was about to exit the barn when she heard footsteps. Ducking behind the door, she waited. Soft murmurs sounded. Whoever it was, they weren't alone.

Shit.

Slowly sliding one hand beneath her jacket, she released the snap on the shoulder harness and withdrew the Beretta. *Better to be safe than dead.*

The footsteps began to move away.

She crept toward the doorway. A quick glance told her there were two people moving around to the back of the barn. With her back against the barn, she edged closer.

Crrrack!

She froze.

Not a gunshot, Jasi. Tree branch.

She heard the distinct sound of one person hushing another as she continued inching her way alongside the barn. When she reached the rear of the barn, no one was there. She'd lost them.

Determined to pick up the trail, she shone the light over the fence. The section directly behind the barn revealed an opening big enough for an average-sized adult to climb through, and it was completely obscured from view. From the other side of the fence, she heard soft rustling noises in the bushes.

Gotcha!

She climbed through, keeping a watchful eye on the woods before her. Nothing moved, and she could no longer hear the crunching of footsteps. Moving with haste, she slipped through the forest, eager to catch up to her prey.

She spotted them several yards ahead. Two shadowy figures, one slightly taller than the other. They were smoking. She could see the fiery end of a cigarette as it passed between them.

What are they doing out here in the middle of the night?

She looked at her watch. *3:27.*

With furtiveness, she followed them, staying a few yards behind at all times. The deeper she proceeded into the forest, the more she kicked herself for not bringing Brandon. She resisted the urge to call him on her 'com. She wasn't in any danger. At least not yet.

One of the shadows ahead giggled. This was followed by ardent kissing sounds.

Good God. They're making out.

Somewhat relieved, Jasi ducked behind a spruce. This wasn't a case of something deadly and nefarious after all. Then again, why would anyone from Sanctuary sneak off into the woods unless their union wasn't blessed by Father Jeremiah?

She moved around the tree, her feet trampling the dry brush below.

"Who's there?" a young male voice demanded.

Eric. The boy from the river.

Jasi stepped forward just as someone else darted past her. Rather than follow the fleeing shadow, she kept her flashlight aimed on Eric's chest.

"You're that cop," he said, his face twitching with panic.

"CFBI, actually."

"What are you doing out here?"

"I could ask you the same thing." She moved the light over him, thankful to see he carried no weapons—only a cigarette.

"Couldn't sleep so I went for a walk. What's it to ya?"

She took a few steps closer. "No one's supposed to go past the fence. We both know that."

"I know what to do if I come across a bear." He sneered at her. "Do you?"

She shrugged and raised her gun to her hip. Eric clamped his mouth shut.

"Who was with you, Eric?"

He shrugged. "Nobody."

"I saw someone else."

"You saw no one but me. Got it?" There was fear in his voice now.

"Does Father Jeremiah know about your late night strolls?"

"You can't say anything to him," Eric cried out, hands raised, beseeching.

"Who are you trying to protect?"

Silence.

"Who, Eric?"

"Just a friend. I can't tell you who."

A waft of pungent smoke entered Jasi's nostrils, and she coughed. The kid wasn't smoking regular tobacco.

"You know pot's illegal, right?"

"What pot?" Eric tossed the joint on the ground, pulverizing it with his running shoe.

She let out a frustrated sigh. "Perhaps we should go visit Father Jeremiah and discuss the ramifications of illegal substance abuse."

"No! Please…you don't understand…"

She softened her voice. "Then help me understand, Eric."

Eric's gaze floundered back and forth as he visibly struggled with what to tell her.

"Listen, kid, I'm here on a more serious matter than pot and kissing," she said. "And I have no intention of turning you in to Father Jeremiah if you don't give me reason to, but if you and your...uh, *friend*...have been wandering these woods at night, you may have seen something. Something we need to know."

"I seen nothing. I swear."

"What about your friend?"

"Nothing either."

"Were you out here the night of the murder?"

"You mean the incinerator chick?"

Jasi's jaw twitched as she eyed him.

"No, we all stayed inside," Eric said. "Bear on the loose."

"Yet we have the same warning tonight, and here you are."

"No hunters out tonight."

She flicked a look around her. "How did you know that?"

"No lights in the trees. I looked out the window first."

"Did you see lights in the trees that night?"

The kid shrugged. "Maybe." When she stepped closer, he said, "Okay, okay! Yes, I saw lights."

"How many?"

"I dunno. Maybe like four."

The crackling of brush told them that someone was coming.

"I gotta go!" Eric said, scurrying off into the trees.

Minutes later, Jasi had a bright light in her face.

"Jasi!" Ben hissed. "Are you okay?"

"I'm fine. What are you doing out here?"

"I saw you on the monitor, tracking two people. Did you find them?"

She gave a nod. "One of the boys—Eric—and his girlfriend."

"Who's that?"

"Well, from the pot they were smoking, I'd say Amanda. Her mother, Hannah, has a prescription, and I'm sure it's not difficult for Amanda to confiscate some."

"I thought this Amanda girl was engaged to one of the older men."

"You can't stop love. Even if it's puppy love." She grabbed his arm and steered him in the direction of Sanctuary. "Let's head back."

"You heard about the multiple graves we found?"

"Yeah. You and Natassia ID the bodies yet?"

"Still working on it. Natassia got a read off a female vic. And I had a few flashes from a male."

"What did you two see?"

He filled her in.

"You think the button came from the killer?" she asked.

"I think it came from someone who was there when he was buried, someone who..." Ben went quiet. He tapped his earpiece, indicating he was listening to something. After a few seconds, he whispered, "Shit."

"What's wrong?"

He beckoned her to duck low behind a cluster of bushes and they turned off both flashlights. "Someone else is in the woods, watching us."

"You sure?"

"Natassia saw him on a camera about five yards from here."

"Who?"

"No ID. As far as she can tell, it's one of the men."

"What do you want to do?"

"Catch him, and find out what the hell he's doing out here."

She raised her gun. "I'm ready if you are."

With flashlights aimed on the forest floor, they headed in opposite directions, intending to circle around and corner their quarry. Above them, the sky had lightened, casting a gray sheen over everything. Another hour or so and it would be sunrise.

She wove between trees and bushes, then stopped. Someone was ahead of her. He'd stopped moving, but she could hear his breathing.

"CFBI!" she hollered. "We know you're there. Come on out."

"Who's out here?"

The beam of Jasi's flashlight captured a masculine face framed by black hair streaked with gray. She recognized him as one of the drummers. His wide brow, obsidian eyes and prominent cheekbones suggested a Native Indian heritage.

She skimmed the light over him, pausing when she noticed his hands were crammed into the pockets of a lightweight jacket. "Slowly take your hands out of your pockets."

The man frowned. "You think I have a weapon?"

Ben stepped from behind a cedar. "Do what she says."

The man withdrew his hands inch by inch and raised them chest high. "See?"

"Who are you?" Ben demanded.

"Name's Henry." He flicked his chin at Jasi. "She can search me if she wants. I don't mind."

Ben ignored him. "What are you doing out here?"

"Saw the lights."

"So you came to investigate?"

"Saw someone leaving Sanctuary grounds and—"

"I thought anyone could leave when they want," Jasi cut in.

Henry waved his hands deliberately, and when she gave a nod, he lowered them. "Look, part of my responsibility is ensuring the safety of everyone at Sanctuary. We already had one unfortunate death."

"Yes, very unfortunate," she muttered.

"Woods aren't safe."

"I know, I know. A bear is causing havoc."

Henry gave a nod. "You shouldn't be wandering around out here. Neither of you. The bear has killed before." He stared into her eyes. "Hate to see you become its next dinner, Agent McLellan."

She shivered. Was this a subtle threat?

"How'd you know my name?" she asked.

"Father Jeremiah told us about you two. We haven't met before, but I saw you at the barbecue. And after, at the sweat lodge. You find it enlightening?"

"I found it hot." *No way I'm going to share my visions of Emily with him.*

Henry considered this for a minute. "Things can get hotter if you poke your nose where it doesn't belong."

Ben stepped in between them. "While there's an official investigation being conducted, we *belong*. Don't forget that."

"Yes, sir, Mr. CFBI man," Henry sneered.

"Let's all head back," Jasi said.

"I'll continue my walk, Agents. I'm sure I saw more lights than yours."

She grabbed Henry's elbow. "There's no one else here." Steering him towards Sanctuary, she added, "And it's your responsibility to make sure we get back safely."

The man remained quiet.

Following Henry, Jasi made a mental note to check the guy out thoroughly. She glanced at Ben, lifted a brow in Henry's direction, and he nodded. He was thinking the same thing.

They reached the fence and stepped through the gap.

"By the way, Agent McLellan," Henry said, "what were you doing in this barn earlier?"

"Just looking around."

"This barn's past its usefulness. We've been meaning to tear it down, but nature's beating us to it." He gave the barn a cursory glance, then looked at Jasi. "Would be a shame if it collapsed while someone was in it.

Another not-so-veiled threat?

When they reached Christiansen's lodge, Henry said, "Have a good evening, Agents." He took off across the field in the direction of one of the cabins.

Ben let out a grunt. "He's not the friendliest fellow."

"I'll keep an eye on him." Jasi said. "We can question him more thoroughly once we get his background check."

"I have a question for you. What in God's name are you doing leaving Sanctuary without Brandon?"

"I thought I'd get samples from the ATVs, and I'd return to the cabin safe and sound. I wasn't planning on venturing into the woods." She gave him an innocent smile. "Until I saw Eric and Amanda, and…well…you know the rest."

"Go to bed."

"Goodnight, Ben. And thanks for having my back."

He leaned down and kissed her cheek. "I'll always have your back."

She watched him scurry across the field and jump the front gate, thankful that Matthew had made Ben her team leader so long ago. Though Matthew had helped refine her psychic skills, Ben had trained her to become a better CFBI agent. They'd been friends a long time.

Soon Ben will be off running his own team again, and I'll have mine. But what about Natassia?

Once Jasi received her official promotion as team leader in a couple of weeks, Natassia would be given a choice. She could follow Ben or stay with Jasi. But of course Natassia would choose Ben. They were in love.

Love…

Jasi smiled. Brandon would stay with her. She'd make sure of that. Maybe it would just be the two of them.

Two is a good number.

She strode toward her assigned cabin, praying that Brandon was still asleep.

16

A seedy hotel in downtown Vancouver, BC

I watched the news broadcast and cursed beneath my breath. I'd done everything to destroy any evidence, even if I'd broken a cardinal rule.

"CFBI agents are on scene now," the reporter said in his overly dramatic way. "The name of the deceased is not being released at this time, but we can confirm this was a woman in her mid-twenties. Cause of death is yet to be determined."

All this hush-hush business made my pulse quicken. Had they linked me to the woman's death? Were they coming for me? Would they knock down the hotel door or catch me when I'm sleeping?

I wandered over to my briefcase, opened it and lifted the false bottom. Her photo stared up at me. I stroked it with one finger. "My lovely prize."

I recalled the night I'd killed her. I remembered every second if it— the blood pounding in my veins as I stalked her, the intense ecstasy of the chase that almost provoked me to orgasm, the look in her eyes when I'd cornered her, the sweet nectar of her blood.

"I knew I'd win you, my love."

She had sunk to the ground, a wounded animal, and I was honored to put her out of her misery.

"You were worthy of my pursuit."

I considered my options. I could return to the sanctity of my home or I could remain in this flea-infested dump of a hotel, where no one would ever think to look for me. At least until things had settled.

I picked up the newspaper. The front page was all about the body found in the incinerator at Sanctuary. My one mistake. I should have followed the program and buried her in the woods.

The phone rang, and I jumped. Only two people knew where I was staying.

"Yeah," I said into the receiver.

A familiar voice greeted me. He wasn't happy. I had screwed up.

"I know," I said.

Then I found out how badly I'd messed things up.

"They found the bodies in the forest?" I stammered. "But how is that possible? You promised they'd be taken care of, that no one would ever find them."

I listened for a few minutes, my heart sinking as I realized the implications.

"So are you saying that's it, it's over?"

I didn't like the answer.

After I hung up, I allowed my rage to ignite.

The television screen flickered to an image of the agent in charge of the investigation. Agent Jasmine McLellan.

"Just my type," I said.

Staring into her luminescent green eyes, I licked my lips. I was hungry. And not for food.

"Agent McLellan," I murmured. "I wonder how fast you can run."

17

Sanctuary, outside Mission, BC

Jasi awoke to the clamoring of a bell and the bitter scent of smoke.

"Here." Brandon shoved an Oxy-Mask into her hands. "Put it on."

She slipped the mask over her face. "What's happening?"

"One of the outbuildings is on fire." Already dressed, he shoved his feet into his boots. "I'm going outside to help."

"I'm coming too."

Minutes later she was dressed, her data-com tucked into a pocket on her breast, set to record all audio and everything the camera captured. Outside, she looked for Brandon, but all she saw was a stream of people racing across the field toward a crackling fire. There was only one building that resided on that part of the property. The red barn.

Or what was left of it.

She took in the murky plumes of smoke that clawed their way into the azure sky high above the sizzling mass of wood and metal. The residents had formed a bucket brigade, passing pails of water from one of the horse troughs to the base of the fire. Men tossed the water into the flames—to no avail.

"Jasi!" Standing a few yards from the fire, Brandon waved at her, his face and clothes streaked with soot. "Over here!"

Ignoring the wary glances from the residents as they took in her face mask, she strode toward him. Her breath caught in her chest when she saw two bodies on the ground, their clothes scorched and the skin on their arms blistered.

"Oh my God. Who?"

"Eric and Amanda," Brandon said, his voice cracking.

"Are they—?"

"They're alive. For now. Both are unconscious. I've notified Ben, and he's calling for a helicopter. There's one monitoring the crime scene and woods. It'll be here any minute." He took a few steps, then paused. "I'm going to examine the scene. Stay here."

Jasi knelt in the grass and felt for Eric's pulse. It was faint and irregular. Amanda was even worse off. Neither teen responded when she leaned over and called their names. She wished she'd brought another mask or her can of OxyBlast. The teens were in desperate need of oxygen.

"Father Jeremiah!" someone yelled.

When she lifted her head, she saw a wild-eyed Giles Christiansen running toward her.

"Lord help them!" he cried as he reached the unconscious teens. "Lazarus!"

Christiansen dropped to his knees on the ground beside Eric and Amanda, while Lazarus obediently hastened to his side. Seconds later, a grief-stricken Hannah latched onto her husband's arm for support, her tear-stained face as white as fresh snow. A blond-haired man in his forties joined them.

Eric's father?

She'd seen him around but hadn't officially met the man. *Amos something.*

"How did this happen?" Christiansen demanded.

"I think the roof collapsed on them," Lazarus said, "when they were inside the barn."

"What were they doing in there?"

"Smoking, I believe," Kenneth O'Brien called out as he joined them. He pulled a crumpled pack of cigarettes from his pocket. "I found these in the grass by the door. If they dropped a lit smoke, that place would go up like that." He snapped his fingers for emphasis.

Christiansen moaned, his mouth contorted in pain. "They disobeyed the rules, and God has punished them for their sins."

Jasi resisted the urge to throw up.

"No God did this," Brandon said, reappearing at her side.

One look in his eyes and Jasi knew exactly what had happened. Someone had deliberately set the barn on fire—with Eric and Amanda inside.

When Brandon gave her a subtle nod, she stood, her worst fears confirmed.

She lifted her mask. "Hannah! Keep an eye on Amanda and Eric. And check their pulse and breathing." The Oxy-Mask settled over her face once more.

The woman bobbed her head, her sobs increasing with each

movement. Eric's father put his arm around the woman's waist.

"The kids are safe with her there," she said to Brandon.

She moved away from the crowd of people, and he followed. When they were a safe distance from the smoke, she tested the direction of the wind and removed the mask.

"You sure this was intentional?" she asked.

"Everything's been set up to look like an accident—*if* you don't know what to look for."

"But you do."

"Based on the singed grass, there was a trail of gasoline running around the outside of the barn and up the back wall. No way that's an accident." He held up his data-com. "I have the pictures to prove it."

"Who do you think is responsible?"

"I can't say for sure." He peered over her shoulder. "Who'd want to hurt these kids?"

"All roads lead back to Sanctuary."

Jasi followed his gaze to where Christiansen hovered over the teens. Was the man's anguish genuine? Or was it all a well-rehearsed act? Could the great Father Jeremiah be responsible for the attempted murder of two teenagers now fighting for their lives?

"This fire's going to burn itself out," Brandon said. "It's a good thing it's far enough away from the other buildings. It won't spread anywhere else. But everything inside?" He groaned. "It's all gone. Including the ATVs. And we forgot to get soil samples last night."

"Actually, I got them while you were sleeping."

He grabbed her arm. "What?"

"If you promise me you won't freak out, I'll tell you what happened."

From his furrowed brow and pinched lips, Brandon wasn't happy with her, but he stayed quiet, so she described her midnight escapade into the woods.

When she told him how she'd seen two shadows darting off into the forest, he gaped at her. "So let me get this straight. You went out into the forest with no backup?"

"I had my gun."

"And you discovered you were following Eric and Amanda."

"They'd snuck off to be together. I could hear them kissing. At that point, I knew I wasn't in any danger. When I made myself known, Amanda took off before I could question her. But I *was* able to speak with Eric."

She told him everything the boy had said.

Brandon's mouth curled in fury. "You're lucky you followed two kids and not Sheral Downham's killer."

"You're right, but I only followed them after I was sure I knew who it was. They're teenagers, Brandon. No danger there."

"Tell that to all the victims of crimes perpetrated by teens. You could've run into serious trouble out there."

Jasi crossed her arms over her chest. "I evaluated the situation and determined I was safe. Then Ben showed up. By the time we ran into Henry—"

"Who the hell is Henry?" Brandon began pacing, visibly infuriated.

"One of the drummers from the sweat lodge. He followed me into the woods. Said he was concerned about me." She swallowed hard. "I was in no danger. Ben saw him on the camera, and you know the rest. No harm, no foul."

Brandon gripped her shoulders. "Listen, Jasi, you've got to stop barging into situations like a bull in a china shop."

"When have you ever seen a bull in a china shop?"

Brandon released an exasperated groan.

"I won't break," she whispered.

"No, but I will, if anything happens to—"

An intermittent chopping noise prevented them from further discussion. The helicopter had arrived.

Within minutes, Brandon and another agent had Eric and Amanda bundled up on backboards and secured inside the chopper. Christiansen gave Hannah and Eric's father permission to accompany the children to the hospital.

"I must stay behind," Christiansen told Jasi. "I have to care for *all* my people."

"Aren't you worried about the kids?"

"They're in God's hands now. And Hannah and Amos will watch over them. There's nothing more I can do for them. If it weren't for your partner..." He released a heavy sigh.

"What do you mean?"

"Your partner, the other agent? He saw Eric and Amanda inside the doorway of the barn. He went in after them and brought them out."

Jasi's stomach churned. *Oh God...*

"He's lucky the whole building didn't come down on top of him," Christiansen added, his voice tinged with something close to spite.

"I think we're all lucky," she said, holding his gaze. "But don't worry. We'll find out how this happened."

"Lazarus assures me it was a foolish accident. The children were smoking. Imbibing in alcohol or tobacco is not allowed on Sanctuary grounds. For that matter, Eric never should have been alone with the girl.

She's promised to another. His parents will not be pleased with him."

Now she understood why Eric and Amanda would risk sneaking off into the forest or down to the river. They were Romeo and Juliet. Young love. Forbidden love.

"Like I said, we'll find out what happened today. Count on it."

Christiansen hobbled off, shoulders slumped, his steps unsure.

In the center field, the helicopter lifted into the air and soared off over the trees. Jasi watched it leave, praying the teens aboard would regain consciousness. Maybe then she'd finally be one step closer to discovering the truth about Sanctuary.

A few of the men, including Lazarus and Henry, stood guard over the fire. She watched them shoo some of the younger children away, while the women gathered like hens and whispered to each other.

"Are you going to do your thing here?" Brandon asked her.

"Later. Too many people around. We'll come back later after the flames have died down."

"You sure you don't need your mask?"

She sniffed the air. "The direction of the wind has changed. It's pushing the smoke east. I'll be okay as long as I don't get too close."

"Keep the mask on hand anyway. I'll feel better." He gave her a concerned smile. "Okay?"

"Yes, sir. Now let's have a shower and change into some fresh clothes. Then we can go get them dirty again." She laughed when his brow arched suggestively. "No, I'm not suggesting we'll be rolling around in the grass. We have a body dump to visit."

Brandon's smile turned into a grimace. "All work and no—"

"We'll play later." She squeezed his hand. "I promise. Once we're outta here."

"Promises, promises."

Back in the cabin, they took turns in the tiny shower stall, much to Brandon's disappointment. There was no way they would have fit inside together without doing some serious damage to each other.

"Let's check in with Ben and Natassia first," she suggested as she dried off with a stiff cotton towel that threatened to exfoliate three layers of skin. "Jesus, the women here must hang the towels to dry outside."

Brandon stepped from the shower and tucked a towel around his waist. "What, you don't like towels dried in fresh mountain air?"

"God, no," she said, fastening her bra. "Give me Bounce in the dryer any day."

He laughed. "I learn something new about you every day, Jasmine McLellan."

"Then you probably know how much I hate wasting time."

"Me too." His towel dropped to the floor.

She eyed his body, taking in the ripples of muscle, tanned skin and droplets of water that trickled down his abdomen. She almost forgot what she wanted to say. "Hurry up and get dressed. You're distracting me."

Laughter followed her from the bathroom and into the central room. She got dressed, sealed the smoky clothing she'd worn earlier in an evidence bag and scribbled her name on the front. Checking her backpack, she discovered she only had two pair of jeans and a couple of blouses left.

At this rate, I'm going to need more clothes.

Her data-com rang. Natassia.

"I was about to call you," Jasi said. "What's the plan at your end?"

"I'm heading to the hospital as soon as my ride gets here. I'll see if I get anything from the kids." Natassia paused. "Have any ideas regarding the fire?"

"Brandon says we have an arsonist on our hands."

"And what about the kids?"

"Whoever set the fire knew they were inside."

"Oh my God."

"I know. It's horrible." Jasi lifted her head when Brandon entered the room. He was nude. She hissed in a breath. "Okay, I have to go."

Brandon moved toward her, kissed her lips, then walked away.

She swore he knew exactly what he was doing to her. *The tease!*

18

Natassia awoke just after four-thirty in the morning when the van door squealed. She didn't even have time to clear the sleep fog from her brain—or notice that Ben was gone. Thinking he was an intruder, she almost clobbered him over the head when he climbed inside. He quickly told her about Jasi and their adventure in the forest. Then she took over watch, while Ben slept up front in the passenger seat.

Two hours later a harsh bell outside alerted them that something was wrong.

From the van's doorway, they instantly spotted the problem. A building was on fire at the far end of the property.

"I'll call the Mission Fire/Rescue Service and Matthew," Ben said.

"I have to check on Jasi and Brandon," Natassia shouted as she ran toward the gate.

As soon as she saw her other team members, she heaved a sigh of relief. She waved, but neither Jasi nor Brandon noticed her.

"Brandon called," Ben said when she returned to the van. "They're fine. But two of the kids were inside. Eric and Amanda. They're breathing but unconscious. We'll be airlifting them out any minute."

"Should we go help?"

"Brandon assured me the fire has been contained. It'll burn out soon. We've been ordered to keep monitoring things in case our killer, or the arsonist, decides to flee during the chaos."

"Could be they're one and the same."

"That's a definite probability. It's too much of a coincidence that Jasi spoke with Eric last night, and then this happens. Someone wants to shut those kids up."

Natassia's mouth narrowed. "Which means at least one of those kids knows something."

"For now, no one leaves Sanctuary."

"Got it. Any indication what started the fire?"

"Someone set it. Brandon believes whoever did, knew damn well the kids were inside."

"Jesus!" She stared at the black sky. "How's Jasi handling all the smoke?"

"She has a full container of OxyBlast and her mask. She'll be fine."

Ben handed her a cup of coffee from the thermos. It was barely warm, but she drank it anyway.

"Matthew is sending the kid to pick you up," he said.

"Jay?"

He nodded. "He'll drive you to Mission Memorial. Let's hope you get a read from one of the kids."

"I'll wait outside, watch the gate and fence."

Natassia had been pacing outside the fence for about fifteen minutes when a cobalt-blue sedan with Washington plates rolled toward her, spitting rocks behind it. She didn't recognize the vehicle. She furtively aimed her 'com in the car's direction and captured the image.

The car stopped when it reached her. An attractive man in a pale gray suit that matched his hair climbed out of the back seat and gave her a polite nod. "I'm here to see Father Jeremiah."

The look he gave her suggested he expected her to physically open the gate for him.

"I'm afraid no one is allowed inside Sanctuary at this time." She flashed her badge. "CFBI."

The man examined her badge. Then his gaze strayed to the smoldering fire. "What happened here?"

"A fire." She wasn't giving him any more information until she knew who he was. "Can I see some identification, please?"

"Of course." He fished inside his jacket and pulled out a wallet. Removing his driver's license, he passed it to her.

"Oliver Gathmann," she read aloud. She scanned the card with her data-com, then handed it back. "What brings you all the way from Washington, Mr. Gathmann?"

"I have business dealings with Father Jeremiah and happened to be in the area."

"So you're not here about the murder?"

The man's jaw flinched. "Murder?"

"The dead woman in the incinerator."

Gathmann raised a hand. "I know nothing about that, Agent Prushenko. I have interests in a few organizations and have invested in many. Sanctuary happens to be one of them."

"What do you do?"

"Construction. Houses mainly."

A helicopter hovered overhead for a few seconds then veered off toward the field inside the fence and landed.

"Was someone hurt?" Gathmann asked, gripping the bars of the gate.

"Two teenagers."

Gathmann's face went white. "Are they going to be okay?"

Natassia took in the man's pallor. "We hope so. You, on the other hand, don't look so hot. You need some water?"

She reached for his arm, but he brushed her hand away. "I'm okay. I'll be on my way." He walked back to the waiting sedan and opened the door. "Agent Prushenko?" He glanced over one shoulder, his expression unreadable.

"Yes?"

"I do hope you find out who's responsible for the murder and the fire."

She narrowed her eyes. "So do I, Mr. Gathmann."

Natassia watched him enter the car and waited until it had vanished from view before heading back to the surveillance van. She was halfway there when she spotted a familiar SUV. Her ride was here.

"Agent Prushenko!" Jay shouted from the vehicle.

The vehicle pulled to a stop and all four doors opened, spewing out five CFBI agents, all armed and dressed in bulky flak jackets.

"These are agents Derek Norman, Vijay Singh, Kaye Killgore and Kristen Howe," Jay said. "They're assigned to guard the property while we're gone."

Natassia shook the agents' hands. "We appreciate the help."

"Is it only you out here?" Agent Killgore asked, the confident look in her eyes betraying her petite stature.

"No. My partner, Agent Ben Roberts, is in the van monitoring the situation. We have two agents inside Sanctuary—Jasmine McLellan and Brandon Walsh. So how are we doing this?"

Agent Norman stepped forward. "Singh and I will be watching the fence. Killgore and Howe will be conducting searches of the buildings on the property, along with your agents."

"Sounds like you have your orders. Jay, are you ready to go?"

"Yes, ma—Agent Prushenko. You want the keys?"

"No, you drive. I might run us into a ditch." When he gave her a questioning look, she added, "The sleeping quarters in the van leave much to be desired."

She strode to the van, yanked the door open and ducked her head inside. "I'm leaving now. Matthew sent us backup for the fence and two agents to assist with the cabin searches."

"Okay," Ben said. "See you when you get back. Good luck."

"We could all use some luck right about now."

Twenty minutes later, Natassia and Jay pulled into the parking lot of Mission Memorial Hospital, located off Lougheed Highway on Hurd Street. Built in 1965, the hospital featured the latest in technology, including emergency services, and though it was an older building, it was well kept and easy to get around.

In the ICU, Natassia showed her badge to the nurse on duty. "We're here to see Amanda Christiansen and Eric..." She paused, realizing she didn't have the boy's last name.

"The two kids brought in from Sanctuary?" the woman behind the desk asked.

"Yes. Can we see them?"

"I'm afraid neither of them can have visitors at the moment. And it wouldn't do you any good, anyway."

Natassia's mouth thinned. "Really. And why's that?"

"They're still unconscious."

"I'd like to see them anyway."

The nurse opened her mouth to argue, but Jay held up his badge and puffed out his chest. "We're here on official CFBI business, ma'am. We'd appreciate your assistance."

"Of course. Follow me."

The woman scurried off down the hall, her shoes clicking sharply on the tile floor. "We put them in the same room. The parents are taking a break in the cafeteria." She opened the door and Natassia and Jay entered.

There were three beds in the room. Only two were occupied. Both Amanda and Eric were hooked up to ventilators and beeping monitors.

Natassia sucked in a deep breath. "Will they be okay?"

"We'll have a better idea tomorrow. Amanda has been in and out of consciousness. We expect her to wake up later tonight possibly. Eric, on the other hand..." The nurse shrugged and shook her head solemnly.

"I'd like to sit with them for a bit," Natassia said. "Jay, get me a coffee."

After the kid left with the nurse, she made a beeline for Eric, but after over five minutes of touching his hand and face, she realized his brain was too amped up on drugs for her to read him.

Apprehensive, she pulled a chair up to the girl's bed, figuring she'd get the same result. "Hi, Amanda. My name's Natassia. I'm hoping I can help you." She stroked the girl's hand. "You're in good hands. Relax…there's nothing to fear. You're safe."

As she touched Amanda's hand, she thought about Sanctuary, picturing the forest and meadows. Something peaceful.

"Amanda, what do you know about the bodies in the woods?"

The air around her grew thick, and she fought to breathe.

In seconds she was in…

Amanda ran through the woods now, her pale blue dress flowing behind her. She laughed. Someone was chasing her. Eric. She couldn't see him, but he wasn't far behind her.

"You can't catch me," she teased.

"Yes I can," Eric replied.

She headed farther into the woods. It was dark, and she only had a flashlight to guide her, but she knew the route by heart. They'd traveled it every week, always in the wee hours of the morning when no one would catch them.

She veered around the wide trunk of an ancient cedar and began the climb that led to the rocks at the base of a small mountain ridge. There were caves here and there, and they'd found one that was uninhabited by wolves or other animals.

Their special cave.

He knew where she would go, of course, and she knew he'd catch her eventually. This was all part of the forbidden game.

Then they'd kiss.

Her mouth lifted into a wide smile. She loved Eric Finnegan with all her heart. And one day he'd tell her he loved her too.

As she scrambled up the hill, she scraped her knee on a rock and let out a small cry. "Stop being a baby, Amanda," she mumbled to herself. "You're gonna be married in a couple years. To an old man who won't put up with no baby for a wife."

She tried not to think of her impending marriage to Mr. O'Brien. It made her want to cry. And run away.

Once she'd asked Eric to run away with her, but he said he couldn't. His dad wouldn't let him and he didn't want to disobey Father Jeremiah. Bad things happened when someone did that.

She thought about the lady she'd seen in the woods a few nights ago. She'd followed her, watched her take pictures of the ground and the trees. She'd trailed the lady to the river, lost her for a moment, then followed her back into the woods.

"You shouldn't be out here," she'd whispered, half-hoping the lady would hear her.

Then she'd heard the beast. She'd seen it once before, about a month ago, a beast from Hell that could change its shape and size. It always went hunting in the middle of the night. She'd followed it a month ago, but it had disappeared, which was really weird because they were climbing the rocks and there was nowhere to go. 'Cept down.

But she never found a body when she climbed down.

"I see you," Eric called, interrupting her memory. He was much closer now.

She squatted behind a boulder and put a hand over her mouth to stifle her giggles. She could hear rocks moving, so she knew he was almost upon her.

Then everything went silent.

She waited.

After a minute, she peeked around the boulder. No sign of him. "Eric?"

No answer.

"Eric! You can catch me now. I don't wanna play no more." She stood up. "I'm over here."

Something moved behind her and she jerked her head.

A huge beast loomed over her, and she felt its hot, rotten breath on her face.

"You're not supposed to be here, girl," the beast said in a low growl.

Heart pounding in her chest, she took off down the rocks, skidding and falling as she went. She didn't think about Eric or their special cave. She had to get home.

Before the beast caught her.

Run, Amanda, run!

As she ran, she heard an earsplitting alarm...

Natassia was jolted from the vision when the door burst open.

"Step aside," the nurse barked as she wheeled a crash cart toward the girl in the bed. "She's coding!"

Natassia pushed past two nurses and a doctor and exited the room.

"I've got your coffee," Jay called out as he strode toward her. "How goes it?"

"Something's happened with Amanda." She pushed her nose up against the glass window, hoping to see what was happening behind the curtains in Amanda's room. "They're using paddles on her."

Damn it! I didn't even get a chance to find out about the fire.

She prayed the girl would be okay.

Ten minutes ticked by before the nurse came out of the room. "We've got her stabilized, but she needs to rest."

Natassia gave her a card with her 'com number on it. "If anything changes with either of them, I want to be notified immediately."

The nurse took the card and returned to her station.

Jay passed Natassia the cup of coffee. "What now?"

"We go back to Sanctuary and take a little walk in the woods." She glanced down at his polished shoes. "Got any hiking boots?"

"In the trunk."

"Good boy."

Jay blushed. "I'm twenty, actually."

"Ah, the innocence of youth."

"You can't be that much older than me."

"Not much," she lied.

"I didn't think so, ma'am."

Her smile thinned. "What did I tell you about that 'ma'am' business?"

"Sorry…Agent Prushenko."

"You're forgiven, Jay." She snickered at his discomfort. "Now let's find the SUV and get out of here."

19

Ben skimmed through the background reports as they were ejected from the printer. Most of the residents were clean, no arrests. A couple had the odd DUI or small drug possession charge. There were a handful of citations for Public Intoxication and one weapons charge for not securing a proper hunting license. Reports on Giles Christiansen's wives and some of the other Sanctuary members raised no red flags.

The girl, Katie, turned out to be a runaway named Katherine Yang. She was from Surrey, and had been in and out of trouble since she was twelve. Her parents knew she was at Sanctuary. They'd given her their blessing and washed their hands of her.

He taped four reports to the van wall—Giles Christiansen, Lazarus (AKA Paxton Helling), Kenneth (AKA Kent O'Brien) and Henry (AKA Horton Edgars). Christiansen's file held no secrets. The CFBI had been watching him, yet the man looked clean on paper. Helling had a stack of unpaid parking tickets, mostly while driving the Sanctuary van. O'Brien, the man engaged to Amanda, had one major red flag. A woman had filed attempted rape charges against him several years ago, but the charges had been dropped. And Edgars had been brought in numerous times to dry out on a cot in the local jail.

Ben was stumped. Nothing in the reports tied any of the men to possible murders.

The printer spat out over two dozen missing persons reports. He divided the stack into male and female, then perused each pile. He matched almost half with the DNA reports from Divine Ops, DNA taken from the graves in the forest.

Why them? What happened to the others?

A dozen bodies suggested a serial killer, yet there were differences in the methods of murder. Some had been shot, some stabbed and a couple beheaded.

On the opposite side of the wall, he taped up the photos of each of the victims found in the woods. He added Sheral's photo at the top, stepped back and studied their faces. *What do they have in common?*

The victims varied in height and weight, hair and eye color, but they had two commonalities. They were attractive and healthy looking, no matter what their personal demons were or what had led them to seek out Sanctuary.

Was Christiansen seeking to create a picture-perfect community? Was he recruiting the beautiful and handsome to merge with his existing family? And why were these victims discarded so horrifically? Had they balked at the idea of giving all control to Father Jeremiah?

He groaned and rubbed his eyes. "What am I missing?"

He thought about his vision. *Where the hell does a small black rodent fit in?*

Nothing made sense. He felt like they'd been going in circles. Or like they were always one step behind figuring this out.

He examined his watch. 7:35 AM. *Time to visit Father Jeremiah.*

Ben slid into the driver's seat, started the engine and turned the van around. As the vehicle meandered toward the gate, he rolled down the window and inhaled. The air was still heavy with smoke residue. He squinted. The fire seemed to be out, and he saw three men heaving buckets of water over the smoldering embers.

A man approached and walked behind one of the brick posts. Seconds later the gate doors squealed open.

Ben parked in front of Christiansen's lodge, climbed out and locked the van. He climbed the steps to the porch and knocked. Seconds later a black-haired, pregnant woman answered the door. Grace Christiansen. He recognized her from one of the background report photos.

"I'm here to see your husband," he said, presenting his badge.

"Please come in," Grace replied. "Jeremiah is in the sitting room."

Ben took in the rustic charm of the place and the handcrafted tables and chairs. It would make a great B&B.

They found Christiansen seated at a desk, going over paperwork.

"Husband, you have a visitor," Grace announced.

Christiansen looked over his shoulder, saw Ben and shuffled the papers into a bottom drawer. Then he stood. "You're one of the CFBI agents who's been watching us, I take it."

"Agent Roberts." Ben held out a gloved hand.

Jeremiah crossed the room. "Welcome." His grip was firm, and it lingered as if a warning. To his wife he said, "Leave us."

The woman dutifully left the room.

"How can I help you, Agent Roberts?" Christiansen asked.

"I have a few questions for you."

"Would you like to walk the grounds, or would you prefer to stay inside?"

"Inside is fine."

"My home is your home."

Ben cleared his throat. "Mr. Christiansen—"

"I prefer 'Father Jeremiah.'"

"Mr. Christiansen, this is an official investigation," Ben said, his jaw clenched. "We'll stick to legalities. Your legal name is Giles Christiansen. You never changed it."

Christiansen gave him a miffed shrug. "Fine."

"We have a number of reports of missing people who were last seen at Sanctuary. That concerns me, considering what we found in your woods."

"Technically, they're not mine." Christiansen strolled to a window and parted a curtain. "My property ends about five yards from that fence line. The land beyond is untamed wilderness. Crown property. Part of that area backs onto a park." He took a few steps away from the window. "Anyone could access that land."

"We found tire tracks in the forest near the area where we found the other bodies." Ben watched the man's face, but it barely registered anything, not even sadness.

"Can't see how a car could get in there."

"The tracks belonged to an ATV."

Christiansen's face went through a barrage of emotions, from disbelief to anger to fear. "You're suggesting that someone took one of our ATVs into the woods to bury innocent victims? No. I don't think so. And I guess you won't be able to prove it now that both ATVs have been destroyed in the fire."

"We already have proof."

Christiansen's composure cracked, along with his condescending smile. "What proof?"

"We took a sample of the soil from one of the tire treads. The report came in this morning. It's a match to the soil from the gravesite."

Christiansen attempted a laugh. "There's dirt all around us. How can you be certain it's from that specific area?"

"Our techs analyze everything from composition to vegetation to insects, but in this case it was an easy match. We found traces of sodium hydroxide, otherwise known as lye, on both ATVs and the ground where the bodies were dumped. I don't suppose you have lye here."

"I'm sure you already know the answer to that, Agent Roberts. We use lye for a variety of purposes—as a drain cleaner...for making soap. It's possible someone spilled some on the ground and the ATVs picked it up that way."

"Possible, except that there were also traces of DNA in the samples we took from the tires. And we already have one positive match from one of the bodies." Ben watched the man, taking in his fidgeting hands and inability to stand still. "We're left with two conclusions, Mr. Christiansen. Either someone killed these victims to protect Sanctuary, or someone is setting you up."

"It has to be the latter. No one here would do such things."

"How many of your members own guns?"

"Two."

"Rifles or handguns?"

"Rifles. For hunting purposes."

"Who?"

"Lazarus and Henry. But neither of them would do something like this. They aren't killers. And in case you're wondering, the RCMP already tested both rifles for gunshot residue. Neither one has been used recently. And the bullets don't match the wound on the woman from the incinerator."

How the hell had Ben missed *that* report? "You have any enemies?"

Christiansen let out a grunt. "I'm sure I do. We live a different life out here, away from technology and impropriety. Not everyone agrees with our lifestyle."

"Any phone calls or threatening letters?"

"No. And no one has stormed our gates either."

"What about people you've exiled?"

"I don't keep track, but I can give you a few names."

Christiansen strode toward the desk. Seconds later, he handed Ben a piece of paper with three names.

"All three of these people are in the Missing Persons Database," Ben said. "I received a list this morning."

"They were exiled from here. Where they went after, I have no idea."

"Tell me about these three."

"Cooper Prescott stayed with us a week but was caught stealing from the cabins. He was black—"

"Ebonic. That's the politically correct term nowadays."

"PC terms aside, Agent Roberts, Cooper was exiled about four months ago. Raylene Mackenzie was exiled last year because she refused to stay on her medication. She was schizophrenic and volatile, and many of the people feared her. And Nora Finnegan left us about two months ago."

"Wait, I know that name." Ben checked his 'com. "We have a DNA match to one of the bodies in the woods."

"I'm sad to hear that. Nora was a tough case. Her daughter, Paige, was killed in a hit-and-run, and Nora took to drugs to escape. She came here over a year ago. Took some time but finally got clean and was doing great. She became our van driver, heading into town for groceries and odd tasks. Then we discovered she was using the Sanctuary van to deal drugs. This was especially hard on her family."

"How do you know that?"

"Her husband is Amos Finnegan. He and Eric, their son, came here hoping to reunite with Nora. But she was already gone by then. I guess now we know why she disappeared."

"Why didn't Amos and Eric go back home?"

"They found a home here and maybe a connection to Nora."

Ben observed the man for a moment. Christiansen seemed forthcoming enough, even saddened by Nora's death.

"What happened after you discovered Nora was dealing?"

"She was exiled. That's when Lazarus took over the driving."

"Anyone else exiled in the past month?"

"Honestly, there've been too many who came for a few days and left. I don't recall them all."

"I understand there was another woman—Jennifer Phillips."

"Oh yes. Jenny was given a choice to repent or leave. She was exiled about a week ago. I don't recall what day exactly."

"And her crime?"

"She slept with one of the men. We do not condone premarital sex."

"Maybe you should punish the men," Ben said dryly. "They seem to be getting off. Literally."

"I deal with my people as I see fit, Agent Roberts." Christiansen dropped the pen on the table for emphasis. "Are we done?"

"Can I get a glass of water?"

Christiansen blinked, taken aback. "Certainly. I'll be right back."

Once the man was gone, Ben removed his gloves and scooped up the pen. It was an expensive one, with gold plating and a rifle emblazoned on the side.

The images came fast—a long metal cylinder and a bank vault door. *Money again?*

"Here you go, Agent Roberts," Christiansen said when he returned.

When he handed the glass to Ben, their bare fingers touched, rewarding Ben with a final vision—bloody hands. The message in that was obvious. The man had blood on his hands. But whose?

"What is involved when you exile someone, Mr. Christiansen?"

"It's very simple. The person to be banished is told to meet us by the gate and bring only the clothes they are wearing and whatever they came to Sanctuary with."

"And by 'us' you mean…"

"Our community, with the exception of the younger children. Exile must be a public statement. It helps us maintain order and peace."

"What happens next?"

"Lazarus drives them into the city and leaves them there."

"Into Mission?"

Christiansen shrugged. "Mission, Port Coquitlam, Vancouver—they decide."

"So you dump them in the city with only the clothes on their back and a few possessions? How are they supposed to survive?"

"That is no longer my concern. Those who are exiled have lost the right to my compassion."

Ben curled his mouth in disdain. "Doesn't that go against the preaching of forgiveness?"

"Agent Roberts, we often must do what is best for the whole, not for the one. At Sanctuary, we give everyone an opportunity to change their lives, but those who cannot walk God's path must leave, so as not to blemish the ones who are living in the light of the Lord." Christiansen glared at him, his words dripping with bitterness. "I understand you live a life of darkness with what you see and do, but that is not the fate of those at Sanctuary. We don't live by your rules but by God's rules."

"And your God tells you to exile people who come here seeking help?"

"We are all tested. Some of us are found wanting."

"And they're discarded," Ben said, standing. "Thank you, Mr. Christiansen. This has been very enlightening."

"Grace!" Christiansen shouted, impatience written all over his face.

His wife scurried into the room.

"Show Agent Roberts to the door."

"That's okay, Mr. Christiansen," Ben said. "I can show myself out."

Back in the surveillance van, he released a slow growl. Men like Christiansen—ones with God complexes—infuriated him beyond reason. However, one good thing had materialized from his visit. Christiansen's composed demeanor was swiftly disintegrating.

And I'm going to find out what he's hiding.

20

Jasi and Brandon had been at the forest gravesites for over an hour, but without a victim whose death was caused by fire, Jasi's psychic gift was useless. And her profiling skills resulted in the same conclusions as Ben's—multiple victims, multiple forms of murder, possible multiple killers. Some bodies had been coated with lye and only miniscule particles of bone remained in the graves. Soil, lye and DNA samples had been taken from all graves earlier in the morning and then rushed to Ops.

"We may as well head back," she told Brandon.

"What next?"

"We'll brainstorm with Natassia and Ben."

In the trees a few yards away cracking and snapping could be heard. Someone was approaching, and they weren't being quiet about it.

Two of the agents reached for their handguns.

"No guns," Jasi warned. "Whoever this is, they're not trying to be covert, so it's not our guy. Could be a hiker from the park."

The bushes parted, revealing a young man in his early twenties with copper hair and an innocent-looking face covered in freckles.

She didn't recognize him from Sanctuary.

"A-hem!" she said, clearing her throat.

"Whew!" The kid bent over to catch his breath. "You startled me."

"And you are?"

He fumbled around in his jacket, attempting to withdraw a black wallet. It dropped on the ground instead. "Oops, sorry about that." He scooped up the wallet, dusted it off and handed it to her.

"Agent Jason Anthony," she read. "What are you doing out here?"

"Agent Prushenko told me to find you guys and guard the crime scene." He took a few steps and stumbled over a tree root.

"Lucky us." To the other agents, she said, "Report to me immediately if anyone other than RCMP or CFBI comes here. Last thing we need is the media lurking in the bushes."

Agent Anthony snickered.

"You sure we should leave him here?" Brandon whispered. "He looks a little green. And I don't mean in a *new* way."

She studied the kid, who was doing his best to not look at the human remains scattered on the forest floor. She heaved another sigh. "Agent Anthony, you're with us."

"But Agent Prushenko said—"

"*I'm* the agent in charge."

"Yes, ma'am."

"That's Agent McLellan."

The kid hung his head. "Sorry."

She strode off, with Brandon at her side and Agent Anthony stumbling along behind them.

"Agent Anthony, have you been inside a cult before?" she asked.

"No, ma—no."

"They have their own way of living, so we'll do our best to respect that. But if you do see anything out of the ordinary, pull me aside and let me know."

"Does that go for out here too?"

She stopped dead in her tracks and faced him. "Why? Did you see something?"

"Well, it's more what I didn't see."

"Continue."

"All this forest here is supposed to be bear country, right? But I grew up on a farm, and bears were always on our property. I'd see bear poop and clawed trees everywhere I went, not to mention dead animal carcasses."

"What's your point?" Brandon cut in.

The kid scratched his head. "You see any carcasses, bear poop or clawed trees anywhere around here?"

"No, but this is a massive forest."

"I thought they said there were bears in the area and that's why they stayed inside the night the woman in the incinerator died."

"He's right, Brandon," Jasi said. "We haven't seen any indication that a bear has been in these woods."

"Why would they lie about the bear?" Agent Anthony asked.

"That's what we're going to find out. Good work, Agent Anthony."

The kid blushed.

"He wasn't made an agent for nothing," she said to Brandon.

Making their way back to the surveillance van, Jasi opened the side door and almost collided with Ben. "We're back."

"Come on in. Natassia just got back a half hour ago. We're going over more documents." Ben glanced over her shoulder. "Who's he?"

"Hey there, Jay," Natassia called out before Jasi could answer.

Agent Anthony waved once. "Uh…hi, Agent Prushenko."

Ben stood aside as Jasi and Agent Anthony entered the van.

"I'll stay outside," Brandon said. When Jasi gave him a questioning look, he added, "It's a bit crowded in there."

She left the door open for fresh air and so Brandon wouldn't feel excluded.

"What did you get from Christiansen?" she asked.

Ben filled her in and showed her the paper with the names of the three exiles. "They match missing persons cases. And a DNA match came in five minutes ago. Cooper Prescott."

She flinched at the man's surname. It was the same as her best friend's. "He's one of the bodies in the woods?"

Ben nodded. "Christiansen said Prescott left Sanctuary four months ago."

"He didn't get very far." She sucked in a breath. "Any relatives in the area?"

"He's originally from Halifax. Most of his family lives on the east coast. He's survived by his father and one brother. I'll notify the family."

Comforted by the fact that she wouldn't be conveying more bad news to Cameron, she peeked over her shoulder at Agent Anthony. He was typing up a report on the laptop.

She lowered her voice. "Ben, did you see anything when you talked to Christiansen?"

"Two hits off a pen with a rifle emblem on the side," he said. "I saw a metal cylinder and a bank vault. After I touched his hand, I saw blood on his hands."

"That's certainly telling."

"The bizarre thing is he doesn't really fit the profile of a serial killer. Sure, he's arrogant and persuasive, but he doesn't exhibit the cold-heartedness normally associated with psychopathy. In fact, it's the opposite. Giles Christiansen seems to genuinely care about people."

"I'd care too if people were investing six figures so I can live by my own rules."

"How the blood fits in exactly, I don't know yet."

Jasi thought of something. "Natassia, how did things go with the kids?"

Natassia eyed Agent Anthony, who was still reading. "Amanda and Eric had a special cave somewhere near the gravesite. And she followed

Sheral one night, but I'm not sure when exactly. She saw something else in the woods too. She called it a 'beast.'"

"Human or animal?"

"I'm thinking human."

"Excuse me," Agent Anthony interrupted from the back of the van. "But if those two kids were unconscious, how do you know all this?"

"She woke up for a minute," Natassia said. "Right before she coded."

Jasi knew Natassia was lying, but the kid needed a believable explanation.

We'll have to be more careful.

"Agent Anthony, can you do me a favor?"

"Uh…okay."

"Go outside and watch the road for any vehicles headed our way."

The kid hesitated. "But there are two agents out there already."

"They're guarding the gate. I want you to walk down the road to where it splits. If you see any vehicles, call me." She handed him a card with her 'com number on it.

"Okay." He scrunched his face in confusion but did what he was told.

After he'd left, Jasi let out a slow breath. "The kid may be young, but he's extremely alert."

She told them about Agent Anthony's keen observations in the woods.

"No bear feces or claw marks anywhere?" Ben asked.

Jasi shook her head. "And he noticed this right away. We'll have to be careful around him. As far as he's concerned we're just regular CFBI agents."

Brandon poked his head in the doorway. "You're anything but 'regular,' Agent McLellan."

"You need something to do?" she asked.

"Oh yeah."

"Incorrigible." She looked at Ben and Natassia. "See what I have to deal with?"

"Don't expect us to feel sorry for you," Natassia said. "Have you seen the bed here?" She pointed to the cushions at the back. "How's the cabin?"

"Believe me, I'd feel safer in here than at Sanctuary."

"Has someone threatened you?" Ben demanded.

"Not directly. Every now and then someone says something that resembles a warning." She shrugged. "I could be reading too much into it."

"We have Christiansen's detailed financials," Natassia said, changing the subject. "Want to go over them? Maybe you'll see something we missed."

"Sure." She glanced at Brandon. "We'll sit up front."

Brandon opened the passenger door and climbed in, while Jasi slid into the driver's seat.

"Here." Natassia handed her a manila folder.

Jasi opened the folder and gave half of the documents to Brandon. She studied the first page in her pile. It listed every person or company who had donated money to Christiansen's cause, one for which he'd actually obtained charitable status. Beside each donor was the total to date they'd given to Sanctuary.

"What are you thinking?" Brandon asked.

"Money seems to be a common element in two visions. Ben saw six zeroes when he touched the headless body in the woods and then a bank vault when he picked up Christiansen's pen. Big money is involved somehow. I think we need to focus on the major investors. That would coincide with official looking documents too."

She scrolled through the list of investors, calling off each name while Brandon looked for the coordinating report. She recognized a few names from the news. There were six major investors.

She picked up the ten-page report on the first investor and flipped through the pages, noting various photographs of a dark-haired man hobnobbing with influential leaders in the community.

One photo made her breath stop.

She handed the papers to Brandon. "Becket Hawley, philanthropist and proud VPD supporter. You see him all over the news. If he's not traveling, he's attending high-profile events." She pointed to the photo. "Here he is at a police convention standing next to Pop, back when my father was still a cop. And there's Uncle Paxton next to Pop."

"Brothers?"

She shook her head. "Uncle Paxton is one of Pop's oldest friends."

"Maybe they can give us some insight into Hawley."

"I'll call them once we're done with this list." She set Hawley's report aside.

The second report was on Van Harvard, a popular motivational speaker, who raked in big bucks selling his money-making schemes and spiritual enlightenment camps.

The third report was on a man she'd never heard of.

"Either of you know about an Oliver Gathmann?" she called out.

"Who?" Natassia said, moving behind her.

"Oliver Gathmann. He's an investor. Have you heard of him?"

"I *met* him. He was snooping around Sanctuary's gate this morning."

Jasi's head jerked up. "Did you question him?"

"Yeah, but he didn't give me much."

"You think he was here checking up on his investment?"

"Absolutely. He also gave me the impression he wanted to find out what we know."

"Why wouldn't he just pick up the phone and call Christiansen?"

"That's the question of the day."

Jasi surveyed the report. "Says here he owns a company that builds earthships."

"I've heard of those," Brandon said. "Earthship homes are usually built into a hillside or berm."

"Who'd want to live in a house that's underground?"

"Environmentalists. With solar and wind power, and using sustainable resources and natural heat from beneath the surface of the earth, you could live completely off-grid. No more utility bills."

She scowled. "I'll keep my loft apartment and my bills, thank you."

"You want Gathmann brought in for questioning?" he asked.

"He was in a vehicle with Washington plates," Natassia said. "He's probably across the border by now."

"I'll call Matthew," Ben said, joining them. "We'll get a warrant to track Gathmann's GPS."

"Let's take a closer look at Mole Tech while we're at it," Jasi said.

Ben's eyes flared. "What did you say?"

"We'll look at his company."

"Mole Tech, you said."

"Yeah?"

"Mole. A small black animal?"

Ben's vision!

"When Ben touched the body in the forest, he saw six zeroes," she said. "I think that's in reference to money, and the signature I think relates to contracts. And the black animal? A mole. Oliver Gathmann is somehow connected to at least one body in the woods."

"Doesn't mean he killed anyone," Natassia said. "He didn't strike me as the serial killer type. Too meek. No signs of a lurking psychopath."

"Maybe not, but he's still linked to this."

And we're going to figure out how.

21

With the Oxy-Mask in place, Jasi strode across the field and made her way to the abandoned barn ruins, while the residents of Sanctuary shared lunch in the larger barn. Brandon followed close behind. A few feet from the embers, she removed the mask and took two deep breaths of OxyBlast.

"Shake 'n Bake time," she murmured.

"Why do you say that?" Brandon asked.

She chuckled. "I don't know. I guess it puts me in the mood." She saw him raise a brow and added, "To read a fire."

Standing inches from the rubble, she inhaled deeply. *In...out—*

The connection yanked Jasi into the arsonist's mind.

The dawn sky told me I'd better hurry. Everyone would be awake soon.

I followed them to the dilapidated barn and moved stealthily around the side, stopping to listen from time to time.

They were in there. I could hear them.

"I think we should tell someone what we saw," the girl said in a frightened voice.

"No one will believe us," the boy replied.

"But we can't ignore it."

"We have to, Amanda. If they know we know, we could be exiled. Or worse."

I spied on them through a small knothole in the back of the barn.

Something had to be done. Their meddling would ruin everything.

Perhaps I could take a shovel to the backs of their heads. A few good whacks should be enough. But how do I make it look like an accident?

I pulled out a pack of cigarettes, intending to light one up to calm my nerves. Smokes weren't allowed at Sanctuary, but I didn't have to follow the same rules as everyone else. Hell, I made the rules.

I stared at the cigarettes and the pack of matches.

I looked at the barn, taking in the dry, weathered wood. There was enough gasoline inside that it would practically cremate everything inside.

Including those damned kids.

I looked over my shoulder. I could do this. Everyone was sleeping.

A reel of rope hung outside the barn. With a pocketknife, I sawed off about three feet. It would do the job. Creeping around to the front of the barn, I secured the doors with the rope. They never even heard me.

There was a full can of gas in the smaller shed. After retrieving it, I poured gas all around the bottom of the barn. I splashed the rest of the gas up the back and side walls.

"We should go back," the girl said.

"Wait."

There was silence for a moment. Then I heard kissing sounds.

At least they'd die happy.

I lit the match.

As the vision faded, Jasi grabbed Brandon's arm for support. "Whoever did this had the cigarettes that Kenneth found and a pack of matches on him."

"So if we find a pack of matches, we'll find the arsonist."

"And he'll be up on attempted murder charges before he can take his next puff."

"You think he's our killer?"

"No. I didn't get the same intensity from him as I did when I touched the remains. We're definitely looking at a killer who had a partner."

"We've planned a cabin-by-cabin search for today. At least now we know what to look for. What about the kids? Learn anything new?"

"Amanda and Eric knew more than they've told us. They saw something, and Amanda wanted to tell someone. That's what they were discussing in the barn."

"Any word from the hospital?"

She shook her head. "Still unconscious. There's a female agent on guard. As soon as they wake up, she'll be able to question them."

"Back to the van?"

"Yeah. Then we'll gather every agent we can spare to assist with the cabin searches. But before we do that, we'll secure the residents in one area."

"I can take care of that now, since they're all in the barn having lunch." With determination, Brandon set off across the field. "See you later, Jasi."

She made a beeline for the van, noting some new faces hovering outside it.

"We've rounded up some help," Natassia said, introducing her to Agents Norman, Singh, Killgore and Howe.

Ben taped a map of the cabins on the side of the van and circled an area with a green highlighter. "Agents Norman and Singh, we'd like you to search these cabins." He outlined a section in blue. "Killgore and Howe, this is your area."

"I'd like these cabins," Jasi said, highlighting a few cabins in yellow. "Natassia, you're with me."

"But what about Brandon?"

"He's ensuring no one goes back to their cabins and that they remain in the big barn where he can watch them."

"I'm going to stay here and collect your data," Ben said. "Anyone find anything, make sure you bag it and tag it. We don't want anything else to go missing."

"Some evidence walked away?" Agent Norman asked, frowning.

"Before we were assigned here," Ben said. He told them about the missing bracelet. "We're specifically interested in locating the bracelet, a mini-com belonging to the incinerator victim and a pack of matches, which we believe may have been used by the arsonist. If you find any of these items, call Agent McLellan immediately."

"Above all," Jasi added, "don't allow anyone—other than one of us—inside a cabin while you're searching it. For *any* reason."

"What about personal searches?" Agent Norman asked.

"We're saving that for after. Don't expect a warm welcome though. These people take their privacy very seriously. Okay, let's move out."

They split up into their respective teams and headed for their designated areas. On the way, Jasi filled Natassia in on her vision.

It took most of the afternoon to search every cabin on Sanctuary grounds, and by four o'clock Jasi was exhausted. They'd scanned every inch of every building on the grounds and had turned up squat. Now they were in the final cabin, the one Lazarus and Henry shared.

Frustrated, she let out a groan. "My God, Natassia. Are we ever going to get a break here? I feel like everyone is conspiring against us. We have missing evidence, no real suspects and no clear motive."

Natassia glanced up from the sofa she'd been peering under. "Something's going to click, Jasi. Trust me. It always does."

Jasi knew she was right, but it did zilch to calm her exasperation, especially when every inch of her being told her the answers were all here, probably right in front of her nose.

What am I missing?

She leaned against the wall of the cabin, scrutinizing every detail of the room. For two single men, they kept the place quite clean. No dirty socks or underwear lying around. No dirty dishes in the sink. They'd even decorated it with paintings of forests and sculptures of woodland animals.

"Found something," Natassia called out, holding up a pop can.

"I don't think pop is against the rules here."

"Except that's not what's in this can." She upended the can and three cigarette butts dropped onto the coffee table."

"Same brand as the ones found at the fire."

"So either Lazarus or Henry is a smoker."

Jasi clenched her teeth. "Then one of them tried to kill those kids."

She pulled out her 'com and called Brandon. When he picked up, she said, "Make sure Henry and Lazarus don't go anywhere. We'll be right over."

Jasi and Natassia arrived at the barn minutes later and were greeted by absolute silence. The members of Sanctuary sat at the tables. No one seemed to be very happy.

Christiansen stood slowly, his mouth pursed in anger. "Agent McLellan, what's the meaning of this? Why are we being detained here like criminals?"

She glared at him. "Have you seen what's left of your old barn or the wounds on Eric and Amanda?" She gazed around the room until her eyes settled on Lazarus and Henry. "You two, come with me, please."

"What did I do?" Henry asked as he stood.

"We have a few questions for you." Jasi indicated that they step outside, and Natassia followed her while Brandon remained behind.

Lazarus's eyes darted from Christiansen to Henry and then to Jasi. "Fine. Ask away."

Once they were outside, Jasi said, "Agent Prushenko, would you please search these gentlemen."

"Now wait a minute," Lazarus sputtered. "I never gave you permission to touch me."

"This," Jasi held up a warrant, "gives me all the permission I need."

Henry held up his hands in surrender. "I got nothing to hide."

While Natassia gave Henry a thorough pat-down, Jasi kept her eye on Lazarus. A bundle of nerves, he twitched and shuffled as though he had something to hide. The more she watched him, the more she was sure he did.

"You have anything you want to say?" she asked him.

He licked his lips but kept silent.

"I've got this one," she said to Natassia. "Take Mr. Edgars back inside."

After they'd gone, Jasi looked at Lazarus. "Follow me."

"Where we going?"

"You'll see."

Grabbing his arm, she steered him toward a picnic table near the old barn ruins. "Two kids almost died here today."

"They shouldn't have been smoking."

"Remove your jacket and empty your pockets."

The man blinked. "What?"

"You heard what I said. And set the contents on the table."

He hesitated at first, but did as ordered. A few pieces of paper, chewing gum wrappers, a folded five-dollar bill…and a gold pen.

"Nice pen," she said, picking it up.

"Just something a friend gave me."

Why did the pen seem familiar? *Ben!* This was the one he'd described. He'd gotten a read from it.

"Father Jeremiah has one exactly like it," she said.

"Naw, I left it in his house. Just got it back. What's the big deal? It's only a pen."

The visions Ben had seen were connected to Lazarus, *not* Christiansen.

"Anything else on you?"

The next item he pulled from his pocket made her gasp. "You have a cell phone? I thought those weren't permitted here."

"Sometimes Father Jeremiah needs to call me when I'm in town."

She picked up the phone. There were no numbers stored in the address book. She pressed redial. No one answered, and no machine picked up.

"Who did you last call?" she asked.

"Can't remember."

She inspected the caller ID for incoming calls. Only one number was listed, and it wasn't the same as the one she'd just dialed. She hit 'call.' It was picked up after the second ring.

"Yeah?" The man's voice was low, grating.

"Who is this?" she demanded.

Click.

Fuming, she yelled, "Who called you, Lazarus?"

"I have no idea."

"Turn out your pockets!"

He obeyed. Nothing but a few wisps of lint.

"Can I go now, Agent McLellan?"

The black buttons of his dress shirt drew her attention. One was missing.

Lazarus knows about the graves in the woods. He was there.

"Pants!" she ordered.

"What?"

"Turn out your pant pockets."

He gave her a steely glare, then glanced over her shoulder. "Oh, look who's here."

She turned, half-expecting to see Giles Christiansen, but no one was there.

Ah, shit.

Something slammed into her back, pushing her to the ground before she could react. Footsteps retreated away from her.

Lazarus was on the run.

"You've got nowhere to go," she hollered as she scrambled to her feet.

She scoured the area, catching a glimpse of his pale blue shirt. He'd climbed through the hole in the fence and was sprinting into the woods.

"Shit!"

She drew her gun from the holster and ran after him.

"Lazarus! Stop running or I'll shoot!"

But he didn't listen.

She dodged cedars, tree roots and slippery moss, all the while cursing herself for letting her guard down. How could she have fallen for the oldest trick in the book?

And now she was chasing him through the forest with no backup.

She flicked a button on her data-com. When Brandon answered, she told him what had happened.

"I'm on my way," he said.

Breathless, she continued following the path of freshly broken branches. Lazarus was nowhere to be seen.

Where is he?

Lazarus had circled far from the gravesite so she couldn't get help from the agents there. He was leading her deeper into the woods and farther from Sanctuary and Brandon.

There!

A wisp of blue caught her eye.

The trees thinned up ahead and she spied a rock ridge rising dozens of feet above her. This was the area Natassia had described, where

Amanda had seen the "beast." She slowed her pace, watchful of every possible hiding place.

Then she saw Lazarus. He was climbing the rocks.

What is he doing?

Amanda had talked of a cave. Was that where he was heading?

She began the ascent after him. When she reached a clear view of the man, she let off a warning shot to his right. "Stay where you are!"

"Back off, Agent McLellan," the man shouted. "You have no idea what you're getting mixed up in. This goes much higher than me." He kicked a mound of rocks and sent it down on top of her.

She dashed behind a boulder. From this vantage point, she spotted a clear trail that would lead her up and around. Lazarus wouldn't even see her coming.

She picked her way through the rocks, the ground evening out so she could increase her pace without worrying about stumbling. When she peered between two boulders, she saw she'd gained on him.

A little bit farther...

Minutes later, she stepped from behind a moss-covered boulder. With his back to her, Lazarus stood maybe ten feet away, near the edge of a steep precipice. One wrong step and he'd stumble over the side.

"Lazarus," she said softly, aiming her gun at his back.

He spun around, and she heard stones skip down the side of the cliff.

"Stay back," he said, his eyes wide with panic as he raised his hands.

"I can get you a deal."

His mouth curved into a smile. "No deals for me."

"If you tell me who's involved, I can get you a reduced sentence."

"These aren't people you can rat out. I won't last a day in any prison."

"There's always witness protection—"

He laughed. "You don't get it. These people...they're judges, lawyers, police officers and businessmen—men with big money and even bigger egos."

"You're talking about a conspiracy?"

"I'm talking about an organization. A *hunt club*."

Jasi felt as though someone had slapped her across the face and woken her up. Finally, all the signs, all the clues, tumbled into place. The contracts, six-figure payments, the metal cylinder—a hunting scope.

She wanted to throw up.

"You're hunting people out here."

Lazarus sneered at her. "Uh, no. Not me personally. I only arrange for the financing and handle the...carcasses...after the hunt."

She took a step forward. "Let me bring you in, and you can help us. These victims' families need closure."

Lazarus shuffled a few inches closer to the edge. "Either let me go or I'll jump."

She sucked in a breath. "I can't let you go, Lazarus. You know that."

"Then you give me no choice."

"No!"

As she ran toward him, Lazarus lifted his arms, leaned back and vanished. When she reached the edge and peered down, she saw him sprawled across the rocks about forty feet below. He wasn't moving.

It took her less than ten minutes to descend and reach his broken body. Blood and brain matter dotted the rocks around him. As she leaned over him, spit oozed from his mouth and she heard wheezy breathing. She touched his neck. His pulse was thread and slow. Collapsed lungs, broken bones, spinal injuries—Lazarus wasn't going to be alive for long.

"You're dying, Lazarus. But you've got a chance to make things right. Tell me who's involved."

He mouthed something indecipherable, grabbed her hand and pressed something into it. Opening her hand, she saw a pack of matches.

"You tried to kill Amanda and Eric?"

Lazarus's eyes drifted shut.

"Please! For all the victims." Her ear was inches from his mouth. "Tell me who's involved. Give me something!"

With his final breath, Lazarus whispered two words.

22

Brandon stormed past the rubble of the old barn, cursing beneath his breath.

"What the hell are you thinking, Jasi?"

She'd taken off after Lazarus into unfamiliar territory with no backup. The guy probably knew these woods like the back of his hand.

He ducked through the fence opening, activated his 'com and set it to trace Jasi's tracker. A beep alerted him that she'd been found, and he released a sigh. Following the display on the 'com, he moved through the trees, watchful for an ambush.

He quickened his pace when the small moving dot slowed then stopped.

Damn it! Why isn't she moving?

Panting, he jumped fallen logs and dodged tree roots and prickly bushes.

When he reached the edge of the woods, he was greeted by a ridge covered in sharp boulders and moss-covered rocks. He paused to get his bearings. The 'com indicated Jasi was ahead of him. But that could only mean one thing.

He shielded his eyes from the sun and looked up. Surveying the rocks, he began to climb. He'd only progressed a few feet when he heard a dull thud a few yards away. Edging to his left, he picked his way through the rocks.

He saw Jasi leaning over Lazarus's body.

"Jasi!" he called, running toward her. "Are you all right?"

"I'm fine."

"What happened?"

"He jumped."

He knelt by Lazarus and felt for a pulse. "He's dead."

"A four-story drop will do that to you."

"Why'd he jump? You could've taken him in. He's our killer, right?"

"He's our arsonist, but I don't think he killed anyone." Jasi handed him the matches and sat down on a flat stone, her hands on her knees. "This is so much bigger than one murderer, Brandon. We're dealing with multiple killers. A clandestine organization. Lazarus arranged it all."

"What kind of organization kills innocent people?"

"One of the sickest kinds—a *hunt* club."

He hissed in a breath. "You mean the kind that hunts humans for sport?"

"Exactly. And according to Lazarus, these hunters are in positions of power. Lawyers, judges, police—you name it."

"Did he give you any names?"

"No."

She told him about the cell phone, the voice on the other end and the two words Lazarus had told her before he died.

"Makes no sense," Brandon said.

"I know."

"How do you want to handle this?"

She glanced down at Lazarus. "We need to get a recovery team in here before the wildlife gets to him."

"On it." He reached for his data-com and dialed Matthew's number. A few seconds later, he hung up. "He's sending two agents from the gravesites. They'll be here in five minutes. They'll take it from there."

Jasi stood slowly, stretching her arms above her head. "I just want this case to be over. I feel like we've been going around in circles for weeks."

"It's been a couple of days."

She scowled. "Feels like much longer."

Bending, she rummaged through Lazarus's pockets. "Nothing. Damn it!"

"I think we need to regroup with Ben and Natassia, go over everything we know."

"Let's get Agent Anthony in on this too. The kid has sharp eyes."

A rustle in the bushes indicated they had company. Two CFBI agents greeted them with a wave.

Brandon watched as Jasi issued orders. Her confidence was sexier than ever, but her vulnerability made him love her even more. He saw the hurt in her emerald green eyes, and he knew she was struggling. She'd promised Emily she'd find her, and time was running out.

He had his own thoughts about Emily. Jasi had been seeing her since she was young. He wanted to protect Jasi from what he suspected she'd find—the girl's remains. After all, she'd first appeared to Jasi as a girl with strangulation marks around her throat.

He recalled that popular television series from years ago, one he'd never watched but his sister had been hooked on. Was Jasi communicating with the dead?

Is she a ghost whisperer?

Upon reaching Sanctuary, Brandon took Jasi's arm and led her to the barn where all the residents were waiting. "We have to find out who else is involved in this conspiracy."

"What do you think Lazarus meant about 'white Jaguar'?" Jasi asked.

"Someone involved must own one."

"Aren't they expensive?"

"Very. A car like that could run you anywhere from sixty to a hundred thousand."

Jasi smiled. "Which means not everyone has one. Ben should be able to find it." She activated her 'com and set it on speakerphone. "Call Ben." When he picked up, she told him about Lazarus, the hunt club and the white Jag.

She hung up and looked at Brandon. "Maybe the vehicle registrations will turn up something on our suspects."

"There's one thing that's been bothering me about all this."

"What's that?"

"I get that Lazarus wanted to escape, but why did he head up the ridge? Why not hide in the forest or try to reach a main road that would take him out of here?"

"I don't know. I wondered the same thing." Her 'com rang. "Hey, Ben. What have you got for us?"

"I checked vehicle registrations for everyone at Sanctuary, their relatives and the investors. No one owns a white Jaguar."

"Maybe they rented it," Brandon said.

"I had the same thought, so I searched for car rentals in the area. No one in Mission has a Jaguar of any color. And there is only a couple in the Vancouver area and none of them are white."

"Damn," Jasi said.

"Matthew's sending out teams to watch the investors. If anyone else makes a move, we'll know." Ben signed off.

Outside the barn, Brandon said, "They're not going to open up if you tell them about Lazarus right away. I suggest we ask our questions first."

"I agree. Let's see if anyone here gets spooked by the mention of a 'white Jaguar.'"

He squeezed her hand. "We're getting close, Jasi."

"I hope so."

He kissed her cheek. "And when this is over, I'll help you with Emily."

Jasi blinked back tears. "You know, not every guy would believe a gal who talks to ghosts."

"I'm not every guy." He hoped she realized he meant it. "Besides, I've heard schizophrenia is common with psychics."

She jabbed him in the ribs with her elbow. "Not funny."

He smirked. "It kinda is."

"Come on. We've got killers to catch."

Brandon entered the barn and noticed the spacious room was calm and orderly. Every chair was occupied. A handful of residents stood near the dessert table, chatting quietly. Two of Christiansen's wives, Hannah and Grace, were wrapping up the leftovers, while Jeremiah sat at the head table soaking in his followers' admiration, smiling as though he hadn't a care in the world.

"Look at him," Brandon whispered. "King of the world."

"Hopefully king of a cellblock by the end of today," Jasi replied.

He couldn't agree more.

Christiansen stood and made his way toward them. "We have had a blessing today."

"What do you mean?"

"My wife, Rachel, gave birth to a healthy son."

"How is your wife?" Jasi asked.

"This was a difficult pregnancy for her, but she is on the road to recovery."

"I'm happy to hear that."

Brandon held out his hand. "Congratulations on the birth of your son."

"Thank you."

When Jeremiah shook his hand, Jasi hissed in a breath. "You've got blood on your hands, Mr. Christiansen."

The man blinked in surprise. "My apologies. Birthing can be a messy process."

"You assisted?"

"I try to assist in every birth here."

After Christiansen left, she motioned Natassia and Agent Anthony to join them. While Jasi told them about the hunt club and Lazarus's death, Brandon eyed two of the men sitting next to Christiansen—Henry Edgars and Kenneth O'Brien.

Were they part of the conspiracy?

Henry caught his eye and scowled.

The feeling's mutual, buddy.

Returning to the conversation, he reminded Jasi about Lazarus's final words.

"Are you sure that's what he said?" Brandon asked.

"Positive. I leaned down and he said it clear as can be—'white Jaguar.'"

"Excuse me," Agent Anthony interjected. "What did you just say?"

Jasi blinked then repeated her words.

The young agent's pale brows shot up. "Holy crap! Uh...sorry. I mean—never mind. You have to follow me back to the van. I read something in one of those documents. I know I did."

"I'll stay behind and keep the natives in line," Natassia said with a sigh.

"He better not be leading us on a wild goose chase," Jasi murmured to Brandon.

"If he does, I'm sure he means well."

Agent Anthony bolted across the field, and Brandon and Jasi followed.

23

Agent Anthony reached the surveillance van first, and he was inside before Jasi could warn Ben. When she climbed inside, she took one look at Ben and made a face. *Oh damn.*

"Didn't you ever learn to knock?" he said to Agent Anthony.

The kid quaked in his boots. "I-I..."

"Sorry, Ben," Jasi said. "Agent Anthony is a little overzealous."

"He thinks he saw something in one of the reports," Brandon added.

Ben clenched his jaw, his eyes narrowing. "Are you suggesting we missed something, Agent Anthony?"

"N-no."

"Then what are you suggesting?"

Agent Anthony drew a deep breath. "Agent McLellan recently came across new evidence. When I heard about it, I remembered I'd seen that reference in one of the investor reports."

"Whose?"

"I don't recall his name, but I'm sure I can find it."

Ben stepped aside. "Have at it."

"Agent McLellan," Agent Anthony said, rifling through various reports, "you thought Lazarus was talking about a car, but he wasn't. He was talking about the famous 'White Jaguar.'"

He glanced up and was greeted with blank stares, including Jasi's.

"Don't any of you watch reality shows?"

"I get enough reality from this job," Jasi said.

"There's a show called Wild Huntsman. It's about *extreme* hunting, filmed all over the world, with legendary hunters hunting in harsh conditions, searching for that rare trophy to place on their walls."

She let out an impatient huff. "What's a TV show got to do with our case?"

"Last season, they had this guy on it. He's hunted in the Serengeti, the Amazon, New Zealand—"

"Agent Anthony…"

"Got it!" He waved a paper in the air then handed it to Jasi.

"Becket Hawley?" she said, skimming over the report.

She was about to ask him how Hawley was connected when she saw a paragraph on Hawley's income. Last year he'd been paid a substantial amount to appear on a television show—Wild Huntsman.

"So Becket Hawley was on a hunting show. That only tells us he likes to hunt."

"He doesn't just *like* to hunt, he's a crack shot. He killed an elephant at a half mile away." Agent Anthony's voice grew excited. "Know what Hawley's nickname on the show was?"

When the answer hit her, Jasi smirked. "White Jaguar."

"I have a list of Hawley's known associates," Ben said. He flipped through a folder until he found the page. "He's definitely well connected."

"Any judges, lawyers or police officers?" she asked.

"All three."

She felt her heart skip a beat. They were closing in on the people responsible for the gruesome murders. "Let me see who the police officers are. I'll call Pop and see if knows anything about them."

Ben handed her the paper and she scanned the names. She was familiar with two of the judges on the list. They'd presided over some of her previous cases. One lawyer she recognized from his television advertisement. He was heavy into tort law.

She reached the list of police officers. It was short—five names. The last one made her do a double-take.

"Oh God…"

Brandon looked over her shoulder. "Isn't that the same guy from the photo of the police convention?"

"I was hoping that was simply a random event." But as she stared into the eyes of a man she thought she knew so well, she shivered. "I have to call Pop."

She left the van. Walking down the road that led away from Sanctuary, she dialed Pop's number.

When he picked up, she blew out a breath. "You're home."

"Where else would I be, lass?" her father said, his Scottish brogue thicker than usual, which suggested he'd been drinking.

"Pop, I need to ask you some questions, and I want you to promise me you won't ask why."

"Okay…"

"What do you know about Becket Hawley?"

"Becket? He comes from old money and likes to travel and hunt."

"Have you ever heard any whispers about him, anything he may be involved in?"

"You mean illegal activities?" Pop paused. "Well, there was some ruckus a few years ago, allegations he was involved in illegal game hunting in Africa. And I know he's smuggled in a few trophy heads, ones that never would've passed customs."

"Did Hawley ever invite you to go hunting around the Mission area?"

Pop laughed. "Mission? Don't know why he'd bother. Not much of a thrill there. But if you really want to know about Becket, you should ask Paxton."

Jasi bit her lip. "How well does Uncle Paxton know him?"

"Oh they've been friends for years. Paxton and Becket went to college together. Paxton was the one who helped Becket when the smuggling charges came up."

"Has he ever taken Paxton hunting with him?"

The elongated silence was palpable.

"Pop?"

"Jasmine," he said finally, "what's this about?"

"Pop, you promised to let me ask the questions."

She heard him sigh. "Ach, I've heard them making arrangements from time to time, but I don't know if they were hunting, playing cards or grabbing a pint. Want me to call Paxton and ask—"

"No, Pop," she said, gripping the 'com tightly. "I'll give him a call."

"Listen, Jasmine, whatever you're thinking, you're wrong. There's no way Paxton is involved in your case. I've known him for nearly thirty-five years. He's a fine cop and a finer friend. He was there for me after your mother..." His voice cracked. "And before that, when your mother was in the hospital. I was out on a call, and he saved her life."

"What? When was that?"

"Two years before you were born."

"How come you never told me?"

"Your mother, she had...woman problems. I didn't think you needed to know that. It didn't seem that significant."

Jasi gritted her teeth. "Everything about my mother is important, Pop."

"When you come for dinner, I'll tell you all about it. You got my word. But Paxton is a decent man, so don't you be going 'round thinking otherwise."

"I have to go now, Pop. I'll call you later. Say hi to Brady for me."

After the call disconnected, she massaged her forehead and thought about her mother, imagining her lying alone in a hospital bed. How could Pop have kept this a secret all these years?

"Is everything okay?"

Brandon walked toward her, his expression solemn, worried.

"Pop says Uncle Paxton knew Hawley and may have hunted with him."

"That doesn't mean Paxton is involved in the hunt club."

"I have a horrible feeling, Brandon." She paced the road, back and forth. "If Uncle Paxton is mixed up in this, it's going to kill Pop. He thinks Uncle Paxton is a hero."

"What do you want to do?"

"I'm going to call him."

"Paxton?"

"Yes." He started to walk away, but she grabbed his hand. "Don't go."

"You sure?"

"I need someone to keep me calm." She activated her 'com. "Call Paxton Helling."

"Jasmine?" a deep voice said.

"Uncle Paxton, hi. How are you?"

"Good, good. How've you been? I haven't seen you in a while."

"I'm keeping busy."

"And your dad?"

"Pop's fine. Listen, I'm calling because your name came up on a case I'm working on."

"Was I a former investigating officer?"

"No. We're questioning a few people, and it seems you're associated with one of them. Becket Hawley."

"Becket Hawley?" Pause. "You're saying he's part of an investigation? What kind?"

"I can't really discuss the particulars of the case, Uncle Paxton. I'm sure you understand. I was hoping you'd be able to tell me what you know about him."

"I don't know Becket very well."

"Really? Pop seems to think you're friends."

"I wouldn't call it that. We went to school together, college actually."

"Ever gone hunting with him?"

"No, hunting's not my thing. Sometimes our paths have crossed at events, but we've never hung out together. Other than that, I don't think there's anything else I can tell you. Sorry I can't help."

"One more thing," she said. "Pop mentioned you saved my mother's life."

Another long pause. "That was a long time ago. I'm surprised he said anything."

"She ended up in the hospital," she pressed.

"It was a sad time and not the outcome anyone expected."

"What do you mean?"

"You need to talk to your father about this."

"But, Uncle Paxton—"

"Jasmine." His raspy growl made her jump. "I'm sorry, but I can't talk to you about your mother. Have a chat with your father. I have to go now. I have a meeting."

She scarcely had time to say goodbye before he hung up.

Shoving the data-com into a pocket, her eyes met Brandon's. "Well, that wasn't very productive. I think I pissed him off."

"What did you get from him?"

"Just discrepancies and more questions." She shook her head. "Uncle Paxton says he never went hunting or did anything with Hawley. He made out like he and Hawley were nothing more than casual acquaintances, but Pop is under the assumption they were chummy and played cards together."

"That's good to know."

"It's just that..." She was halfway to the van when she came to an abrupt halt. "Something doesn't feel right about all this."

Brandon tucked his arm around her waist. "You're exhausted. Maybe a quick nap would do you good."

"I can't sleep, Brandon. There's too much going on in my mind."

"To do with your mother?"

"That too. Uncle Paxton said it was a sad time when she ended up in the hospital. That no one expected it." She stopped walking and glanced up at him. "I think she had cancer. But why didn't Pop ever tell me about this?"

Her eyes welled up with tears, and he brushed one away with his thumb. "I think you should ask him."

"I plan on it. Not that it changes anything."

"Jasmine?" Ben called from the van doorway. "Matthew is sending a team to bring in Becket Hawley for questioning."

"We may finally get some answers," she said to Brandon. "Come on."

Back in the van, Jasi didn't waste any time. "Where are they taking him, Ben?"

"CFBI headquarters. Matthew will let us know as soon as they have him."

"Okay. In the meantime, we need to do a thorough check on Paxton Helling. He's a cop with VPD, and in the interest of full disclosure, he's a friend of my father's."

"You want financials too?" Ben asked.

"Everything you can find. I'm hoping, for Pop's sake, we won't find anything incriminating."

"What if we do?" Natassia asked.

"Then we do what we have to do."

Ben's data-com beeped.

"It's Matthew," he said. He listened for a minute, then disconnected. "Hawley isn't at his home or office."

"Shit. He's not making this easy."

"We were able to track his cell phone."

"You get a location?"

"What do you think?"

"Where?"

"Some dive hotel in Mission, of all places."

Jasi frowned. *What is Hawley doing in Mission?*

Ben's 'com beeped again.

"I'm putting Matthew on speaker," he said.

"We have a team in place outside the EZ Sleep Motel," Matthew said. "All exits are covered."

"Did anyone get a visual on him?" Jasi asked.

"We've confirmed Hawley is inside, and it looks like he'll be there a while. He just ordered Chinese." Matthew cleared his throat. "Jasmine, I can send a helicopter if you want in on the takedown."

She caught Brandon's eye. "I'll need an extra seat, Matthew."

24

EZ Sleep Motel, Mission, BC

The helicopter dropped Jasi and Brandon a few blocks away, and an unmarked police car drove them to the motel. The rundown building covered in flaking baby-blue paint and graffiti suggested the rooms were paid for by the hour. Not a place one would typically expect to find a millionaire like Becket Hawley.

Jasi confirmed the time. 8:12 PM.

She and Brandon joined the agents hunkered down in the parking lot behind a rusty RV that looked as though it hadn't moved in several decades.

The dimly lit street and parking lot were dead quiet.

"Agent Norman," she said, surprised to see one of the agents who had assisted them at Sanctuary.

"I was reassigned," he said, giving Brandon a nod.

"Fill us in."

"Becket Hawley's in room 109." Agent Norman handed her a pair of binoculars. "That red Ford Fusion parked in front is his rental car."

"He make any calls?"

"Only one. Wang Ho's Chinese Restaurant. His supper arrived about thirty minutes ago."

"Anything suspicious about the delivery?"

"I don't think so. He paid the delivery guy and went back inside." Agent Norman's gaze drifted to the hotel window. "He looked out the window about ten minutes ago, but there's been no movement since."

"You sure he didn't see any of you?"

"Positive."

"And there's no way out of that room other than the door."

"Not unless he's Houdini."

Becket Hawley was no magician. Intuition told her the man was a demented serial killer who enjoyed hunting down his innocent prey.

"You and your partner want to go in first?" Agent Norman asked.

"Yeah." She withdrew her gun from her shoulder harness. "You and your team follow us in. But send a couple of agents to the back alley to watch the bathroom window, if there's one."

Agent Norman issued the command to his team.

"Ready?" she asked.

Brandon and Agent Norman nodded.

Squatting low, she moved between the vehicles in the parking lot, inching closer to Hawley's room. *Who's hunting who now, asshole?*

Brandon crouched beside her, and muted rustling behind her indicated the backup team had moved into place.

She studied her target. Room 109. Curtains drawn, only a faint yellow glow inside. She hoped Hawley was sitting on his bed, wolfing down his chop suey and fried rice, and she hoped he choked on it when they broke down the door.

She motioned for Brandon to veer left, while she continued toward Hawley's rental car. Sliding a jackknife from her pocket, she stabbed the back tires. The hiss of air that followed ensured Hawley wouldn't get far if he happened to make it past them. She sprinted around the side of the car. When she was positioned on the right side of the door to Hawley's room, and Brandon was in place on the opposite side, she raised her fist.

Everyone halted.

Pressing her ear to the door, she heard the theme song for *Dexter.*

How fitting.

She held up three fingers and mouthed the countdown. *Three...two...*

On *one*, Brandon kicked the door in.

"CFBI!" she shouted, moving inside. "Becket Hawley, you're—" She froze.

Apparently she'd been wrong. Hawley did have one magic trick up his sleeve. He had somehow vanished from his carefully guarded room.

"Shit!" Seething, she yelled, "Search the room!"

Agents swarmed the place. They searched the closet, bathroom, under the bed—everywhere—but Hawley was gone.

"Check the back alley and every room and car on this lot," she ordered. To Agent Norman she said, "You're with us."

"Listen, Agent McLellan, we did everything—"

"Then how the hell did he escape without anyone seeing him?"

"I'm not sure. We had the entire motel covered, front and back."

She groaned in frustration and strode into the bathroom. Gripping the edge of the sink, she glared into the mirror. "Where are you, you bastard?"

"We have an APB out on him," Agent Norman called out.

Her senses tingled. Hawley was nearby. She could feel him.

Her gaze wandered from the shadows under her eyes to the reflection of the motel room. A cheap pressboard dresser sat in the far corner near the window, and above it was…a crawlspace hatch.

He couldn't be…

She strode out of the bathroom. As she moved closer, she spotted a stress fracture on the dresser's surface. Next to it, in the dust, was a fresh shoeprint.

Gotcha!

"Everyone stand back."

"What are you doing?" Brandon asked.

"Hunting."

Agent Norman and Brandon stared at her as though she'd lost her mind.

She pointed to the dresser then up at the hatch in the ceiling. In a firm voice she called out, "Becket Hawley! If you don't show yourself, I'm going to shoot the ceiling until one of my bullets finds you."

No answer.

She aimed the Beretta and pulled the trigger. A bullet ripped through the drywall, sending a small plume of white dust into the air.

"Hawley?"

Silence.

Then she heard him. Hawley was making his way across the ceiling. She aimed at the center, near the light, and fired three times. Another cloud of dust detonated around her. A piece of the ceiling broke away, tumbling to the ground and revealing a hollow area.

"I've got two full clips, Hawley. And you've got nowhere to go but down."

"Are you sure you want to do this?" Agent Norman said. "You might kill him."

She shrugged. "His choice."

The next two bullets tore out another chunk of drywall and the lighting fixture from the ceiling. The ceiling began to buckle.

"Agent Norman," she said, "you shoot the left side. Brandon, you go right. Let's put this guy out of his misery."

"Okay, okay!" a voice screamed. "Don't shoot me. I'm not armed."

Jasi aimed her gun at the ceiling and waited.

This time Hawley was anything but quiet as he moved toward the nearest opening. When his head emerged, his hair was covered in cobwebs and dust. He raised his hands. "See? No gun."

"Come on down," she said, watching his every move.

"Ah, Agent McLellan," the man said, scurrying closer to the edge. "I was hoping—"

"Watch out!" Brandon yanked her out of the way just as the entire ceiling came crashing down.

After the dust settled, Becket Hawley was sprawled facedown in the rubble, blood oozing from a gash on his arm.

She moved to the man's side and touched his wrist. "He's still alive."

Hawley moaned.

"What's he saying?" Brandon asked.

"I think he wants us to turn him over."

She cuffed Hawley. Then they rolled the man onto his back.

"I couldn't breathe," he said, panting. "Thank you."

"Don't thank me yet. You're under arrest." She holstered her gun, activated the voice record on her 'com and read him his rights.

Brandon inspected Hawley's pockets. "Look what I found." He held up a cell phone. "Outgoing numbers have been wiped clean."

"Any incoming calls?" she asked.

"Only two in the last three hours. One is a private number."

"Call the other one."

A minute later, Brandon said, "It went to Lazarus's voice mail."

"He set this whole thing up you know," Hawley said. "You want to know who's involved, talk to Lazarus."

"That's not possible."

"Why?"

"Lazarus killed himself."

Hawley didn't even miss a beat. "Guess there'll be no rising of the dead this time." He tried to stretch his arms and let out a groan. "I think my ribs are broken. I need a doctor."

"We'll consider calling one if you cooperate. Who does the private number belong to?"

"What do I get if I tell you?"

She straddled him, digging one knee into his chest. "You get to breathe. Tell me who's in the hunt club."

"Can't do that."

"Then give me one name. Is Giles Christiansen involved?"

"Who?"

"Father Jeremiah."

Hawley laughed. "That nutcase? He was oblivious, too occupied with his creepy cult following to see what was going on right under his nose."

Jasi gaped at him, stunned. "But he *had* to know why you were paying him."

"Lazarus handled the business side of things, our *investments*. Told Father Jeremiah they were for the cult, out of the goodness of our hearts. And the guy believed every word."

"You're saying *Lazarus* is the brain behind the hunt club?"

"The kid was smarter than he looked—brilliant actually. He planned the hunt club, found the members and organized our events. And he came up with the whole bear sighting thing to keep everyone confined inside the fence."

"And the victims?"

Hawley shrugged. "No one anyone really missed. Poor bastards were half dead anyway. They just didn't know it yet."

"Some of those *'poor bastards'* were on their way to recovery and living decent lives," she shot back. "How could you pick on the weak?"

"But we didn't. The greatest challenge in hunting is stalking an animal that is physically fit, one you have to track, corner and then put down."

The coldness of his words cut right through her.

"We gave them a chance," he said. "The rules were clear. One hunter, one 'huntee'. If they made it past the fence and onto Sanctuary grounds, they'd live. It's the ultimate game of survival."

"And how many made it."

"None. Every hunter hit their target. Some with rifles, some with handguns, a couple prefer knives and one likes to pretend he's Arrow."

"What about Oliver Gathmann?" she asked.

Hawley's gaze clouded over. "He built cool buildings for a few of us, but he wasn't a hunter. He didn't know how to track his prey, how to instill panic in their hearts and make them run for their lives." He looked deep into her soul and stripped away her breath. "Not like me."

She stifled the urge to rip him apart, her hands fisting his shirt.

Then he smiled. "Now how about that doctor?"

"I don't think so."

Hawley studied her for a moment. "You're a wounded soul, aren't you?"

She released him and stood quickly. "You don't know anything about me."

"But I do. We have mutual acquaintances."

"If you're talking about my father or Paxton Helling, I've already talked to both of them."

"I don't know your father well, but Paxton and I, we go back a long way. We have a special arrangement."

"What kind of arrangement?"

Hawley clamped his mouth shut.

"Did Paxton participate in the hunt club?" she asked, dreading the answer.

"He's too virtuous for that."

She swallowed hard. "But he knew about it."

"He found out by accident. He's always poking around where he shouldn't be. I should've killed Paxton when I had the chance." Hawley's tone was devoid of emotion.

"Why didn't he turn you in then?"

"I gave him some incentive not to. And Paxton has his own secrets to protect."

"So you blackmailed him."

"We blackmailed each other. It was a mutual agreement. A kind of...stalemate."

"What could you possibly have on Paxton?"

"That, my dear Agent McLellan, is for me to know and you to find out."

"Oh, I will. Trust me."

"Next time you see *Uncle* Paxton, ask him about your mother. He was obsessed with her abilities."

The Beretta was back in her hand and pointed at the man's face in seconds.

"Jasi," Brandon warned.

Ignoring him, she leaned in close to Hawley. "What about my mother?"

"It must have been very difficult for little Jasmine to find her body."

Jasi released a growl. "What the hell do you know about that?"

Instead of answering her question, he said, "I know you're a psychic."

She pressed the gun against his head. "What are you talking about?"

"Your mother was also gifted. A psychic, like you."

This couldn't be true. Pop would have told her.

But he didn't tell me about the hospital visit.

"Tell me what you know, Hawley."

"I'm not saying another word unless you cut me a deal."

"The only deal you're getting," Brandon cut in, "is that you get to leave here alive and not in a body bag."

"He's right," she said between clenched teeth. "Talk!"

But Becket Hawley was done talking.

Jasi wanted to wipe the smug grin off his face. As the man's words replayed in her mind, she tried to make sense of it all. Her mother had been a psychic.

Could my mother see into the mind of an arsonist? Or did she have another gift?

Jasi straightened and brushed off her hands as though she'd touched something slimy. She couldn't bear to look at Hawley. He was the keeper of secrets, and she fought the overpowering urge to promise him anything—even his freedom—for the answers she so desperately wanted.

Her data-com rang. "I'll take this outside. I need some fresh air."

Brandon followed her.

Outside room 109, she set her 'com on speaker. "We've got him, Matthew."

"Thank God."

"Brandon and I are going to head back to Sanctuary."

"Before you do, there's something you need to know."

She glanced at Brandon. "What?"

"Hawley owns a fishing lodge in Oregon, near Klamath Falls. A team went in about half an hour ago and searched the place."

"What did they find?" Brandon asked.

"At first glance? Nothing. Until someone noticed a discrepancy in the design of the building. Hawley had a kind of panic room installed, but it's not like anything you've ever seen."

Jasi swallowed hard. "How do you mean?"

"We found a number of heads mounted on the wall. Seven were human."

"Jesus. Hunting trophies."

Hawley was the hunt club member who had decapitated his victims.

Including Sheral Downham.

"Two other things," Matthew said, his voice ominous. "There was a melted yellow mass on the mantle below the heads. We suspect it's the missing amethyst bracelet you've been looking for. And we found blueprints inside the room that confirm Hawley's lodge was built by a Washington company connected with this case."

"Let me guess—Mole Tech."

"You got it."

"Oliver Gathmann, the CEO, showed up at Sanctuary this morning," she said, "but he's probably back in Washington by now."

"Not quite, Jasmine. RCMP pulled Gathmann's body from Davis Lake ten minutes ago."

"Davis Lake? That's not far from Sanctuary."

"Or the EZ Sleep Motel."

"You think Becket Hawley killed him?"

"Gathmann was shot, one bullet to the base of the skull. Whoever killed him was in the hills, almost half a mile away."

"Jesus," Brandon said. "How many people can make a shot like that?"

"Only one I can think of," Jasi said.

Her stomach churned as she returned to the motel room. Hawley watched her every move. When his eyes met hers, they narrowed, and a slow smirk spread across his face.

"Agent McLellan," he said. "I think it's time to do some bargaining."

"Unless you're going to give me the list of hunt club members, you've got nothing to deal with."

"You'll want to hear about this. Trust me."

25

Natassia, Ben and Agent Anthony were already waiting when the RCMP transport helicopter landed in a grass clearing near the gravesites in the woods. Brandon disembarked, followed by Agent Norman and his team.

Jasi was last, her mind still reeling from Becket Hawley's final revelation. It had cost her. She'd have to speak on the man's behalf at his trial, but if what Hawley had told her was true, it would be a small sacrifice.

"You get it?" she asked Ben.

After a search of Oliver Gathmann's office at Mole Tech, Matthew's team discovered a number of blueprints for concealed earthships and secret chambers, many of them owned by other investors, including motivational speaker Van Harvard and Judge Cyrus Timmons. Only Mole Tech and the owners knew these existed. Lazarus had arranged for the construction of one of these earthships. Who paid for it exactly, and whether Christiansen knew anything about it, was yet to be determined.

Ben unrolled a blueprint. "There's an entrance somewhere in the rocks on the ridge." He indicated the entrance marked by a solid slab of rock. "The problem is the blueprint doesn't specifically say where. The earthship—"

"Let's call it what it is," Jasi interrupted. "A bunker."

"The bunker is vented in multiple places," Ben said. "And a generator inside provides all power. There's even a clean air filtration system installed. Some of you will navigate the upper ridge in search of vents or anything that suggests a possible bunker."

"Amanda thought she saw someone disappear around here," Jasi said. "They must have gone inside."

"That also explains where Lazarus was running to," Brandon added.
She nodded. "Exactly."

"What about the X-Disc?" Natassia asked. "Why didn't it pick up on the bunker?"

"Rock's too thick," Ben said.

"Agents Howe and Killgore," Jasi said. "I want you on that chopper. Tell the pilot to fly as low as he can over the ridge, and radio me if you see anything."

"Got it," Kaye Killgore replied.

"Agents Norman, Anthony and Singh, I want you up on the top of the ridge right away looking for vents."

"Do we search on the way up?" Agent Anthony asked.

"No. Just get to the top. The sooner we find the vents, the sooner we know we're in the right area." To Ben, Natassia and Brandon, she said, "The four of us will be searching the rocks from the ground up. I want every inch of this area searched. We're looking for a solid rock door. Ben, how do we get inside?"

"According to the plans, there's a key tucked in a hole drilled into the rocks to the right of the door and about waist high."

"Okay everyone, fan out," she ordered. "Keep your 'coms on my frequency and flashlights on high. We don't want to miss anything."

They split up into their designated teams, and the search was on.

As they headed for the rocks, Brandon pulled her aside. "Jasi, are you sure you don't want to go after Paxton? We can handle things here, you know."

"This can't wait. Paxton can. Matthew has him under surveillance. And Paxton is our best bet at catching the others in the hunt club." The crisp night air sent a shiver up her spine. "We have to hurry, Brandon."

An hour into the search they'd turned up nothing but scratches and bruises.

Jasi heaved a sigh of frustration. "We know it's here. Keep looking." She activated her 'com and connected to Agent Norman. "You guys see anything?"

"Nothing."

Her watch indicated it was almost 10:30 p.m. Clouds had rolled in, obscuring the sliver of moon that hovered above them. Even with flashlights in hand and the helicopter flying overhead with its search beam on high, the rocks around them presented a maze of possible injury.

"You sure you don't want to wait until morning?" Brandon asked. "We could start out at first light."

She shook her head. "You heard what Hawley told me. We have to find this bunker before it's too late."

"Agent McLellan!" Agent Norman's voice sounded over her 'com. "We've got something."

"Give us your location."

He read out the coordinates. "I think I see your flashlights. Keep heading south."

Jasi and Brandon made their way over and around boulders and crevices, using the GPS system on her 'com. Every now and then she peered up, hoping to catch a glimpse of light from Agent Norman and his team.

"Over there," Brandon said, pointing up and toward her right. "See them?"

"We're closing in on your location," she told Agent Norman. "How many vents do you see?"

"Three. They're spaced out approximately twenty feet apart, heading further south from my current position."

"Call Natassia and Ben," she told Brandon. "Tell them to meet us. And tell Agents Anthony and Killgore to meet us inside the bunker."

While he followed behind, she continued picking her way across the rocks.

Ten minutes later, she reached an area of rock that seemed out of place.

"Looks like someone's done some blasting around here," Brandon said, sliding his hand along the surface of one boulder. "Some of these have been sheared clean."

"The bunker door has to be around here somewhere."

While Brandon aimed both flashlights on the rocks, Jasi inched along a small shelf, feeling the wall of rock as she went. "They wouldn't have made it easy to find. The entire purpose of the bunker was so they could hide what they were doing."

Another five minutes and Jasi's hands were raw.

"How about we trade places?" Brandon said.

"I'm smaller."

When he let out a grunt, she laughed. "I just meant that it's easier for me to walk along this shelf."

Lights winked a few yards away, moving closer. Natassia and Ben.

"What do you want us to do?" Ben asked.

"The vents are above and to the south," Jasi told them. "Natassia, see if you can make your way about twenty feet from me. You keep heading south. Ben, make sure she has plenty of light."

As Natassia and Ben set off, Jasi shouted, "Check your GPS for

Agent Norman's position. He's right above us."

She thought of what Hawley had told her, and panic rose in her chest.

What if Lazarus booby-trapped the bunker?

"We have to be careful, Brandon. We don't know what we're walking into."

She watched as he shone the flashlights over an area of rock not far from Natassia and Ben's position. Shadows fought with the light, making it challenging to see any detail.

Something twinkled.

She almost missed it. "Wait! Go back."

Brandon skimmed the rocks with the light. "Did you see something?"

"I thought I did, over..." She squinted. "There!"

A tiny shimmer reflected back at them.

"There's something metal in that boulder." She sprinted toward it, praying she was right, while Brandon maintained a close target on the sliver of metal. As they drew nearer, she let out a laugh. "It's the key!"

Brandon messaged the other teams. "We found the key."

Sure enough, a long metal key protruded about half an inch from a hole in the rock. Unless someone knew where to look, they'd never see it.

She removed the key and held it up to the flashlight. "It's custom made."

"Wonder why they didn't go with an electronic keypad," Brandon said.

"Maybe they wanted to ensure that any hunt club member could get inside. This way they didn't have to worry about anyone forgetting a passcode."

"True. And in the case of generator failure, they could still access the bunker."

"The door has to be to the left."

She hopped over a slippery rock slab that obstructed her path. With caution, she touched the smooth rock face. It emitted such a chill that she shivered. She stretched higher, trying to discern if there was any kind of seal or door frame.

A gasp escaped her mouth when she touched a clean horizontal and then vertical ridge. "I found the edge of the door."

"Wait for us," Ben called a few feet away.

Seconds later, Jasi found the keyhole, which had been cleverly concealed by a thin wedge of rock that swiveled to one side.

Once Natassia and Ben reached her side, she looked at Brandon. "Ready?"

She slipped the key into the keyhole and turned it. The locking mechanism made a loud clunking sound, then the door hissed and swung out about three inches. Behind the door, lights hummed and flickered.

When Brandon pushed the door open, Jasi battled temporary blindness as brilliant light encompassed her. She stepped inside and followed a narrow passageway until it opened, revealing a spacious room.

"Wow," she said. "This is unbelievable."

The room was set up like a living room, with two sofas and two recliners. A small poker table and four chairs sat next to a well-stocked bar. The opposite side of the room housed a computer desk and a high-end laptop. Further down a central hall, a compact kitchen with every modern convenience was visible.

"Quite the opposite of Sanctuary and its lack of technology," she said. "Natassia, check the computer and copy any data on it."

"Are you suggesting I hack into someone's computer without a warrant?" Natassia winked. "I'm on it."

"We don't have a choice. If this place does have a self-destruct mode, I don't want to lose any evidence. And if we're lucky, that computer will lead us to every single hunt club member." She inhaled deeply.

"You ready for this?" Brandon asked.

"I am." She straightened. "I'll keep an eye out for sensors and possible explosives. Everyone else stay behind me until I say otherwise."

As she strode down the hall, her eyes darted left, right, up, down, scouring every inch of wall and floor.

So far, so good.

"There's a bathroom down here," she called out.

A quick peek inside told her the bathroom was empty.

Further down the hallway she came to a door. She opened it. "Storage closet."

"Looks like a bedroom on the other side," Brandon said over her shoulder.

"I thought I told you to stay back," she snapped.

"I tried that. But we're a team. Where you go, I go."

With a sigh, she motioned for him to follow. They entered the bedroom. Four bunk beds, a desk and a bookshelf.

"What if Hawley was lying?" she said.

"It's possible. But why? How would he benefit?"

She shrugged. "I don't know."

"We'll keep looking," Brandon assured her.

The hallway ended with a set of double doors.

Maybe this is it.

She examined the doors. "They don't appear to be wired."

Hesitating, she eased open one of the doors. "Shit. It's another damn closet."

This one had multiple shelves with electronics, batteries and boxes of ammunition. But it was what was on the inside of the doors that captured her attention—two rifles, a crossbow, a Japanese katana and a dagger, all displayed like works of art.

"Hawley said each hunter could select the weapon of their choice. Most had their favorites."

She sniffed the rifle barrels. "They've been fired recently."

She slipped on a pair of latex gloves and lifted the sword from its wall mount on the door. "I think if we swab this, we'll find blood. Same with the dagger."

Using her data-com, she took photographs of the closet and weapons.

"Let's rejoin the others," she said.

As soon as they returned to the living room, she saw Natassia sitting dutifully at the computer. "Any luck?"

"Oh yeah. I'm in."

"You *are* good," Brandon said.

Natassia raised her head. "Was there really any doubt?"

Brandon chuckled. "No."

"Anything to be worried about?" Ben asked Jasi.

"If this place is rigged, I can't see it. And we looked everywhere. The floor is solid rock so no worries about IEDs in the floor. No motions sensors. No cameras."

"You find anything else?"

"An assortment of weapons, most likely the ones used on each victim. We need swabs and finger prints."

"I have an evidence kit in my backpack. Just point me in the right direction."

"Straight down the hall. Doors at the very end. You can't miss them."

Agents Anthony and Norman entered the bunker.

"Where's Agent Singh?" Jasi asked.

"He's flagging all the vents," Agent Norman said. "And taking readings to ensure we won't have to worry about biohazards."

A shudder raced up her spine. "Biohazards?"

"It's just a precaution."

"How about you make sure the door stays open?" She shuddered. "I'd feel a lot better if I knew we had a quick escape route."

Agent Norman gave a nod. "Done."

Her eyes wandered over the room and sadness crept over her, threatening to pull her under. She'd been hoping for one ray of light, one small miracle…one blessed reward. But that wasn't going to happen.

"Here," Brandon said, placing the blueprint in her hand.

"I don't get it," she said with an exasperated groan. "We've searched every nook in this place. Hawley lied."

Behind them, Agent Anthony cleared his throat.

She whipped around. "Yes?"

"It's just that…I…uh…well—"

"For crying out loud, Jay," Natassia snapped. "If you've got something to say, say it. We don't have all day."

"Natassia's right," Jasi said.

The kid sucked in a breath. "The floor plan for this place doesn't match the layout we're looking at."

"How?"

Agent Anthony took a few steps closer and held out one hand. "If you give me the plan, I'll show you."

She passed him the blueprint and watched as he spread it out over the poker table, anchoring the corners with four heavy glass tumblers.

"Here's where we are," he said, pointing. "There's the bathroom, bedroom and the oversized storage closet at the end of the hall."

"Okay." She squinted. "I don't see the problem."

"Here's where that other closet is." He indicated an area of the living room. "It was added later."

"But that space is huge."

"Exactly. There's something behind the—"

Jasi didn't wait for the kid to complete his sentence. She rushed toward the smaller closet, threw open the door and felt around the wood shelves until her fingers came into contact with a lever.

She pulled on it.

A whirring sound accompanied a soft vibration, and a sliver of space could be seen on the right side of the back wall. There was no light behind it, only a rush of warm, pungent air.

"This is it," she said. "The moment of truth. And no matter what we find here, Hawley and his cohorts are going down hard."

She pressed the door, stepped inside and was devoured by darkness.

26

Hawley's words echoed in her ear. *"Agent McLellan, what if I told you we still had one little rabbit kept in quarantine?"*

"What do you mean?" she had demanded.

"Lazarus already selected the woman for the next hunt."

"Who?"

"I think he said her name was Jenny. I don't know—I never paid attention to their names. But I guess I screwed things up. Not something I'm proud of. I thought the incinerator would run for hours and there'd be nothing left of my prey except ash. Oh, and the head. A real prize that one."

The sheer bliss in his eyes made her shiver. She wanted to bash his face. The man was a demented psychopath.

"Get back to the other woman, Hawley. Where is she?"

"Lazarus kept her in our lair. But once the RCMP and you all showed up, he had to leave her there."

"Are you saying there's a victim who is still alive?"

Hawley smirked. "Well, she *was* a few days ago. I can't promise anything now. Who knows what tricks Lazarus had up his sleeve. He could have the place wired with C4 or on zero oxygen."

"Oh my God."

"You'd better hurry, Agent McLellan. I suspect time is running out."

Now as she stood in the shadows, she wondered whether Hawley had told the truth. The room seemed empty. Nothing moved. Not one sound.

No sign of life.

She gagged at the nauseating stench that lingered in the air.

"Brandon," she called. "I need light."

In the doorway, Brandon visibly held his breath and tucked a flashlight into her hand. "Careful."

"Don't worry. I'm not taking another step until I know what to expect. Whatever you do, you stay here. That's a direct order."

"Staying right here," he repeated.

She could tell by his clenched jaw that he wasn't happy.

"Brandon, I'll call you as soon as I know it's safe."

"Be sure you do."

She flicked on the light and aimed the beam in a slow sweep over the room. Boxes of food were stacked in one corner, blankets and pillows next to the food.

She aimed the light at the floor by her feet. No drop-offs, no wires, no surprises.

"I'm going in further," she said.

A metal shelf with canned goods separated the room into two areas.

She peered into the void behind it. "I think I see something."

Heart pounding in her chest, she stepped behind the shelf and shone the light across the room. A few feet away from where she stood she found the source of the odor. A bucket. Someone had used it as a toilet.

She inched forward, holding her breath, as the beam from the flashlight illuminated a heap of what looked like laundry in the far corner.

She heard a faint sound. "Hello?"

Nothing.

"I'm with the CFBI," she said. "Come on out."

A blanket on top of the pile moved, subtle but there.

With quick strides, she crossed the room, grabbed a corner of the blanket and peeled it back. "Oh Jesus."

A woman dressed only in panties and a bra lay sprawled on her back on the concrete floor. She was in bad shape, barely conscious. Her lips, eyes and cheeks were discolored, cut and swollen. Both arms were dotted with what looked like handprints. Her short hair was so caked with sweat, dirt and blood that it was impossible to identify the color.

"She's here!" Jasi felt for a pulse. "And she's alive!"

She glanced up and found Brandon beside her.

"Let me take her," he said.

When they emerged from the hidden room, he placed the woman on the sofa, while Jasi tried to rouse her.

"Everyone, stay back," she said. "We don't want to frighten her."

Bruised eyelids twitched.

"That's it. Open your eyes."

The woman whimpered.

"We're with the CFBI. You're safe. I promise."

The woman's eyelids fluttered. Her left eye opened. It was filled with fear.

"Jennifer...Jenny?"

The woman's mouth opened and closed, and her swollen eyes streamed with tears as she struggled to speak. With a scared moan, she pushed up on her elbows.

Brandon placed a gentle hand on her shoulder. "Don't try to sit up all the way. You could have internal injuries." He positioned a pillow under her head for support.

Natassia handed Jasi a glass of water. "She's dehydrated."

Jasi held the glass of water to the woman's cracked lips. "I know you're thirsty. It's been at least two days since anyone's been here. Drink."

As the woman sipped, she said a silent prayer. Finally something had gone right. Though it would take weeks before Jennifer Phillips's injuries were healed, and probably years of counseling, she'd survived. Not everyone had. Some of the victims' families would have closure, but not all.

The woman pushed the glass away.

"You should drink more water, Jennifer."

"My..." Her voice was hoarse from dehydration and most likely screaming and crying.

Jasi leaned closer. "Take your time."

"Name..."

"Your name?"

"Share..."

As the pieces fell into place, Jasi gasped. "Oh my God."

"What's wrong?" Brandon asked.

"This isn't Jennifer Phillips."

"Then who is she?"

"Sheral," the woman rasped. "Downham."

Jasi looked at Brandon. "Cameron's reporter friend."

A multitude of emotions swept through her, from disbelief to joy to relief. She'd found Cameron's friend. *Alive.*

"I'll radio the chopper," Ben said.

"Ms. Downham?" Jasi said, kneeling on the floor. "Can you talk?"

"Yes, but it hurts."

"I only have one question for you. Everything else can wait until you've seen a doctor."

"Ask."

"Do you know who beat you and imprisoned you here?"

Sheral cleared her throat and winced. "Brad Pitt."

"You mean Lazarus."

"Yes."

Jasi rose, but Sheral grabbed her arm. "A native guy was with Lazarus. Harry, I think."

Henry.

"The helicopter's waiting in the field," Ben said.

"Wait," Sheral said, her mouth trembling. "What happened to Jenny?"

"We don't know," Jasi said. "She's missing."

"She's troubled but sweet."

"Sounds like you two became friends."

"I gave her a bracelet as a sign that I believed in her."

Jasi blinked. "The amethyst one?"

"Yeah." Sheral attempted a smile. "I fastened it on her wrist and told her to leave Sanctuary and never come back. Do you think that's what she did?"

Jasi didn't have the heart to tell her the truth. There'd be time for that later.

"You gave your friend a special gift—hope."

Sheral took another mouthful of water.

"We need to take you to the hospital." Jasi turned to Natassia. "You get everything?"

"I've copied the entire drive. Now what?"

"You and Ben head back to Sanctuary and arrest Henry—Horton Edgars. Agent Norman and his team can secure this bunker and collect evidence. Brandon and I'll go with Sheral to the hospital."

"What about me?" Agent Anthony asked.

"You can accompany Natassia and Ben. After they arrest Henry, drive him to Mission PD. Think you can handle that?"

"Yes, I do," the kid said, puffing up his chest.

Jasi caught Natassia's eye. "Do you think he's capable?"

"He's definitely ready now."

Jasi almost laughed when the kid's eyes virtually popped out of his head.

"P-pardon me, Agent Prushenko?" he stammered.

"No pardon needed. You did good." Natassia patted his back, then swiveled on one heel until she faced Jasi. "Not everyone noticed that the blueprints didn't match the interior layout. Checking for a secret chamber within the bunker was all Agent Anthony's idea."

"Agent Anthony?" the young man repeated, dumbfounded. "If you really want to call me Jay, that's okay, Agent Prushenko."

"I was goading you on purpose. When Matthew assigned you to me, he told me to make things difficult for you. He wanted to know you've got the balls for this occupation. Not everyone's cut out to be a CFBI agent."

"So...all of this was just for show?"

Natassia shrugged. "I was following orders. But I have to admit, you made an easy target."

Blushing, Agent Anthony turned to Jasi. "So...have I got the—um, I mean, did I pass?"

"What do you think?"

He grinned. "I passed. Yeah, I did. Does this mean I get to work in the field permanently now?"

"Hey, don't rush things. One step at a time, remember?"

"Come on," Natassia yelled from the doorway. "We don't have all night."

Jasi gave the kid a small push. "Go get Henry, Agent Anthony."

Like a devoted puppy, he sprinted after Natassia.

27

Friday, July 19, 2013
Mission Memorial Hospital, Mission, BC

The doctor attending to Sheral Downham had a kind face and silver hair, but his expression was unreadable as he made his way across the ICU floor to the waiting room.

"What's her prognosis?" Jasi asked, standing.

"She has mostly superficial wounds, bruised ribs and severe dehydration. There is some damage to her right retina, but I'm confident it'll heal on its own."

"What about internally?"

"No damage to her kidneys or any other organs." The doctor paused then lowered his voice. "And the rape kit was negative."

"How long will she be in here?"

"Maybe a week. Once she has her strength back and her injuries have healed, she'll be able to go home."

"Can we see her?"

"Yes, but I don't want you getting her wound up. Emotionally, she's very fragile, and she needs rest." He glanced at his watch. "It's after midnight and technically visiting hours are over, but I can make an exception for the CFBI. You have five minutes."

When they entered the hospital room, Jasi was relieved to find Sheral Downham awake and drinking water, although a padded bandage covered both eyes.

"Ms. Downham?"

Sheral stared at them. "CFBI, right?"

"Right."

"You have to take my statement or something."

"I'm sorry. I know you're exhausted."

"That's okay. You need answers."

"Yes. We do."

Jasi pulled a chair close to the bed and took a second to take in the woman's appearance. Sheral's hair was the color of straw, not the rich brunette hue from her photograph. Someone had recently washed it, probably to take a closer look at her scalp in case there were injuries there. The paleness of her freshly cleaned skin made her appear almost luminescent, except where she was marked by bruises.

"Do I look that bad?" the woman asked, her voice still rough.

"You look far better than you did a couple of hours ago."

"No camera work for me for a while."

Silence invaded the room.

"My partner and I have a few questions for you," Jasi said finally. "Are you up for it?"

"Shoot."

"We know you went into Sanctuary to investigate a string of disappearances," Brandon began. "Did you get caught? Is that why you were beaten and captured?"

Sheral blew out a breath. "Yes, but that's only part of it. I discovered something sinister at Sanctuary."

"The hunt club?"

"You know about it?"

"Yes. We know Lazarus was behind it."

"He's a sick bastard. And so are the others."

"Was Giles Christiansen involved?"

"At first I was sure he was. But when I was being held, I never saw him or heard him. And no one else mentioned his name."

"So if he's guilty of anything—"

"Then it's not the hunt club," Sheral finished.

"Do you know who all is involved?"

"No. I never saw their faces, other than Henry and Lazarus." Sheral trembled. "But I know there were others. A few nights ago—I don't know how many—Lazarus told us there was a bear sighting. We had to stay indoors so they could hunt it."

"You didn't believe him?"

"Not one bit. There was something evil in his eyes, like…a hunger, greed. And it wasn't for a bear. So I waited until I heard them walking across the field, him and Henry. Then I followed them."

"Into the woods beyond the fence."

"Yeah. All I had was the light from my mini-com and a bit of moonlight to guide me. In hindsight, it wasn't a smart move on my part. I stayed several yards behind them, praying I wouldn't get caught. But luck wasn't with me." She shook her head slowly. "I saw them meet up with another man. And then I saw a woman being dragged from the bushes. They told her to run and that if she made it back to Sanctuary, she'd live."

"You filmed this on your 'com?"

"Yes. But you can't make out any faces. I have no idea who that woman was. She didn't make a sound. She just took off, away from me, and the man with the rifle ran after her, laughing like it was all some perverse game..." Her voice drifted away.

"What happened next?" Brandon asked.

Sheral shivered. "While the other man hunted down that woman, Lazarus and Henry spotted me and came after me. I had no idea where I was or what direction I was heading in until I came to the river. That's where I hid the mini-com."

"Where exactly?"

"In the marsh. There's no current. There's a tree uprooted on the shore and its branches hang over the water. I tied some string to it and tied the other end to a waterproof bag I kept the 'com in. It's far enough away from the swimming area and upstream from where the women wash laundry. I knew no one would find it there."

"Is that why they beat you? Did they know about the camera?"

"The flash went off, and they saw the light. When they caught up to me, they found nothing on me and demanded to know where I'd hidden it."

"And they tortured you until you told them."

Sheral shrugged. "I never said a word."

"You're a brave woman, Ms. Downham."

Jasi had to agree with Brandon.

"What happened after that?" she asked.

"I was unconscious. When I awoke, I was in that room. They left me there with no food or water. I tried to open some of the cans, but I was too weak and I couldn't find anything sharp enough to pierce the cans. After a while, I gave up and crawled into the corner. I think I had a fever."

"Emotional trauma and the injuries you sustained will do that."

"Next thing I knew, you found me. Thank you, Agent...I'm sorry, I forget your name. Must be all the drugs they're pumping into me."

"McLellan. Jasmine McLellan."

"And your partner?"

"Special Consultant Brandon Walsh."

"Correction," a voice sung out behind them. "That's *Agent* Brandon Walsh now."

Natassia stepped into the room. "Matthew called a minute ago. The

Director has approved Brandon's promotion to full agent with the CFBI, with all the lovely perks." She winked at Brandon. "Including an appointment to get your navel tracker injection. Lucky you. Congratulations."

Jasi hugged Brandon. "Agent Walsh, congratulations."

Sheral Downham laughed. "Sounds like you all have something to celebrate."

"We should let you get some rest now," Jasi said, pausing near the door. "By the way, Cameron Prescott is on her way to see you."

"You know Cameron?"

"She's a good friend."

Sheral lifted her bruised chin. "She sent you looking for me, didn't she?"

"Like I said, she's a good friend."

Jasi followed Brandon and Natassia from the room. In the hall, they stopped at the nurses' station.

"I'd like an update on the two kids from Sanctuary," she said after showing her badge to the night nurse. "How are they doing?"

"They're both fully conscious and alert," the man said, "and there's no permanent damage from smoke inhalation. You can come back tomorrow if you want to see them."

"Thank you."

Brandon pulled her close. "Well, what next?"

"Now, Agent Walsh, we go visit an old friend."

28

Uncle Paxton's mobile home was situated on an oversized lot on the west side of the well-maintained park. One of the older models, the two-bedroom trailer had a concrete porch out front and a spacious cedar deck in the back. Uncle Paxton and Pop had built the deck one summer, when Uncle Paxton was still married and Jasi's mother had been alive. A cherry tree that Brady used to climb adorned the front yard, raining tart cherries that Jasi and her brother would eat until they were sick. The backyard had been Jasi's favorite—a lush wilderness of fruits, vegetables, flowers and plants. A blue metal gate led from the backyard into a wooded area that ran all along the back of the trailer park. Uncle Paxton used to take her there to pick wild blackberries, the hinges of the gate often screeching to let them pass.

Two lots away, Brandon pulled the SUV up to the curb across the street.

Jasi stared out the window. "It's not the same place I remember."

The trailer and yard were more rundown than she remembered, as though Uncle Paxton had given up on them. The once-beautiful cherry tree that had been the cause of countless stained faces had been hacked down, its parched, dead stump a permanent reminder of its former glorious existence. The banana-yellow paint on the exterior of the house was faded and peeling. The roof was in desperate need of new tiles, and the concrete front porch had a crack through the left side, causing it to sag forlornly. Fresh dents and gashes in the single door of the garage at the end of the driveway were telltale signs that someone had used it recently for target practice.

"Seems pretty neglected," Ben said from the back seat.

"Uncle Paxton used to take such pride in his home. I don't know what happened."

"His divorce, maybe?" Natassia suggested.

"Could be. I don't remember his wife. She left him when I was young."

"What about your mother?" Brandon asked.

"What do you mean?"

"Did she like him?"

"She'd invite them over for dinner, and they'd go out with her and Pop. They were all friends."

"Can you do this?"

She gave a hesitant nod. "I think so."

Beside her, Brandon squeezed her arm. "I know this isn't easy."

"Pop is going to be devastated."

She could already taste Pop's disappointment, anger and betrayal. He'd be crushed to discover his oldest and dearest friend was mixed up in a murder conspiracy. And Uncle Paxton? Prison was the worst possible place for a police officer.

She couldn't think of that now. She had a job to do.

Behind her, Natassia said, "Perhaps Hawley lied? Maybe he only said those things because he knew Paxton and your father are friends."

"What would he gain? Hawley says he has proof."

Her 'com rang.

"Warrant is in," Matthew told her when she picked up.

"Okay. We're ready to go in."

"Jasmine, I know Paxton Helling is a family friend, but don't let your guard down. He has everything to lose now."

"I hear you." When she disconnected the call, she turned to her team. "*No* one gets hurt tonight. Keep sharp."

"You sure he's home?" Ben asked. "There aren't any lights on."

"And there's no car in the driveway," Natassia added.

"I called the station on the way to the hospital," Jasi said. "They said Uncle Paxton took a week off with no warning. He's a homebody usually, unless he's with Pop. I can't imagine he'd be out on the town." She glanced at her watch. "Almost ten o'clock. It does seem unusual that he'd be in bed already."

Doubt made her stomach clench. If Uncle Paxton wasn't home, they'd be forced to wait for him or hunt him down.

Across the street, streetlights emitted fingers of brilliance that caressed each trailer along the road, except for Uncle Paxton's. The light near his house was burnt out. Was Uncle Paxton watching television, unaware that his life was about to irrevocably change? Or was he spying on them, waiting in ambush?

She shivered. *How far down the convoluted rabbit hole does Uncle Paxton's involvement go?*

Hawley had suggested that Uncle Paxton knew about the hunt club, that he chose to pretend it didn't exist. Hawley also said Uncle Paxton had buried leads and evidence that would have led police, RCMP and the CFBI right to Hawley's door.

"Okay, let's do this," she said finally. "Brandon and I'll head around back. Ben, you and Natassia take the front. I'll call you when I'm in place. Then we go in fast and clean. Stay sharp and be safe."

They climbed out of the SUV and dashed across the street, staying behind parked vehicles until they reached the house. Ben ducked under the large bay window in the front, and Natassia stood to one side of the front door. They gave Jasi the thumbs-up and waited.

With her gun at her side, Jasi sprinted down the driveway and through the opening into the backyard and crept onto the deck. Brandon was right behind her, and she pointed to a window at the far right, Uncle Paxton's bedroom. He proceeded toward it, while she approached the sliding doors. Peering inside, she saw a kitchen in disarray but no sign of Uncle Paxton.

Brandon moved toward her. "No one's in the bedroom, as far as I can tell. The bed's unmade."

"He has to be here."

She gave a gentle tug on the door handle and was surprised to find it unlocked. Uncle Paxton was usually more safety conscious.

She texted a quick signal to Ben.

"Now," she said, yanking open the sliding door.

"Paxton Helling," Brandon shouted. "This is the CFBI. Show yourself."

They stepped inside, the front door crashing in a second later.

Weapon raised, Jasi darted toward the wall that separated the kitchen from the hallway. As they swept through the living room, she took one look at the stack of newspapers, dirty dishes, empty pizza boxes and beer bottles on the coffee table and knew that something was wrong. Uncle Paxton had always been proud of his home.

She lowered her gun. *He's not here.*

"Master bedroom's clear!" Brandon shouted.

Ben joined her. "As is the second bedroom."

A minute later, Natassia joined them. "His car is still in the garage."

Jasi turned on a lamp in the corner of the living room. She inspected the closet near the back door. Something caught her eye—a rectangular imprint in the dust on the floor. She tried to recall what Uncle Paxton had kept in the closet, but any memory was gone.

"Search every room," she said. "We're looking for anything that may indicate where Uncle Paxton—*Paxton*—may have gone."

Once they finished searching the house, they reconvened in the living room.

"Most of the drawers in the master bedroom have been emptied," Brandon said. "And the closet is half empty too."

"Damn it. Paxton is on the run."

"What do we do now?" Natassia asked.

"We can wait here," Brandon suggested. "See if he comes back."

"I don't think he'll be returning." Jasi picked up the newspapers. "All of these are turned to updates on the murders at Sanctuary. He was holed up in here, following the story closely."

"Any idea where he is?"

"No, but I have a feeling Pop may know."

She wandered into the kitchen and stared out the window for a minute. Pulling her data-com from her jacket pocket, she said, "Call Pop."

Within seconds they were connected.

"What's up, lass?" Pop said.

"Have you heard from Uncle Paxton?"

"What's going on, Jasmine? What has Paxton gotten himself involved in?"

"I promise, I'll explain everything later, but right now it's important that I find him."

"Is he in danger?"

She paused.

"Jasmine?"

"He's in a dangerous situation."

She heard Pop sigh on the other end. "He called me a wee while ago, Jasmine, after you first talked to me."

"Did you tell him I was looking for him?"

"Well…I might have said something."

She muffled a groan. "What did you tell him?"

"Just that you were asking questions about him and were looking for him. He laughed and said he'd come find you. Why don't you head up to Maple Ridge?"

"We're already here. He's gone."

"Oh." There was an extended pause. "You said 'we.'"

"My team is here at his house. Is there anywhere you can think of that Uncle Paxton would go? Another friend, perhaps? Or a relative?"

"Paxton kept to himself the past few years. He didn't socialize much outside of his buddies on the force. Work and fishing, that's what he lived for."

Fishing. Something twigged at the back of her brain.

"Where'd he go fishing?"

"All over."

"You ever go with him?"

Pop chuckled. "You know me and fishing rods don't agree. I'd rather buy me a salmon than spend four hours waiting on the daft fish to bite."

"Wait!" She made a beeline for the closet and yanked open the door. "Now I remember. Uncle Paxton used to keep a tackle box and fishing rods in the closet by the back door. That's what's missing."

"There was one thing…" Pop's voice faded.

"What?"

"A couple years back I was visiting Paxton, and I saw a floor plan for a building. When I asked him about it, he got all fidgety and locked it away in the wall safe."

"Where?"

"The bedroom wall, behind a picture."

She strode into the bedroom, her 'com pressed to her ear. A photograph hung above the side table to the left of the bed. She yanked the picture off the wall and a small safe was revealed. Tossing the photo on the bed, she spun the dial then gave up.

"Any idea what the combination would be, Pop?"

"No, lass. Paxton didn't share those things with me."

"We'll have to wait until someone can get inside."

"Wish I could've been more helpful."

"You have been, Pop. Sorry, but I have to go."

"Jasmine, I—"

"I promise, later we'll talk." She hung up before he could say another word.

Brandon leaned against the doorframe. "A safe, huh?"

"You know how to break into it?"

"Not my forte."

"Natassia!" she hollered.

When Natassia jogged into the room, Jasi jerked her head toward the safe. "Can you open it?"

"If it were keypad access, I could probably hack it, but this is old-school. You'll either need the combination or a safecracker."

Moving the photograph to one side, Jasi sank down on the edge of the bed and stared at the floor. "Pop has no idea where Paxton is. But he said something about floor plans."

"Think Mole Tech is involved again?"

"Gathmann and his company seem to be involved in everything."

"I put out an APB on Helling," Ben said, joining them. "So far no one's seen or heard from him in two days, except you and your Pop."

"There's a cellphone in the garbage can under the kitchen sink," Natassia said, holding up the mangled remains. "He trashed it and destroyed the SIM card. A tech might be able to retrieve some data, but I highly doubt it."

"Matthew is sending a team to collect evidence," Ben said. "We can leave as soon as they get here."

"Where are we supposed to go? We have no leads, no clues as to where Paxton is headed."

Frustrated, she pounded one fist on the bed, catching the edge of the framed photograph. Glass shattered beneath her hand, and she felt a sharp stab of pain.

Brandon rushed to her side. "Are you all right?"

"It's just a little cut."

"Let me see."

She opened her hand and winced as he pulled a small sliver of glass from her palm. "Okay, that hurts a bit."

"I bet it does. You need a bandage. I'll go check the bathroom."

After he left, Jasi gave Natassia a wry look. "It's really only a scratch. My fault for not paying attention."

"Blame it on the owner's poor taste in design," Natassia said, picking up the photograph from its broken frame. "It's kind of vain to hang photos of yourself in your bedroom." She was suddenly transfixed by the photo in her hand. "Jasi? Didn't you say something about fishing?"

"Yeah. Why?"

"Check it out."

In the photo Uncle Paxton showed off four plump trout as he stood in front of a decrepit burgundy Ford pickup that was parked in front of a log cabin. Behind it was a body of water, a river or lake.

Jasi reached for the picture and flipped it over. In faded pencil someone had scribbled something, but it was hard to make out.

"Looks like 'W-H-O…something…K-E, Maple Ridge.' Wherever Paxton is, he's close."

Brandon returned with a bandage.

"I think he's at this cabin," she told him, holding up the photo.

"I did a property search," Ben said. "The only place he owns is this one."

"Maybe it's under someone else's name. Remember that case we worked on before Sanctuary? The guy who used a vehicle registered to his mother?"

"You know Helling's mother's name?"

"No, but his ex-wife's name is Betty-Ann. He could've registered it under her name and never told anyone about it."

"But why keep a fishing cabin secret?" Natassia asked.

Jasi shrugged. "Seems everyone's full of secrets."

"I hate to say this, but maybe he had his own hunt club going."

"There's something more to this. I feel it."

"You were right," Ben interrupted. "Betty-Ann Spellman, once Helling, is the proud owner of a log cabin on Whonnock Lake. I called her, and she swears she knows nothing about it."

Jasi flicked the photo. "Then that's where we go."

29

They advanced toward the cabin on foot, their flashlights aimed at the potholed gravel road ahead. A fingernail of opalescent moon hung high in the sky, offering only the faintest of light. An intermittent breeze rustled the leaves, as if acknowledging them as they trekked onward.

"It's up ahead," Jasi said in a low voice.

The gravel road ended parallel to the lake's shore, the log cabin now in sight. The yard was clean and landscaped, the grass freshly mowed. A light shone in the living room window and smoke drifted up from the chimney, but inside there was no movement.

They gathered in the bushes behind the cabin to assess the situation.

Jasi pulled out her binoculars and swept the area. "No sign of Paxton."

"Nice cabin," Ben said.

"I guess it explains why his trailer was left to rot. He's living here most of the time." *But why?*

"Seems strange that he wouldn't have told your father about this place," Natassia said. "What's the big deal? So he has a cabin on a lake."

"The big deal is the money spent on it," Brandon said. "This cabin probably cost him twenty times what he paid for his trailer. Not to mention the price of the lot."

"Nothing wrong with living in a nice place."

"On a cop's salary?"

"Brandon's right," Jasi said. "There's no way Paxton could've afforded a cabin like this."

"So where'd he get the money?" Natassia asked.

"Hawley," Jasi said. "He said he gave Paxton incentive not to expose him—hush money. And that's why Paxton couldn't tell Pop anything about this place."

"Look," Brandon said, pointing toward the water. "There's a boathouse over there."

It was hard to make out, but a black blob dotted the shore about twenty yards away. The barest of light twinkled from inside the boathouse.

"You think he's in there?" she asked.

"He could be."

"Then we have a problem. If we storm the house and he's in the boathouse, he could take off across the lake. And if we all head for the boathouse, there's a chance he'll see us from the cabin. We have to split up."

"Natassia and I can take the cabin," Ben said, checking the magazine of his gun.

"We'll check out the boathouse. If we don't find anything, we'll head back to the cabin. If you two see Paxton inside, signal me and we'll come running."

"And vice versa," Brandon added.

With guns at their side, Jasi motioned Brandon to follow her as she made a wide sweep through the bushes toward the rear of the house. A nondescript rental car was parked a few yards away. As they passed by it, she touched the hood. "Cold. Paxton has been here a while."

Darting between the trees, they made their way to the water's edge. The boathouse hovered over the water at the end of a short dock.

"Wait," Brandon said, grasping her arm. "How do you want to do this?"

She glanced over her shoulder at the cabin. From this vantage point, she could clearly see inside, which meant Paxton would be able to see them—if he was looking.

"Chances are he feels safe," she said. "No one knows about this house, so he may not be watching for an ambush."

"Then we walk the plank?" Brandon said wryly.

She chuckled. "Just don't fall off. Ready?"

"Let's do this."

Ducking low, they hurried along the dock. When they reached the boathouse, they crouched low on one side of the door.

Jasi slowly raised her head and peeked into the small window. An oil lamp sat on a wooden table, its flame flickering and illuminating the interior enough to make out a speedboat. A couple of raincoats hung on the wall, one larger than the other.

She looked at Brandon and shook her head. No Paxton.

Something clanged within.

Alert, she signaled Brandon to move to the other side of the doorway. With careful movements, she reached out and tested the doorknob. It was unlocked. Opening the door an inch, she peered inside.

"Me first," she mouthed.

She eased the door open and crept inside, with Brandon right behind her.

No Paxton.

"There's nowhere to hide here," Brandon said.

Jasi looked around her, knowing he was right. There was nowhere a man could hide. Not here. The speedboat was small, no cabin below.

"Check this out," she said.

A gray tarp had been spread out on the floor in one corner. On a table beside it were rolls of duct tape, a knife and a pair of scissors. Next to these were six hefty bricks.

"There's only one reason for this kind of setup," Brandon said.

Jasi stared at him, her eyes wide. "Paxton plans to kill someone and dump the body in the lake."

"You think he's gone after Hawley and that's why he's not here?"

"How? The rental car is still here."

She glanced out the window. "Ben and Natassia are in position. I want you to join them."

"What are you going to do?"

"Make sure he can't escape by boat."

He hesitated, but she gave him a nudge. "Go. I'll be right behind you."

Once the door closed behind him, she jumped in the speedboat and pulled the key from the ignition, tossing it in the water.

What if Paxton has a spare?

Her eyes caught sight of the knife. She didn't know much about boats, but she was sure it wouldn't get too far if she dismantled the control panel.

Minutes later, she stood back to examine her handiwork. *No one's going anywhere in this thing. Time to join the others.*

Rushing toward the cabin, she saw figures moving inside. She headed up the steps to the front deck and knocked on the glass door.

Brandon opened it. "He's not here. We've search both floors."

"Damn."

"Brandon told us about the kill kit in the boathouse," Natassia said. "Maybe he went after his victim."

"But how? His car is at his house and the rental car is—" She cursed. "The truck."

"What truck?"

"The Ford from the photo in his bedroom. He must have kept it here."

"Now what?" Brandon asked.

"You and I'll stay here and search for anything that might indicate who Paxton's target is." She looked at Ben. "You and Natassia take the SUV and head to that gas station we passed. Paxton would've driven by it on his way out, and he might have stopped to fill up."

Ben gave a nod. "If they have security cameras, we'll check them out. Maybe he left us a clue."

She stood in the doorway and watched Ben and Natassia head toward the road. "Call me if you find anything!"

"Will do," Natassia said.

When they were out of sight, Jasi turned to Brandon. "Do you think Paxton's going after Hawley?"

"Maybe—if he doesn't know Hawley's in custody."

"When he discovers that, he'll come back here."

"Unless Hawley's not the one he's after."

Lazarus is dead, and that's all over the news. Hawley already took care of Gathmann. Who else is left?

"Paxton's only connection to this case is Becket Hawley," she said. "He didn't know any of the other investors, and he'd have no reason to go after them."

"Could Paxton be planning a jailbreak? Maybe his plan is to get Hawley out, bring him here, dispose of him so the guy can't talk."

"He's not that foolish. Every officer on the force is looking for him. He'd never get inside the police station, and there's no way in hell he'd make it out with Hawley." She released a sigh. "But maybe he's *that* desperate."

"I'll take the upstairs. With any luck we'll find some answers."

Jasi roamed around the lower level of the cabin. The décor was expensive. Hawley must have paid Paxton a substantial sum. Every object was in its place, a perfect feng-shui atmosphere.

She emptied the drawers in the kitchen. She looked behind every cupboard door. Nothing.

Hawley had said Paxton had a secret, something big.

"I found something," Brandon called.

She left the kitchen and headed toward the stairs. Brandon stood by the loft railing, a leather box in his hand.

"Paxton's gun box," she guessed.

"Yeah, except it's empty. But come see what else I found."

She ran upstairs and followed him into Paxton's lavish bedroom.

"In here," he said, leading her into the bathroom. He opened the cupboard beneath the sink. "What do you see?"

"Toilet paper, cleaners—" She froze. "Sanitary pads?"

"And check the laundry basket."

She did as he suggested. "Bras and panties?"

"Size thirty-two B."

She cocked her head and gave him a wry look. "And you know this just from looking at this bra."

"I saw the tags."

"What is Paxton doing with women's clothing?"

"Maybe he's into it. Wearing it, I mean."

She grimaced. "No, I can't see that."

"You don't want to."

"Of course not. But seriously, there's no way on earth Sergeant Paxton Helling would be caught dead in women's clothing. He's too much of a manly man."

"Perhaps he has a girlfriend?"

"I think Pop would've known about that."

"A stripper, then."

She shrugged. "Why would she leave her clothes here? Whoever this mystery woman is, she's in for a rude awakening when she discovers what he's done."

They searched the remainder of the upper floor but found no clues as to Paxton's whereabouts and nothing further to identify the woman he was seeing.

"I'm going back to the boathouse," Jasi said. "I saw a jacket that looked too small to belong to him. Maybe it's hers. I'll check the pockets."

"Okay, I'll go through the box of files I found in his closet. Most look like income tax information, but maybe there's something there."

She hurried downstairs and went outside via the sliding door. Running toward the boathouse, she went over everything they knew about Paxton. He'd been married once, no kids. Divorced his wife, Betty-Ann, a few years after Jasi's mother had been killed. He and Pop would get together for cards or a hockey game. Other than his involvement with Hawley, he'd seemed to be a great cop.

What could he be hiding?

The question ate at her, twisting at her insides.

In the boathouse, she removed the smaller jacket from the wall hook. It was pale yellow and decorated with daisies—a child's jacket.

She shoved a hand into one of the pockets. "Hmm…what's this?"

She stared in surprise at the small plastic toy in her hand. It was a figurine of a young girl, one she recognized. Years ago, Pop had bought her a dollhouse, complete with furnishings and a happy family of five. She loved that dollhouse and played with it every day. And then one day, she lost a piece. The girl.

Now here it was in her hand.

But what does it mean?

Paxton had sometimes played with her when she was little. She couldn't recall him showing any interest in the dollhouse.

Paxton, Pop, Mom. Her pulse quickened. *What if Paxton and my mother—no! There's no way they had an affair? Pop would've known, and he never would've remained friends.*

Her stomach churned and bile rose in her throat.

What if Pop had found out they were having an affair? What would he do?

With a shake of her head, she exited the boathouse. As she strode down the dock, thoughts raced through her mind. She needed to clear her head.

A picnic table sat in the grass close to the bushes. She made a beeline for it.

"You just couldn't mind your own business," a voice said behind her.

30

She turned slowly. Paxton Helling, the man she'd called "Uncle" for most of her life, had a handgun trained on her chest.

"Uncle Paxton, put the gun down."

"Shut up! Let me think."

She inhaled deeply. "What are you doing? You know this is wrong. You don't want to hurt me."

He shone a light on the ground ahead of her. "Raise your hands and keep walking."

"Where?"

"There's a path behind the table. It leads into the woods."

She mentally cursed herself for holstering her gun. She couldn't grab it now. He'd shoot her before her fingers touched the strap.

"My partner's in the cabin. He'll come looking for me."

"I'll take care of him too."

She shivered. "Why? Just answer me that."

A few feet behind her, she heard the soft crunch of twigs.

Then he said, "I loved your mother, you know."

She wanted to throw up.

"She was the most beautiful woman I'd ever known. And so gifted."

"What do you mean?"

"You know exactly what I mean, Jasmine. She was just like you."

Jasi spun on one heel. "How was she like me?"

Paxton smiled. "She was psychic. She could see the future."

"I don't believe you."

"Your father couldn't keep such things from me. I'm his best friend. I knew all about your mother. Don't you know how valuable that made her? She knew things, important things."

"So you planned to use her. For what? To make you rich? Famous?"

"We could have had everything, Cali and I. Except she refused to see a future with me in it."

"You can't force someone to love you."

He ignored her. "And *you*—I've been watching you, following your progress."

"I know you're a PSI with the CFBI," he added.

"That's a top-secret division."

"I'm a cop. I have access to information. There's not much I don't know." He waved his gun. "Keep moving."

After a few yards, Jasi said, "Did you have an affair with my mother?"

"I would have, if she'd chosen me. I wanted Cali more than anything. Especially after she saw my future."

"Did she see this?"

"She saw a celebration in my honor. I'll be rewarded for my achievements. Nothing can stop that."

Jasi squeezed the doll in her hand, wanting to chuck it at him. "What achievements, Uncle Paxton? All I see is a washed-up cop who's about to commit murder." She paused. "Speaking of which, we saw the tarp and tape in the boathouse. Who's your victim? It can't be me, because you had no idea I'd find you here."

The light on the ground stopped moving.

Behind her, Paxton said, "Turn around."

She obeyed, squinting as his flashlight skimmed her face.

"You look like Cali," he said. "She was always so full of life and joy. She made everyone around her happy."

"Tell me about her. You owe me that much."

"What do you want to know?"

"Did she have cancer?"

"What?"

"When she was in the hospital."

"I don't know where you got that idea."

"You said it was a sad time. What did you mean?"

"I'm talking about the baby she lost."

Jasi gasped. "Baby? Oh God." She gawked at him, praying the baby hadn't been his. "Why wouldn't Pop tell me?"

"He didn't want to dwell on it. It was better that way."

"Better because…"

"Just better. For everyone."

The woods opened up to a dirt road. Paxton's burgundy Ford was parked a few yards away.

"Not many people know about this access road," he said. "It leads around the opposite side of the lake and onto the highway."

With her hands in the air, Jasi paused and faced him. "So you're going to shoot me and take off?"

"I'm going to climb into my truck and leave." He gave her a sad smile. "I'd take you with me, but that would get too messy. Your father's probably going to hunt me down anyway."

"Does he know how you felt about my mother?"

Paxton shrugged. "Don't know. But she felt something for me too. I could tell. We could've had a great life together, me and her."

"My mother saw you as Pop's friend, nothing more."

"You don't know anything."

"I know you're a weak coward who was in love with a woman who never loved him back."

"Go to hell," he snarled.

"I've already been there. The day you murdered my mother."

Paxton blinked, his mouth hanging open.

"I've finally put it together, Uncle Paxton. The clues were there all along, but I didn't want to see them. I was there that day, hiding in the closet. But you knew that, didn't you? Pop told you afterward. That's why you spent so much time with me when I was a kid. You wanted to ensure that I'd never remember that day." She glared at him. "That I'd never see the fun, cool uncle as what he really was—a murderer."

"You think you're so smart." His face contorted into an evil grin. "You have no idea."

"I saw your shoes. I recognized them as being like Pop's, but I never thought they'd be yours. You kept them polished to a mirror shine, but you had a bad habit of kicking the table legs with them, scuffing the tips. That's what I saw that day."

"It doesn't matter anymore. Cali's gone. I hadn't planned it, but she wouldn't give me what I wanted."

"That's what I don't understand. Why did you want me when I was a child and then brush me off when I grew up?"

"I wanted you *and* your mother. We could've done great things together, especially if you had the gift of foresight like she did." He sighed. "But that's not your gift. Once I learned that you only read arson fires, you became useless to me. Sad thing is, Cali never saw her own future. Maybe if she had, things would've been different. I loved her to the core."

Jasi's eyes burned. "You shot her and left her to bleed out on the floor. That's what you call love?"

"You have to let go of the past, Jasmine."

She opened her hand.

"What have you got there?" he asked.

"This doll was part of a dollhouse Pop bought me. I found it in a jacket in your boathouse. Why did you take it?"

Paxton visibly swallowed. "I-I don't know."

"I think you do."

"Enough talking." He pointed the gun at the ground in front of her. "On your stomach."

"So you can shoot me in the back?"

"Just do it.

Releasing a nervous breath, she knelt on the ground and rested her hands on her knees. Out of the corner of her eye, she saw movement in the trees. *Brandon!*

She had to stall Paxton.

"Who's the tarp for, Uncle Paxton?"

He didn't answer. Instead he released the safety on the handgun.

"You're going after him, aren't you?" she pressed. "Whoever this person is. It's not Lazarus because you know he's dead. Did you know the other hunt club members? Gathmann perhaps. He's dead too. So who's your target?"

"You ask too many questions. Trust me, you won't like my answers."

"Try me."

Before he could answer, Brandon stepped from behind a cedar. "Lower your gun, Helling."

"Can't do that. Sorry."

"Don't force me to shoot you in front of her."

"I'm a cop, kid. I'll put two bullets in her before you have me in your sights."

A single blast shot through the air.

Instinctively, Jasi ducked and rolled, pulling her gun from the shoulder holster. When she raised her head, Paxton was sprawled on the ground, one hand clenched to his chest.

Brandon kicked away Paxton's gun. "I only needed one bullet."

Jasi stood, her legs shaking. Pointing her gun at Paxton, she inched closer with caution, taking in the pallor of his face and the red stain blossoming across his chest. "Call it in, Brandon. He needs an ambulance. Tell the paramedics we'll meet them at the cabin."

Brandon lifted the man in his arms, and she led him through the woods.

"Set him down on the picnic table," she said when they reached the front yard.

Paxton moaned.

"I'll find something to help stop his bleeding," Brandon said.

While he went inside, she removed her leather jacket, rolled it up and pressed it against Paxton's blood-soaked chest.

"Why bother?" he asked, his eyes filled with pain.

"Because this is what's right. I'm bringing you in. You're going to pay for your crimes, and you're going to tell Pop what you did." Her voice broke. "He needs closure. We all do."

"You'll never find the closure you're looking for."

"I think we just have. All these years we've wondered why someone would break into our home for no apparent reason, kill my mother and take nothing. Pop blamed himself for not being home that day."

"I knew he was taking Brady out for his birthday ice cream. Your father's so predictable. But I don't think he ever realized how lucky he was. He had the family I always wanted."

"*You* were part of our family," she sobbed. "We all trusted you, *loved* you. You were my Uncle Paxton. I used to play with Barbies on your back deck. Remember? You picked them up at a yard sale just for me."

"Yard sale, yeah."

"Then where'd you get them from?"

He coughed, spewing up blood.

"Where?" she cried.

"Your *sister*."

31

"I don't have a sister," Jasi snapped.

Paxton tried to laugh. "Don't you?"

Her head throbbed. None of this made sense. "You said the baby died."

"That's what I told them. I delivered her. Your mother was unconscious."

"But…what about…a body?"

"Babies are dumped like garbage every day. All I needed was to find one who'd died around the same time and make the switch. With all the chaos, and your father so occupied by your mother, it was easy." He moaned, his body racked by another wave of coughing.

"Where's my sister now?"

"She was a beautiful child, so smart," he rambled. "So much promise."

Jasi gripped his shoulders and shook him. "Where is she?"

"Dead."

That single word made her cry out. "No!"

"She wasn't gifted like you." Bubbles of blood oozed from his lips. "I waited, gave her time to grow into it, but nothing happened. She was just normal, average. In the end, she became worthless to me."

"So you killed her?"

"I chose the wrong sister." His eyelids closed. "I should've taken you."

Sirens screamed in the distance.

Brandon returned with four bath towels. "We can use these."

"His pulse is weak, and he has lost a lot of blood."

Brandon removed her jacket from Paxton's chest and inspected the wound. "The bullet's still inside. We just have to keep him stable until the ambulance gets here." He draped the towels across Paxton's stomach and applied pressure.

"He killed my mother."

Brandon's eyes widened. "What?"

"He's the one I saw. He was in love with her." She debated telling him about her mother's psychic skills. *Another time.*

The sirens drew closer.

"I had a sister, Brandon." She collapsed into his arms. "He killed her too."

He held her close. She knew there was nothing he could say, nothing that would take away the searing pain in her heart. She'd barely had time to mourn her mother, now that she knew the truth, and now she had a sister to grieve for too.

"I don't understand how he could've done all this," she cried. "He was Pop's best friend."

Wordlessly, Brandon stroked her hair and wiped away her tears.

"Oh God..." She gazed into his eyes. "How am I supposed to tell Pop about my mother and sister?"

He kissed her forehead. "You'll find the right words. I know you."

She looked down at the man who had once been her uncle. "I still have questions. He'd better make it."

Flashing lights appeared at the end of the road, moving toward them with speed.

"The ambulance is here," she said.

"You want to ride with him?"

"No. They'll take care of him."

Brandon's brows arched in surprise. "You sure?"

"Positive. I need to stay here. Did you call Ben and Natassia?"

"Yeah. When I went for the towels. They're on their way back. The gas station attendant said he stopped for gas, but he filled a gas can instead of the truck's tank."

"That's a bit odd." She shrugged. "Maybe he already had a full tank."

"Want me to go check?"

"Not yet. Just stay here with me."

They were interrupted by two paramedics. She showed them her badge and led them to the picnic table, where they set up the stretcher.

"What's the name of the victim?" one paramedic asked as he took Paxton's vitals.

"Paxton Helling," Brandon said.

"Exit wound?"

"No."

Jasi filled in the paramedics on what happened and gave them her card. "Have the hospital call me as soon as he's conscious."

As the ambulance drove away, Jasi folded her arms across her chest. Suddenly, she was exhausted to the bone. All she wanted to do was go home, climb in bed and sleep.

Her data-com rang.

"Hey, Ben."

"We're about twenty minutes away," he said. "You okay?"

"I will be."

"Did Helling give you any information on Hawley and the hunt club?"

"Nothing new." She'd tell him about her mother and sister later.

"The team at Helling's trailer found something interesting."

She perked up. "What?"

"A bill of sale for a cabin built by Mole Tech."

"The cabin here at Whonnock Lake?"

"That's the one."

She looked at Brandon. "So Paxton and Gathmann probably knew each other. Interesting."

Ben signed off, and she studied the cabin. Every time she walked by it, electrical charges raced over her body, causing the hair on her arms to stand.

"We can head down the road," Brandon suggested. "Meet Ben and Natassia along the way."

"I agree. I need to get out of here. This place feels…weird."

With flashlight beams on high, they strolled arm-in-arm down the gravel road, chatting about the case, but avoiding anything to do with Paxton Helling.

"Mole Tech sure had their hand in everything," Brandon said.

"Yeah."

He chuckled. "Remember when we said that 'all roads lead back to Sanctuary'? I think we should amend that now to 'all roads lead back to Mole Tech.'"

"Doesn't have the same—" Jasi stopped walking.

"What's wrong?"

She couldn't move her legs. "I don't know."

"Are you feeling okay?"

"Not really." Her throat was raw and her skin itched.

"Maybe you should sit down."

She tried to take a step forward, but a voice in her head screamed, *"No!"*

"Jasi?"

"I want to leave, but something's telling me to stay."

"I don't understand."

She glanced over her shoulder at the cabin. *Why is it reeling me back?*

"We should leave, Jasi." His voice sounded scared.

"There's something here, Brandon. I feel it. I know it. I have to go back."

Without waiting, she ran toward the cabin, barely aware that her legs were finally moving. With every step closer, the pain in her throat subsided. At the back door, she paused and drew a deep breath.

"We've already searched inside, twice," Brandon said.

"We never really looked outside."

"What for?"

"I'm not sure exactly." She shone her flashlight over the house as she walked. Something illusive twigged at her memory. "What do we know about this place?"

"It was built by Mole Tech, and Becket Hawley paid for it."

Mole Tech...

"Why *that* company?" she asked. "Why not any other construction company?"

"Because he wanted to live a green lifestyle?"

She let out a snort. "Did you see his trailer? Anything green about it? No, he didn't care about the environment. He cared about comfort. And did you notice inside—there's no green technology in this cabin other than a few energy efficient appliances."

"You're right. He could've paid far less for a cabin without the environmental perks."

She faced him. "Unless he wanted a different kind of perk."

"What are you thinking?"

Excitement coursed through her veins. "A secret room."

"But if you look at the outside of this place and the windows, you'll realize everything fits. There's no place on the main or second floor for a secret room."

She swept her flashlight across the ground. "Maybe it's not on the main or second floor. Maybe there's a basement. Maybe that's the secret room."

She hurried toward the house, her eyes fixated on a shadowed area near the concrete base of the house. "Some small animal has dug a hole here." She poked at the toe of her boot. "See there? The concrete goes down at least a foot."

Brandon grabbed a rake that was leaning against the house. Using quick movements, he dragged the earth aside. He flipped the rake and jammed the handle into the hole, tilting it toward the base.

"It's at least two feet in and still connecting," he said. "You may be right."

"There has to be an access to the basement inside the cabin." She darted toward the back door. "Are you coming?"

"Wouldn't miss it."

Inside the cabin, she studied the open kitchen/living room area. First, she inspected the closet, tapping on the walls inside and listening for any hollowness. Brandon searched the hall and main floor bathroom.

"I've got nothing," she said twenty minutes later. "I don't understand. It has to be here."

"So where would someone like him build an entranceway to a room he didn't want anyone else to know about?"

"It would have to fit the place, Brandon. That's Mole Tech's forte. Remember the door in the rocks? It was camouflaged perfectly."

"Well, this is a rustic cabin that's been modernized in some ways but not overly so. How could he camouflage a door here?"

She paced across the living room, examining every nook and cranny. Brandon's question kept repeating in her mind.

Without warning, she stopped dead in her tracks.

"You got it?" he asked, moving to her side.

"The answer was in front of us all long, if we'd bothered to look down."

She pointed to the floor. Two long scratches indicated the sofa had been moved often, and she doubted it was for cleaning.

Brandon set to work, swiveling the sofa out along the same tracks.

"There," she said.

An area of hardwood was slightly discolored, the planks dulled by hands.

She knelt on the floor and smoothed her hands along the large rectangular area. Her fingertips touched a rough patch. She pressed down. The floor made a soft popping sound, and the rectangular area lifted on three sides. Inching her fingers beneath the edge, she lifted it a few inches. "Jackpot."

Brandon helped her open the narrow hatch in the floor. Wooden steps led downward into blackness.

"We need a flashlight," she said.

Brandon disappeared for a moment, and when he returned he handed her a flashlight. "Want me to go first?"

"Be my guest."

She followed him down into the gaping mouth.

As soon as Brandon reached the concrete floor, he said, "I'll clear the left side. Any idea what we're looking for?"

"When I see it, I'll know."

They split up, dodging boxes and old furniture.

Down one hall, Jasi came across a box of children's toys, mostly girl stuff. She had to hold back the tears as she thought of the little girl Paxton had killed.

Keep looking.

The further she went, the colder she got. She trembled, rubbing her arms to get her circulation moving. When she reached the end of the wall, she shone the light around her.

Was she losing it? They'd found the hidden chamber. Where was the prize?

She heard water dripping, probably from a waterline. *Drip...drip...drip.* The sound echoed around her, its regular beat mesmerizing her, lulling her.

Something clattered on the other side of the basement.

"Brandon?"

The noise was followed by a dull thud.

Shit!

Someone was in the basement with them.

Jasi clicked off the flashlight. Feeling her way as she went, she slipped between crates and camping gear, edging toward the sound. Several yards away, she saw a dim light on the ground. *Brandon's flashlight.*

She crept closer and slowed her breathing, but it took all her effort to do so. Inching around a wall unit with broken shelves, she peered into the gloom. She covered her mouth with one hand to quell the cry that rose in her chest. Brandon lay on his stomach about two yards away. She couldn't tell if he was breathing, and she had no idea where his gun had gone.

A shape shuffled from the shadows and hovered over Brandon's body, a baseball bat in one hand.

Jasi reached for her gun and stepped from her hiding place. "Don't move any closer." She flicked on the flashlight and aimed it at the shape. "Put the bat down."

A woman with wild-eyes stared back at her. "Oh my God. It's *you.*"

"Who are you?"

"Don't you recognize me? You promised you'd find me."

Jasi gasped. "Emily?"

32

Jasi and Emily sat on the sofa in the living room, while Brandon sat in a chair, a cold cloth pressed against the back of his head.

"I'm so sorry," Emily said for the millionth time. "I thought you were *him*."

"Forget about it," Brandon said. "I've had worse injuries than this."

Jasi squeezed Emily's hands. "I can't believe you're here. That I'm here with you."

Slightly taller than Jasi, Emily's ethereal appearance was even more emphasized by the shadows under her eyes and her pale skin. She was older than Jasi had seen in her dreams, around her age, but those big blue eyes were still hauntingly the same.

"How did you find me, Jasi?"

"Honestly? I think you led us here."

She gave Emily the basics of the case, focusing mainly on Paxton Helling's involvement. "Everything was connected. And for some reason, I couldn't leave this cabin, even when I tried. It was like a powerful magnet kept me here."

"I tried calling you," Emily said. "But everything was fuzzy. Sometimes I could feel you, and it seemed as though you were nearby. I desperately wanted that to be true. I was terrified."

"Which is why you bashed Brandon over the head."

Emily winced. "Sorry. I thought he was coming to kill me. A while ago I heard someone upstairs making all sorts of noise, thumping up and down the stairs, slamming doors."

"That was probably us," Brandon said. "We were searching the place for Helling."

"Uncle Paxton—" Emily's head jerked up. "I can say his name now."

"You called him 'Uncle' too?" Jasi asked, frowning.

"He said my mother and he were close friends. Or they had been before she died giving birth to my sister."

Jasi swallowed hard. "Oh God…"

"It's okay. I've had time to deal with their loss."

"No, he lied to you."

Emily blinked. "About my mother?"

"About everything."

"He told me she was psychic. Every week he'd ask me if I could see the future. He said he loved my mother. 'Cali,' he called her."

"I believe that's the truth, but it wasn't a healthy love."

"What do you mean?"

"Cali was our mother." Jasi waited for the words to sink in.

"*Our* mother?" Emily's eyes widened. "You're my sister?"

"I believe so. He told us you'd died when you were born, but he abducted you." Jasi took a deep breath. "He was obsessed with our mother, with her abilities, and he wanted to control her."

"Like he controlled me?"

"Pop wouldn't let him."

"Pop is your father?"

"*Our* father."

"I often wondered if Uncle Paxton was really my dad." Emily's voice was laced with sadness. "I used to pretend he was when I was little. Until he turned mean." She paused. "If he lied about so much, did he lie about…our mother?"

Jasi blinked back tears. "Mom is dead. When he couldn't have her, he murdered her."

"Oh God, no…"

Jasi told her what had happened that fateful night. When she was done, they cried, mourning their loss together.

When her tears had subsided, Emily lifted her head. "He planned to kill me too."

"Because he thought you had no gift."

"I couldn't tell him about you, about how we communicated. Sometimes I wondered if you really existed or if I were going insane. All he saw was a normal kid who grew up into a woman with zero psychic abilities."

"The joke's on him. I've never met a psychic who could connect with another as completely as you do with me."

Emily smiled. "It's because we're sisters."

A car horn honked outside.

"The rest of our team is here," Brandon said.

Emily inhaled deeply. "I can't wait to meet them."

"I can't wait for you to meet Pop and Brady," Jasi replied, her throat burning with emotion. "I still can't believe this. We're *sisters*."

Emily hugged her tightly. "Just don't forget who's older. Me. By two years. I get to boss you around."

Brandon snickered behind them. "Good luck with that. One thing you'll learn fast is that Jasi isn't one to be bossed around. She can be quite stubborn."

"I believe it."

Jasi pouted. "Hey! Stop ganging up on me."

Laughter filled the room, and the sound of it filled her heart.

"We're going to take you to the hospital in Mission." When Emily opened her mouth to argue, Jasi raised a hand. "No arguments. You need to get checked out." She stood. "You ready to meet the rest of my team?"

"I am."

"Let's go."

Outside, Natassia leaned against the SUV, chatting to Ben. When she saw Jasi, she stifled a yawn. "It's about time you came out."

"Natassia, Ben, this is Emily." Jasi nudged her sister toward them.

Natassia's eyes flared. "The dead girl from your closet?"

"Well, I'm not dead now," Emily said with a wry grin.

Natassia's arms flew around her. "And I'm so glad to hear that. But I don't understand—what...how...?"

"It's a long story," Jasi said. "I'll tell you the whole thing on the way to the hospital. For now, suffice it to say that I found Emily. Oh, and by the way, she's my sister."

The stunned look on Natassia's face was priceless. Her head swiveled from Jasi to Emily as she floundered for words.

"Any sister of Jasi's is a friend of mine," Ben said with a nod.

"Just watch out for her," Brandon said. "She's got a mean swing, especially if she has a baseball bat in her hands."

At Mission Memorial, Emily was taken away by a doctor who assured Jasi she'd come get her the minute they were done. A nurse led Jasi to a room where she gave blood for DNA testing. It was time to find out once and for all if Emily truly was her sister.

Now, sitting in the waiting room with Brandon, Ben and Natassia, she had to resist calling Pop and Brady and telling them the unbelievable news.

The time has to be right. Everything has to be in place.

Ben left for a few moments, then returned. "I have news about Helling."

"Is he dead?" she asked.

"No. He made it through surgery just fine. We have an agent watching him. Apparently Helling has lots to say now that he knows he's headed for prison. He claims he stole the list of hunt club members from Hawley, and that's why Hawley paid him so much money."

She whistled. "Now it makes sense. So Paxton has this list?"

"Yeah. It's in a safety deposit box at an RBC in Vancouver, registered under his ex-wife's name."

"We've got them then." She blew out a breath.

"Matthew's getting arrest warrants. We'll have them all in custody within the next few hours."

She slumped back into the chair, beyond exhausted. Hawley, Paxton, Henry and the other members of the hunt club were headed for prison. Lazarus was dead. Sheral and Emily had been found alive, and their wounds would heal eventually.

Now Jasi could focus on her family. And her sister.

"I know all the signs point to Emily being my sister," she told Brandon, "but I want to be sure before I tell anyone."

"I get it. You don't want to find out later you're wrong."

"That would devastate Pop."

"While you were giving blood, Matthew called," Ben said. "Once Emily is done at Ops, he's giving you two weeks off. You're going to need time with your family."

"Especially since it's grown overnight," Natassia added.

"And Matthew is putting together a little celebration, a kind of 'welcome home' for Emily," Ben said, smiling. "I think we could all use a party."

"Hear, hear," Brandon said.

Jasi's gaze swept over the faces of her friends. She was so blessed to have them in her life. So blessed to have Cameron as her best friend, and Pop and Brady and now Emily for her family.

Emily's doctor returned. "Ms. McLellan, I've finished examining Emily, and although she's suffering from anxiety, she's in good health. She's a bit underweight, but I'm sure with proper nutrition and care, she'll be fine."

"Can I see her now?"

The doctor nodded. "We have the results of the blood work, and I think it's best if we do this together."

Jasi searched for a sign in the woman's eyes, but they remained all business and somewhat sympathetic.

Her heart sank. *It's not true. Emily's not my sister.*

"Ms. McLellan? Are you coming?"

She stood, hissed in a breath and followed the doctor woman down the hall, her boots clicking along the tiles as if counting down the seconds until doomsday.

"Matthew Divine sent over your mother's medical files," the doctor said as they walked. "He's filled me in on your mother's case and on Emily's." She paused, her hand on the door lever to an examination room. "I haven't read the results myself, but no matter what the blood work says, Emily is one very lucky lady to have you in her corner."

When the door opened, Jasi saw Emily sitting on an examination table, fully clothed, her hands twisted in the fabric of her jacket.

"This is it, Jasi."

"No matter what happens, you're not alone. You have me. I'll help you in any way I can."

As the doctor reached for an envelope in the chart pocket on the door, Jasi grasped Emily's hand. She could feel their pulses racing together, hopeful, excited.

The doctor pulled a piece of paper from the envelope and peered over her glasses, her expression unreadable. She lifted her head. "I take it you both want a positive match."

Jasi swallowed hard. Beside her, Emily blinked back tears.

The doctor smiled. "I'm happy to tell you, there is more than a ninety-nine percent probability that the two of you are, indeed, sisters. Congratulations. I'll give you some time to let that sink in." She left the room, closing the door behind her.

Jasi stared into Emily's eyes. "Sisters."

"Yeah."

"It's all true then, what Paxton told me about my mother—*our* mother."

"Mom…" Emily let out a sob. "I'll never get to meet her."

Jasi wrapped her arms around her sister. "I'll tell you everything you need to know about her. I promise. Brady will too. And Pop. Oh God, Pop. He's going to be so shocked and so unbelievably happy."

"Do you really think so?" Emily whispered.

"I *know* so. Now let's get out of here. It's going to be a grueling couple of days. You'll have reports to fill out, questions to answer. When that's all over, we'll bring you…home."

Emily's eyes watered again. "I don't really have a home to go to."

"Yes, you do. As soon as Pop learns about you, he's going to want you to stay with him." She grinned. "You'll probably get my old room. But I don't mind a bit. And you can come stay with me one weekend. We'll have sleepovers."

Emily chuckled. "Sleepovers?"

"Hey, we missed out on those. We've got a lot of catching up to do,

Sis."

"But aren't sleepovers for little kids?"

"Not my kind of sleepover. Mine come with a bottle or two of wine."

There is no greater sanctuary than a home filled with laughter, light, love and life.
Cheryl Kaye Tardif

Epilogue

Monday, July 22, 2013
Vancouver, BC

In a luxury suite at the Fairmont Pacific Rim, Jasi acknowledged the lush extravagance that surrounded her, but nothing was more beautiful than the sight of Cameron, Natassia and Emily. For the first time in her life, she felt complete and whole. She was no longer haunted by the dead girl in her closet, no longer searching for a girl in jeopardy.

She took a deep breath, brushed sweaty palms down the sides of her white lace dress and stared into the mirror. Cameron had done a great job with her tangled locks, and the up-do she'd created made Jasi look elegant, sophisticated.

"This is it," she said to her reflection.

Today was the big day. In a few minutes, lives would be changed forever.

"You ready?" Natassia asked.

"As ready as I'll ever be."

"I'm so nervous," Emily murmured as she pinned back one side of her blonde locks with a cherry blossom clip. The blush-pink dress and natural makeup she wore gave her a healthy glow.

"You look beautiful," Cameron stated.

"Radiant," Jasi said. "Apparently you got the good skin genes, Sis."

Emily joined her by the mirror and they stared into it together. With Jasi's red hair and green eyes and Emily's blonde hair and blue eyes, it was hard to believe they were sisters. But the DNA tests were conclusive.

"You finally came out of the closet," Jasi said, grinning. "So I take it you'll leave me alone now and stop haunting my dreams?"

"We'll see," Emily said with a laugh. "It's not like I can turn it on and off at will."

"Matthew will help you with that. He's ready to take you in for PSI training next month."

"I can't believe how my life has changed."

"Mine too."

Emily kissed Jasi's cheek. "You ready for this, Sis?"

"I am. What about you?"

"Hey, I'm gaining a new family in this. And I have the best sister in the whole world. You can show me the town. We'll go shopping together. Go to movies. What have I got to complain about?"

Behind them, Natassia groaned. "Oh God, you have no idea what you're in for. Jasi's motto is 'work, work, work.'"

"Except when Brandon's around," Cameron cut in.

"Hey, I know how to have fun," Jasi said, pouting.

Natassia snorted. "Lucky for your sister, Cameron and I can show her how to have a real good time."

"As much as I can't wait to continue this discussion," Emily said, glancing at her watch, "it's time to make our grand entrance."

The four women hurried from the suite, a flurry of fabrics and laughter.

With instrumental music playing over the sound system, Jasi walked down the aisle of the private hall filled with family and friends. Grandparents, uncles, aunts, cousins—they were all here for this special day, to celebrate the immeasurable power of love and destiny.

She caught sight of Matthew Divine and gave him a grateful nod. He'd made this extravagant event possible. Ben and Natassia stood next to him. Cameron snapped photos from the center of the room. Jasi's gaze swept to the left until she found Brandon. He looked so sexy in his black suit and lavender dress shirt. He blew her a kiss, giving her the boost of confidence she needed.

Pop and Brady stood next to him, the tears in their eyes threatening to spill at any second. This would be a day none of them would ever forget.

She stepped onto a raised platform that was decorated with blush pink roses and pale blue hydrangeas, took a sip of Arbor Mist Peach Chardonnay and picked up the microphone. "Pop and Brady, please come on up."

Her brother practically leapt toward her, the grin on his face threatening to split him apart. He hugged her, nearly knocking the wind out of her. Pop's greeting was no less enthusiastic.

"First," she said, "I want to thank everyone for coming and being part of this very special day."

Her father confiscated the microphone. "I thought the next time we'd be doing something like this it would be for Jasi's wedding."

"Pop!" She blushed, unable to look in Brandon's direction.

Jasi took a deep breath. *Keep going.* "I like to think that things happen for a reason, but sometimes there appears to be no rhyme or reason to what life can throw at you. Two years before I was born, my mother gave birth to a daughter. Everyone was led to believe this child died, but that's not what happened."

The silence in the room was palpable.

"I won't go into all the details because that's not imperative right now." She hugged her father. "Pop, too many years ago, something was taken from you, taken from all of us. I'm here today to return it to you."

The door at the back opened, and Emily stepped into the room.

"Pop," Jasi said, "this is Emily. Your daughter."

Emily made her way toward their father, her steps timid and unsure.

"My sister was kept from us for far too long," Jasi continued, "and I hope you will all help me in welcoming her into the McLellan family."

Pop held out a hand as Emily reached the platform. She stepped up, blinking back tears. "I can't believe this is happening."

Pop let out a gruff sob as he pulled her into his arms. "My girl."

Brady wrapped his arms around both of them, burying his head into Pop's shoulder.

It was an epic moment.

Warm tears trickled down Jasi's face, but she didn't brush them away. They were joyful, well-earned tears, and as she gazed around the hall, she noticed there wasn't a dry eye in the room. She even spotted Matthew covertly wiping away a stray tear.

She released a pent-up sigh and thought back to the past week's events. Not once had she suspected that everything would culminate in *this*. During her time at Sanctuary, she had begun to question what "family" really meant. Certainly she had witnessed many forms of it deep in the woods of Mission. And with Emily, she'd experienced the inexplicable connections that humans have to each other. Now, as she reveled in her surroundings, she knew she'd always be blessed with family, friends and home.

Jasi gave a nod to Brandon, and he increased the speaker volume. She had selected a special song to dedicate to her sister.

"Emily, this song is for you, from all of us."

As *Compass* by Lady Antebellum played over the room, its celebratory beat and lyrics created an atmosphere of sheer bliss.

When the song ended, Jasi's face streamed with tears. "Like the song says, 'you'll never be alone.'"

Emily hugged her. "Thank you."

Everyone gathered around to formally meet the newest addition to the McLellan clan, and Jasi watched with pride as her sister was accepted into the family. She hadn't seen Pop this happy in…forever. And Brady was doing his best to show Emily his goofy side.

She saw Brandon moving toward her and gave him a wave.

He stepped up onto the platform and muffled the microphone. "I need to talk to you privately."

"Can't it wait? I don't want to miss a single moment."

Brandon removed his hand from the microphone. "I think we've waited long enough, Jasmine McLellan."

The room hushed.

She blinked, her smile subsiding. "What are you talking about?"

He stared at her for a moment, then chuckled. "Well, since you always have to be so stubborn—"

"I'm *not* stubborn."

"And since you always have a way of interrupting me—"

"I don't—" She swatted his hand.

"I guess I have no choice. I'll just have to," he reached into his pocket, "do this right here in front of all these people." He dropped down on one knee, and excited murmurs swept through the hall. "Jasmine McLellan, you're the love of my life—"

"Stop fooling around, Brandon, and get off the floor."

"—who always finds ways to test my patience—"

"Is this a joke? You're not really doing this here? Not now!"

With a flourish, he popped open a small black box, revealing a stunning square-cut diamond ring in white gold.

She gasped. "You *are* doing this here!"

"Jasi, shut up and listen to the poor guy," Ben hollered.

"If this past week has taught me nothing else," Brandon continued, "it has taught me not to take anything for granted. Jasi, you're the one I want to spend the rest of my life with, *my* sanctuary, and where you go, I go." He took her hands. "I already asked your father for your hand."

"And I told him it was about time," Pop called out. "But he has to take all of you. No take-backs!"

Even Jasi had to laugh at that.

"So what do you say?" Brandon asked. "Will you marry me?"

She gazed into his eyes, her hands reaching up to caress his face. "You don't have to be psychic to know the answer to that question."

As her lips met his, she realized that everything she'd been searching for, whether she'd known it or not, was in this room—a loving family, a new sister, the best of friends and the man of her dreams. There was no place on earth she'd rather be than this most divine sanctuary.

~ * ~

If you enjoyed this book, please consider writing a short review and posting it on Amazon, Goodreads and/or Barnes and Noble. Reviews are very helpful to other readers and are greatly appreciated by authors, especially me. When you post a review, drop me an email and let me know and I may feature part of it on my blog/site. Thank you. ~ Cheryl

cherylktardif@shaw.ca

Message from Imajin Books:

This concludes Cheryl Kaye Tardif's DIVINE trilogy. Take a moment and let the story and characters settle in. We know it can be difficult to let go sometimes, so take a deep breath.

We hope you enjoyed every page.

If you enjoyed this book, please consider writing a short review and posting it on your favorite ebook retailer or community library site.

Reviews are very helpful to other readers and are greatly appreciated by authors, especially me. When you post a review, drop Cheryl an email to let her know, and she may feature part of it on her blog/site. Thank you.

cherylktardif@shaw.ca

Message from the Author

Dear Reader,

This is the final book in the Divine trilogy, and I really hope you enjoyed it.

I wanted to ensure that you were not left with any unanswered questions and that you were left with a sense of happy closure, especially on the two subplots. Did I succeed?

Although I have immensely enjoyed writing these books and exploring the characters, I have so many books I want to write so I have to let the series go. I hope you understand, and I truly appreciate all of your emails regarding this trilogy and Jasi and Brandon.

~Cheryl Kaye Tardif

About the Author

Cheryl Kaye Tardif is an award-winning, international bestselling Canadian suspense author. Her novels include *Divine Sanctuary, Submerged, Divine Justice, Children of the Fog, The River, Divine Intervention*, and *Whale Song*, which *New York Times* bestselling author Luanne Rice calls "a compelling story of love and family and the mysteries of the human heart...a beautiful, haunting novel."

She is now working on her next thriller.

Cheryl also enjoys writing short stories inspired mainly by her author idol Stephen King, and this has resulted in *Dream House* (short story), *Skeletons in the Closet & Other Creepy Stories* (collection of shorts) and *Remote Control* (novelette eBook). In 2010 Cheryl detoured into the romance genre with her contemporary romantic suspense debut, *Lancelot's Lady*, written under the pen name of Cherish D'Angelo. And she even has a children's picture book published, *The Elfling Princess*.

Booklist raves, "Tardif, already a big hit in Canada...a name to reckon with south of the border."

Cheryl's website: www.cherylktardif.com
Official blog: www.cherylktardif.blogspot.com
Twitter: www.twitter.com/cherylktardif

You can also find Cheryl Kaye Tardif on Facebook, Goodreads, Shelfari and LibraryThing, plus other social networks.

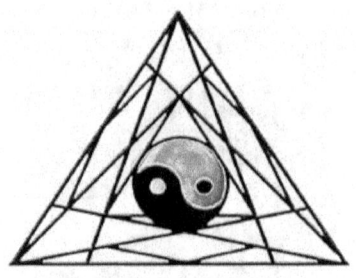

IMAJIN BOOKS
Quality fiction beyond your wildest dreams

For your next eBook or paperback purchase, please visit:

www.imajinbooks.com

www.twitter.com/imajinbooks

www.facebook.com/imajinbooks

www.ingramcontent.com/pod-product-compliance
Lightning Source LLC
Chambersburg PA
CBHW051647260626
47170CB00004B/1380